BREAKING THE SILENCE

Historical Fiction about the Spanish Civil War

MARIA J. NIETO

INK START MEDIA
5710 W Gate City Blvd Ste K #284
Greensboro, NC 27407

CONTENTS

Little is heard about the Spanish Civil War nowadays, which is a pity, because it was one of the defining events of the 20th Century, when Fascism first flexed its muscles, on the way to trying to take over the world. Here, we have a fascinating combination of the perceptions of a young girl, reported by the intelligent old lady she had grown into.

I am a strong believer in the proper use of Point Of View (POV), of presenting the story from within the reality of one of its participants. However, every rule has its exceptions. The POV in this story is always the author's -- the wise old lady's -- but despite this, the world of the little girl is vividly brought to life.

In fact, I shared her grandmother's anguish when little Mari suffered terrible injuries from an exploding shell, cheered on the ordinary people of Madrid fighting against Franco's army, backed by the German air force and tanks -- I was THERE, in the story.

There are many admirable people in the novel. I don't know if they are fictional or historical, nor does it matter. I admire Mari's grandfather, the idealistic worker philosopher. His interactions with the little girl are delightful, and he is a person worthy of respect. Then there is her uncle, sheltering her in a little village, and a teenage Moorish soldier, who all present the best in what it is to be human, in stark contrast to the bestiality of others who rape and torture. The contrast of described horror to their nobility is particularly effective.

Being an obsessive editor, I always find typos and other technical mistakes in whatever I read. I'm very impressed that this self-published book has very few them. It is technically better than many a book from major publishing houses.

This is a powerful book, a book to make you think, and question, and at times, to cry.

And the ending will take you by surprise.

"Little is heard about the Spanish Civil War nowadays, which is a pity, because it was one of the defining events of the 20th Century, when Fascism first flexed its muscles, on the way to trying to take over the world. Here, we have a fascinating combination of the perceptions of a young girl, reported by the intelligent old lady she had grown into."

Dr Bob Rich, author of award-winning books
http://bobswriting.com

Spain, a piece of rock between oceans.
Spain, silent and apart from the rest of the world—
A graveyard
That nurtures its dead with the
Growth of new olive trees and covers
The blood of its children under fresh new meadows.
I am old now.
I cannot see the New Spain—
Busy, hustling highways,
Tourists talking, laughing, eating, drinking
In Madrid's outside cafés.
I only see the heads of my childhood friends,
Decapitated and bleeding,
Starving faces looking up from their graves
While the New Spain eats *jamón* serrano
And manchego cheese.
Spain is an agonizing nightmare to which I return
Every time I forget.
I am old now. It is urgent that I tell you what happened.
Perhaps you will give a silent salute to Spain's
Dead children the next time you visit her.

INTRODUCTION

There is a common grave in Spain where the remains of hundreds of victims from the Franco regime have rested for the past seventy-five years. On this grave, someone has written:

"TO FORGET THEM IS TO LET THEM DIE FOREVER"

After the Spanish Civil War of 1936–1939 ended, Spain was forced to keep silent under the savage and brutal ways of the Franco dictatorship. Those days were a long and painful darkness of night, during which silence was the only protection against torture and death. The children of Spain lived in this silence, learning to become emotionally distant from the suffering and horrors of the war years, soon becoming blank pages for the sophisticated Fascist doctrines of race and religious purity. The Franco regime demanded obedience and, if necessary, that people die for the new dictator and Spain. The children grew up chanting Fascist songs and listening to the Vatican's praise of Franco's dictatorship, calling his brutal methods a "crusade" against atheists and "Reds."

After Franco died, the new Spain was young and unstable. In a fierce struggle not to fall back into another era of hatred and revenge, its people chose to let the civil war history sleep from one generation to another, eventually forgetting its dead heroes. Not all heroes were forgotten. They were the children born too young to fight in the front lines but old enough to have suffered the pain, the hunger, and the horrors of war. Some of these heroes were killed during the war and slept in unmarked graves. Others died later from emotional castration and murder that occurred under the Franco regime.

None of these children were ever forgotten because they were never remembered.

It was only midmorning, yet the hot summer sun had already made temperatures climb in the streets of Old Madrid, making the atmosphere in neighborhoods of narrow cobblestone sticky and uncomfortably warm throughout the city, especially in the streets without trees or shade, where the mansions of long ago had been converted into apartment housing for working families with modest incomes. These old buildings, two or three stories tall, contained numerous spacious rooms attached to large reception areas, where the rich and powerful had once entertained each other. These rooms had long since been divided and subdivided to make apartments for less-privileged families. The outside facades had been left untouched and still maintained the charm of yesteryear, a charm accentuated by sculptures left undisturbed with the passing of time. Strong buildings, living history of the architecture from times when only pampered wealthy families and aristocrats entered and left through these portals, portals that had witnessed the daily passing of elaborate and expensive carriages that transported the elite. That part of the city's history was long gone, and now, especially in the summer, those same streets resonated with the chatter and the laughter of children playing, as well as the voices of women exchanging conversations on their way to the market. On this summer day, when the sun rose to shine on all living things, the streets of Old Madrid were empty and silent. There were no shouts of peddlers pushing carts loaded with fruit and vegetables, no fish vendors promising fresh fish from the Mediterranean off the coast of Alicante, no children playing and laughing.

On this morning, all sounds and activity were gone from the streets as the sun silently stroked the cobblestones undisturbed by human steps. No sounds came from inside the converted mansions other than radios, all tuned to the same station, which continuously played the same music behind closed balconies normally open during the summer months. There was also no sign of life or movement from the windows that faced the courtyards in the rear of the buildings other than the same music from the same radios heard from the balconies that faced the street. Gone was the morning chatter of mothers and children getting ready to go to school and the grumpy voices of fathers barking orders, demanding good conduct and less noise in the home. Gone was the never-ending bickering of siblings. It had all suddenly stopped. If not for the radios, the courtyards felt as if there was no life inside the apartments.

But there *was* life in the apartments. Entire families moved about inside their homes, quietly listening to the radio and waiting for the news that would change their lives forever. They listened hour after hour as a hoarse male voice interrupted the music from time to time with updates from the Ministry of War about an army uprising in Spanish Morocco.

The Second Spanish Republic, weak and unstable from constant disagreements within its own parties, was now trying to explain to the people the efforts being made to stop the uprising by using constitutional methods and asked all citizens to be patient, ordering all local governors to hold all and any distribution of arms to the civilian population.

As the government played hopeless diplomatic games to subdue the enemy, the people of Madrid were asked to wait inside their homes and listen to the radio for updates, unprotected and unarmed. Schools closed; men stayed at home and did not go to work, but toward the noon hour, they left home and gathered in the neighborhood bars to discuss all possible methods of defense in case of an attack. They needed arms, and the government's refusal to distribute guns escalated their fear and anxiety over feeling powerless to defend their families.

While the men argued and discussed the situation in the bars, the women kept the children busy with menial tasks as they listened to the radio and waited for news, while attending to the usual daily chores of cleaning and making beds. On this day, there would be no washing and hanging of clothes across the courtyards, no leaning against windowsills exchanging gossip with other female neighbors up and down the courtyards. It was enough just to pick up and make beds. The rest would have to wait.

As the morning melted into early afternoon, the seriousness of the situation was further established when the men did not come home for the midafternoon meal, at which the whole family gathered daily to share food and lively conversations before retiring for a short nap. After that nap, the men would return to work, and the children would go back to school as the women gathered in front of their balconies, sewing and gossiping with their neighbors. On this day, the women had waited for the men to come home to eat, but as time passed, they realized that they would have to eat alone. They made excuses to the children. Filled with fear and concern, the women decided not to cook a full meal. The courtyards felt strange and empty without the familiar smells of olive oil and garlic that usually filled the courtyards at that time of the day. Instead, the women prepared sandwiches and held a short and almost silent meal, during which only the small children chattered with each other, showing no concern. After eating, the ritual of a nap after lunch was followed; it was almost a religious interlude, when silence in the courtyards and apartments was absolute and strictly observed. Nothing moved at these times; even the buzzing of flies in and out of the windows seemed to stop. That day, the mealtime had been short everywhere, and the usual absolute siesta silence had been transgressed by mothers listening to the radio while children lay in their beds, unable to sleep.

The silence in the courtyards continued throughout the day. There was no chatter and no laughter, just the irritating sounds of radios crackling in between music and the hoarse voices making announcements from time to time into the evening. Eventually, the men returned home, tired and apprehensive after planning to unify and march to the Ministry of War in the morning to demand that they be armed. The smell of discord and uncertainty was in the air that night. A people whose daily lives had been rooted in traditions, good food, and good family interactions now felt frightened without the strength of the familiar and with the possibility of losing or being separated from the loved ones by distance or death.

The streets remained empty throughout the evening. No one strolled to enjoy the cool night air. No one sat in the sidewalk cafés, drinking wine or draft beer and picking tasty appetizers from a platter using toothpicks. No families gathered in the kitchen to share snacks with a bottle of wine after the working day. These were the times in the evening when the courtyards had come alive in the past with the sound of music, laughter, and the chatter of families sharing the day's experiences with each other. All these activities had been replaced in a single day by the silence of entire families listening to radios and waiting.

Before long, the dreaded information arrived: the first unit of the Army of Africa, two hundred Moorish regulars well known for their brutality, was now trying to cross the Strait of Gibraltar and advance through southern Spain toward Madrid, where the Republican government had its headquarters. In response to the advancing threat of rebel troops heading into the mainland and the continued denial of the civil government to arm its citizens, Spain was in a state of chaos. Thousands of workers stormed the streets of Madrid, asking for arms. Women joined in the frenzy by beginning to build barricades in their neighborhoods. The multiple attempts by the Republican government to repeal the uprising by constitutional methods before initiating a counterattack had given the enemy more time to organize throughout Spain and advance from the northern provinces, as well as from Morocco. Thundering cries for arms rose above the night skies of Madrid well into dawn. By the time the sun rose, the government had accepted the Fascist declaration of war, and hundreds of rifles had been distributed throughout the streets of Madrid. Spaniards of all political parties took to the streets, cheering and chanting, drunk with the fervor to hunt and kill those known to sympathize with the Fascist revolt.

As adults filled themselves with the energy that comes with hate and fear, some of the children imitated grown-ups without understanding the meaning of their behavior or language by initiating games and introducing vulgar phrases into their speech. Other children felt lost in the strange new environment of adult behavior that they did not recognize and that made them feel abandoned, thinking that all that was happening was somehow their fault.

One of these children was Mari, a small six-year-old child who lived with her father's family in one of the neighborhoods of Old Madrid, who, the same as thousands of other children in Spain at this time of chaos, woke up one morning to the preamble of what would become an upside-down world of adult confusion and fear. The first thing she noticed upon awakening was that the radio in the dining room was turned on and playing music. This was never supposed to be in the morning, a strict rule set by her grandfather, especially loud music, another no-no in the family. Even for a small child, this kind of intrusiveness was loud and annoying, and later, when sitting in the kitchen and eating breakfast with her grandparents and her deaf aunt, Mari tucked in her chin, curled her fingers around an imaginary mustache, and jokingly imitated her grandfather's grumpy voice asking that the "noise machine" be turned off.

Mari's father and her uncles had left the apartment earlier that morning, and her grandfather, don Juan (*don* spelled with a lowercase *d* as opposed to the capital *D* used for aristocrats and the wealthy), as everyone respectfully called him, was silent and more serious than usual. His seriousness was not a problem; he was almost always serious. His silence was strange; don Juan was never silent when the family gathered to eat. Mealtimes had always given him the chance to expand upon his righteousness as head of the family, as well as on family behaviors that needed correction.

Ignoring her husband's silence, Mari's grandmother Maria talked about a canceled trip to Alicante, where she and don Juan had planned to attend the wedding of their daughter Cristina. "She can get married without us. It would have been good to be there, but I am not sure what is going to happen to the trains if we go to war, and I sure do not want to be caught in Alicante!"

Mari's aunt Pilar, who had been carefully reading her mother's lips, asked, "If you are not going to the wedding, will you attend the women's union meeting in Tetuán?"

"Yes, and I will probably be gone all day, as we have to arrange things with various construction companies for sandbags to begin building barricades. If the boys return home before you go to sleep, make sure they eat something—and watch Mari. There is absolutely no going out to play today."

Mari listened to her grandmother, but all that she really heard was that she could not go out to play. She had made plans to catch frogs with her friend Isabel in a secret stream that fed small gardens nearby. Mari's grandmother was great for ruining things—or was it something Mari herself had done? Not knowing what to think, Mari asked, "*Abuela,* are you mad at me?"

"No." That is all Mari's grandmother said. *No.*

Mari pushed a little. "Abuela, if I can't go out to play, can I go with you this morning?"

"No."

No explanations, no reasons, no excuses, just another no. Later on, when Mari's grandmother left without Mari, it was hurtful. True, her grandmother looked serious and worried, but this was no excuse to leave without her. Mari walked around the apartment for a long time, but finding nothing to do, she finally curled up in bed and sulked. Living with grown-ups was tiresome; they were always either lying or making rules. She thought of maybe changing her plan to join the Spanish Foreign Legion when she grew up and instead join it now. Africa could not be that far away.

It was already afternoon when Mari woke up, but the radio had not stopped playing. The music continued the same as before, interrupted by crackling sounds that were followed by the same hoarse and tired voices. The voices were still shouting words that were hard to understand and often incomprehensible, especially for a child.

She roamed the apartment and found Aunt Pilar scrubbing floors and making beds; Mari's grandfather was in the dining room, chewing on a cigar, a faraway look on his face. Her father and her uncles had not returned from wherever they had gone in the morning, which was not too unusual, and it did not matter, anyway, because when they were home, there was seldom time for her. Sometimes, Alfonso, her father, would tickle her, toss her up in the air, and laugh, but most of the time, he did not seem to know that she was there. That hurt a lot.

From time to time, new noises and angry voices came from the street, together with the radio, making Mari begin to feel anxious and fearful that something was really wrong and that something terrible was going to happen. She felt threatened and alone and needed the safety of an adult who could explain things to her and reassure her that nothing was going to happen to her. Sometimes at night when she felt all alone, if she closed her eyes tightly and whispered the magic word—*Mommy*—a smiling lady with curly black hair and big dark eyes would hold her until she went to sleep. Maybe the lady with the curly hair and dark eyes would help her now. She closed her eyes and whispered "Mommy" three times, but nothing happened. After waiting for a time, it was clear that the lady with the curly hair and big dark eyes was not coming.

Mari went looking for Aunt Pilar but stopped and turned around before finding her. Her aunt was deaf, and as her aunt could not hear what was happening, she probably would accuse Mari of lying to attract attention, as Aunt Pilar always did, the way she did on the day Uncle Chato hid Teodoro, the teddy bear that Uncle Fernando (who lived far away) had given to Mari. Her aunt had shaken her finger at Mari and said that no one had hidden Teodoro. "Look under the kitchen table, and stop fibbing." Well, if Chato had not put Teodoro under the kitchen table, who had? Things were always like that with Aunt Pilar.

Mari went into the dining room, where her grandfather was typing and stood by the door, hoping that he would see her. His attention was on whatever he was typing and nothing else. After evaluating the situation for a short time, Mari went into an internal debate with herself about the chances of a peaceful conversation with her grandfather. True, he liked to explain things to her—and no one else in the family did—and for this, she loved him a lot. Sometimes, he did not mind being interrupted, but there were also times when he *did* mind being interrupted and got angry, but not always, especially if the interruption gave him a chance to tell one of his stories. He loved to talk, and he sometimes could talk forever. That was a problem, especially if he said, "Let me begin from the beginning." That was a sign that his talk would be endless. She decided to give him a chance, so she walked toward her grandfather and asked him about the voices in the street and the radio being on all the time.

He stopped typing and moved his chair away from the table. Placing his eyeglasses on the typewriter, he coughed a little. His granddaughter looked a little pale and scared, so he asked, "Are you afraid of the voices?"

"No," she lied. "I just want to know if that is why I can't go out to play today."

Grandfather Juan smiled and cleared his throat. Short and hefty, this proper middle-aged man with a crew cut and mustache always dressed in a three-piece suit and tie, even when he was home. He straightened his tie, puffed on his cigar to hide a strange need to cry, and leaned forward toward his granddaughter. He said, "Well, my love, do you have time for me to tell you the whole story of how it all began?"

Mari wasn't sure she wanted the whole story, as her grandfather's stories were not only long and grandiose but also sometimes boring, especially when he needed to begin at the beginning of things. Looking up at the ceiling, she thought about the situation. There was no way to sneak out to play in the street. Aunt Pilar probably did not know what was going on and would only make fun of Mari for being afraid. The lady with the dark curly hair and dark eyes was apparently busy. Mari was afraid of being alone. There was nothing else to do. Returning her grandfather's glance, she let out a long deep sigh and whispered, "Yes, *Abuelo*. I have time."

Don Juan ignored his granddaughter's condescending tone of voice. He shifted his legs and smiled at her. He was a proud Castilian who was born in a small village nestled behind hills and mountains not far from Madrid. He was a homemade genius with an eighth-grade education who could already read and write at six years old—an unknown feat in a village where most adults went to school for two or three years but seldom passed beyond learning the alphabet and the ability to sign their names. Forced to leave school to go to work, he had borrowed books from the village priest and read avidly when he was not working in the fields. Karl Marx fascinated him, and he became an informed politician and strong believer in Marxism, mastering the universal language of Esperanto before he was of age with the belief that if all people spoke the same language, it would unite the world.

During his late teens, don Juan felt that his thoughts needed telling, so he began scribbling on every piece of paper he could find. When he started using his father's playing cards to make notes, his father purchased an old, rusty typewriter from the schoolmaster's widow and asked the village's traveling merchant to get his son typing paper from Madrid. From then on, don Juan wrote hundreds of pages using the typewriter his father had given him, the same typewriter he carried from one continent to another trying to educate workers, the same typewriter he had been using when his granddaughter interrupted him that day.

Don Juan kept a smile on his face while he stretched and cracked his knuckles. He liked it when his granddaughter asked him questions; she was a little like him, curious and opinionated. He hoped that someday, she would maybe follow the footsteps of Dolores Ibárruri and work toward ending social class discrimination and abuse in Spain. Dolores Ibárruri was a courageous member of the Communist Party who was teaching the country to finally accept women's thinking as a valuable contribution to mankind, something far more valuable than scrubbing floors. Don Juan liked Comrade Ibárruri, but she was a Communist, and Communism was fast removing itself from the teachings of Karl Marx and would eventually exploit the workers just as did monarchies, fascism, and capitalism.

Don Juan hoped that his granddaughter would someday develop a clinical, analytical, political mind and help Spain become one of the best democracies in the world. Until that time, she could study and learn to be a good disciple of Karl Marx and protect the rights for equality and liberty of the Spanish people and people everywhere.

Looking at his granddaughter, who seemed to be waiting eagerly for him to speak, he thought that perhaps this day was a good one to finally begin her political education. He lifted the waiting child onto his lap, puffed on his cigar, and began speaking with a faraway look in his eyes. "Once upon a time, there was a wonderful land of green meadows and dense forests with endless water cascades streaming from the mountain, keeping everything green. Cows roamed everywhere, and in this land of green meadows and roaming cows lived the strong Happy Farmers. They toiled the earth from sunup to sundown to keep fertile the land handed to them from father to son for hundreds of years and then slowly taken from them by the rich and powerful."

"But *Abuelo*, you said they were Happy Farmers! How could they be happy if their land was taken from them?"

"Ah, Mari, my child, that is a good question. They were happy because, most times, they still had something to eat, even though they had to work very hard."

Mari wiggled, making herself comfortable on her grandfather's lap. She had his full attention, and this made her feel safe and loved, which did not happen very often. She rested her head on his chest and continued to listen.

"The strong Happy Farmers worked hard to feed their families, but what they were given by the rich and powerful was not enough to survive, so their sons worked sixteen hours a day in the city's sweatshops, and their daughters—and sometimes their sons' daughters—worked as maids for the self-declared aristocrats who did not respect women. The aristocrats sometimes even forced these women to have babies and left them without money with which to feed the babies after they were born. But the Happy Farmers hoped someday to be able to have back what was rightfully theirs, and they kept toiling the land for other people without making any trouble for anyone, trying to be happy."

He paused and then added, "But you are right; they must often have been a little angry. They worked the land from sunup to sundown, and their wives worked, cleaning and cooking for the same rich people, and at the end of the summer, they were given such a small portion of the harvest that it was barely enough to feed their families through the winter. But they were good people and made everything feel better for themselves and their families by trying to be happy in the evenings after work when they went home. These once-upon-a-time Happy Farmers always gathered at night and danced in the village streets, clapping their hands at the rhythm of lively guitar music, and because they knew God was very busy making things grow, they only complained and questioned God's love when singing deep wailing songs."

"Were the once-upon-a-time Happy Farmers gypsies?"

"No, my child, but they had a drop of gypsy blood somewhere, because at the beginning of things…"

Mari smiled. She knew that, sooner or later, her grandfather would get back to "the beginning of the beginning," so she prepared herself for a long story.

"At the beginning of things," continued her grandfather, "the land of the Happy Farmers belonged to their ancestors, and this land was separated from the rest of the world in the north by tall, snowy mountains, later on called the Pyrenees. No one knew that the ancestors of the Happy Farmers were behind the mountains, because the mountains were too tall and always covered with too much snow for anyone to walk over them."

Mari interrupted, "Why didn't they fly over in an airplane? Or ski?"

The grandfather rolled his eyes and lifted his eyebrows. "Nobody had airplanes at that time, and they did not know how to ski. Now, where was I? Ah, yes. The mountains were on the north side of the Happy Land; on the south side, there was a narrow, treacherous body of water where two oceans met, now called the Strait of Gibraltar, that separated the Happy Farmers' great-grandfathers from a crazy wild world of all kinds of crazy people doing all kinds of things, each in a different way. The ancestors of the Happy Farmers had wanted to cross over the water and maybe do a little shopping, but the currents were too dangerous to swim across."

Mari could not understand why those people made crossing the Strait of Gibraltar so difficult, and she once again interrupted her grandfather. "Why didn't they cross over in a ship or in a submarine?"

The grandfather's eyebrows lifted again as he let out a big sigh of faked exasperation. "There were no ships or submarines at that time, and because of that, many years passed—hundreds of years—when finally a bunch of ill-mannered people from places on the other side of the mountains, now called Europe, started gossiping and spreading rumors about the Happy Farmers' ancestors.

"People from Europe like to gossip a lot. Actually, that is all they do: gossip and fight against each other. Anyway, the gossip traveled, and soon, a few tough guys followed the gossip, and the ancestors of the Happy Farmers were discovered. But that did not happen until the seventh century before Christ." He stared at his granddaughter. "You do know about Christ, no?"

Mari twisted her face with annoyance. Of course she knew. "Yeah. He was a Jew who got mad at the rabbis. They are like priests, except they have bigger noses. That's how you can tell them apart from the priests.

Anyway, the rabbis were selling lottery tickets in the Jewish temple, and Christ got really mad and asked the pope to make him a Catholic."

At first, don Juan did not move a muscle in his face, but then he covered his mouth, pretending to cough, and took long puffs from his cigar as he tried not to laugh. "Yes, he was a Jew, all right. Who told you about him?"

"Uncle Chato. He knows a lot stories."

Don Juan nodded. Chato was his youngest son. He was fifteen years old, with a fifteen-year-old's imagination. There were four other sons who were fairly tolerable, except the oldest, Alfonso, Mari's father. He had been a cross to bear. He was now a fairly bright thirty-year-old narcissistic rooster without an ounce of common sense or responsibility toward anything in his life. Looking at his granddaughter, don Juan began thinking back to the child's mother, Rosa, now back in New York City and gravely ill. Poor Rosa, she was so young when she married the rooster—too young to have been treated so badly by Alfonso and his mother. Oh, yes. Don Juan loved his son, but he was not proud to be his father, and he deeply disliked Alfonso. Don Juan's wife was just ignorant. His daughters were all right, not particularly bright, but serious and responsible young women, all three of them. Don Juan had always regretted dragging his children through the migrant camps in America, where the whole family picked fruit and where his youngest daughter, Pilar, lost her hearing from a meningitis epidemic in one of the camps. Oh, yes, a lot happened in America, in the state of California, where another daughter, Margarita, then six years old, died as the family was crossing the desert in a truck that broke down every five miles. America had not been the land of opportunity for don Juan or his family.

A strong pull on his tie returned don Juan to the present. His granddaughter was impatiently jumping up and down on his lap. "Abuelo, are you ever going to finish the beginning of the beginning?"

Don Juan nodded his head and smiled. "All right, let us go on. When the ancestors of the strong Happy Farmers were first mentioned or recognized by the gossipy people on the other side of the mountains, they were called Iberians, and, my child, these Iberians were strong, dark, hairy people. They had incredible strength and survival instincts. No one really knew how they got to the Happy Land, not even themselves. They were a little ugly but were good fathers and husbands."

"Abuelo," Mari interrupted one more time. "Did the Iberians ever marry someone in our own family?"

"I am sure they did. Some people say they even married Asiatic people— you know, people with narrow eyes, like the Chinese. They also married a mixed-up people with a lot of problems from Africa called Afrosemites. But, Mari, you do not have to remember all of these names; those people are all dead now. Just remember that the strong Happy Farmers were descendants of many races of people, like the tall, blond, gossipy Celts that came from the north across the tall, snowy mountains, the mountains that no one had dared cross before. Oh, yes, the Celts were intelligent and adventurous! They liked the Iberians and immediately joined them to form a land of Celtiberians, with a peaceful way of life centered on family groups —or what they called clans. They all lived together, and they all shared the land and all the harvests, and if someone sneaked around and did not share something, they killed him. That was the law. And then the Romans came to the Happy Land, followed by the Visigoths. Everyone tried to be the only masters of the Happy Land. It was messy for many years, almost as it is today." [The pure Celtic strain has straight black hair and blue eyes. The blond hair comes from Germanic people like Angles and Saxons.]

"Abuelo, did the Visigoths come to Madrid last night and start all of that noise this morning?"

"No, but some of those people may have been descendants of the Visigoths. The Visigoths were here a long time ago, and I am sure they married and had babies with the Celtiberian women. Many people came to the Happy Land after the Visigoths were here, and it may have been some of their descendants making all that noise in the streets this morning. You see, all of these people, all of those people who crossed the mountains from the north and the dangerous waters from the south later became our great- great-grandfathers, yours and mine."

Don Juan was not sure of the order of things that far back into Spanish history, but his grandchild was listening, and she was no longer afraid. That was all that mattered. He rearranged himself in the chair as he tried to put his thoughts in order and continue his narration. Pilar came into the room and silently placed a plate with two sandwiches next to the typewriter, along with two glasses, one glass filled with highly diluted red wine for her niece, the other one with pure, rich, undiluted dark-red wine for her father. Don Juan looked up and smiled at his daughter with gratitude. She smiled back and left the room as silently as she had entered. The grandfather put down his cigar, and both he and his granddaughter each picked up a sandwich and looked inside the two halves of the crisp, crusty bread. Rich, aromatic, incredibly tasty ham from free-roaming, acorn-eating pigs was stuffed between the bread.

Mari ate, and don Juan joined her. They chewed and swallowed large mouthfuls of ham, nodding their heads as they smiled at each other; the sandwiches were good, and it was a good moment when they finished eating in silence, looking at each other with expressions of mutual love and approval in their eyes.

"Good, no?" asked don Juan.

Mari yawned and nodded her head in assertion, her body sinking a little deeper into her grandfather's chest.

He asked her, "Are you tired? We can finish another time. I don't think that we can get to the history of the street noises and the radios today."

Mari did not answer. Don Juan felt her head drop. His granddaughter was asleep.

He straightened his back on the chair and gently kissed her on the cheek. "Oh, well. Not enough time to tell you about the Romans…or the ravaging Visigoths…or about how the Iberians learned to fight, to change loyalties, to create civil wars, to make and break alliances." Letting out a big sigh, he lifted the sleeping child into his arms and walked outside the room, looking for Pilar, who was reading in the kitchen.

Totally engrossed in the book she was reading and failing to see her father coming toward her, Pilar jumped up, looking at her father with surprise when he tapped her on the shoulder. He spoke to her slowly and carefully annunciated his words. "The kid fell asleep. Either your father is really boring, or your sandwich was really good, or maybe you put too much wine in her water. Anyway, I am looking for a bed."

Taking the child from her father's arms, Pilar walked toward her room. "Let her sleep with me tonight. I think that the loud music scares her. It must be really loud, because the bottoms of my feet have been tickling all day from the vibrations."

Don Juan followed his daughter into the room and watched as she carefully placed Mari's limp body on the bed and then removed the cloth and rope-soled *alpargatas* from her feet and covered the child with a light blanket. Walking out of the room with his daughter, don Juan put his arm around Pilar's shoulder while walking back into the kitchen. "Got any coffee, Pilar? I am going to stay up and wait until your mother and the boys get back. They should get back soon."

Pilar nodded.

"I just hope the streets are safe," don Juan mused. "Maybe I should have gone with her or the boys, but I really don't want to see the mess the government has created. They should have been one step ahead of what Franco was planning to do in Morocco, and if Franco's sons of bitches don't retreat tonight, the boys and I will probably have to join the civilian militia in the morning and try to get some guns."

Pilar placed a cup of coffee next to her father and looked at him with questioning eyes. She asked, "Who is Franco?"

"Oh, he is a brigadier general. He put together the Spanish Foreign Legion in Morocco. He's astute, a strong Catholic born in Galicia and fairly bright for a Gallego. He has been unhappy with agrarian reform and especially with the separation of church and state."

Pilar frowned. "I'll have to read more about him. What exactly were the boys doing today? I did not understand why there was a need for public manifestations in front of the Ministry of War."

"They wanted to show the need for armed civilians in case Franco gets to Madrid before he is stopped by the army." Don Juan sat behind his typewriter and sniffed the strong coffee aroma from the cup his daughter had given him. "Um, the coffee is good. Thank you, little woman." He read the last words he had written earlier.

The Second Spanish Republic has failed to convince some of its citizens that agrarian reform and separation of church and state are steps toward a democratic and long-lasting, peaceful Spain. As a result, Spain is once again about to enter into another of her endless circles of national violence and pain. When are we going to stop being pushed by false gods into devouring ourselves and leave nothing but rotting bones as our only inheritance for future generations? Comrades, fellow citizens, let us not allow this to happen again! We are all sons of this glorious land, regardless of from which province we come: Aragón, Sevilla, Catalonia, Galicia, Asturias—or if we come from Murcia or Valencia. We are all individuals and perhaps distinct in traits and thinking, but we are all descendants of special races with special combinations of strength, honor, and intelligence. We may have sprouted from the earth separately, but our roots travel deep and interlace, feeding from the same soil and drinking from the same water. Our differences in thinking make us stronger, for in spite of these differences, we are still brothers, equal and bonded together by a long heritage of nobility and honor, never enemies!

After he finished reading what he had written earlier that day, don Juan pulled the paper from the typewriter and tore it into small pieces. It was already too late for this kind of logic.

When Mari woke up, she was surprised to find herself in her aunt's bed, and she sat up, expecting to find Aunt Pilar next to her, but the other side of the bed was empty. The loud crackling and music coming from the radio had not changed, but now Mari could also hear many voices singing, shouting, and chanting. This sound came from the dining room balconies that faced the street. The courtyard was still silent. None of the usual neighbors' voices and laughter had returned from the day before. Swinging her legs to one side of the bed, Mari tried to remember why she was in this room, but she could only remember eating a sandwich with her grandfather the night before and falling asleep without finding out why the radios were on all the time making all that noise and why she had not been allowed to go out to play in the street.

Mari was fully dressed, but her feet were bare, which was a strange thing to happen or for her aunt to allow; Aunt Pilar was always finicky and tolerated no sloppiness, especially not wearing pajamas at night. But then, everything had been different the past couple of days, such as her grandmother being gone all day without saying where she was going and not coming home to make lunch for the family. The voices and the noises from the street were also strange.

Mari looked around the room. Everything was bright with the glow of summer streaming through the curtains of a half-opened window. The breeze blowing in from the outside was pleasant and might have made the room feel safe and comfortable if not for the persistent crackling and loud music from the radio, which made everything confusing and frightening. Now more voices were chanting and screaming in the streets. The only place that was silent was the courtyard, with the exception of intermittent whistling-wheezing noises made by something flying and leaving a resonating sound when hitting a solid object.

The sounds were bullets, like the bullets her father fired when he practiced with his hunting rifle. Who was hunting? What were they hunting? Mari shook a little and ran to the kitchen. She watched silently as her grandmother and her aunt prepared large slices of bread-and-sausage sandwiches and wrapped them in newspapers. Working rapidly to finish the lunch for don Juan and his sons, the women did not notice Mari staring at the family with wide eyes.

The men, busy preparing to join hundreds of other workers in a march to the Ministry of War, also failed to see her. They acted as if there was nothing else in the apartment but them—themselves talking and laughing, themselves slapping each other's shoulders, almost as if intoxicated by the sounds coming from the loudly playing radio. They were all dressed in blue coveralls with red-and-black armbands. Each of them wore a pointed military cap with a tassel in the front. Alfonso was loading the old hunting rifle he had owned since his younger days. He stuffed the extra bullets in his pocket. Pascual and Max carried hand grenades, which hung from thick leather belts around their waists, and young fifteen-year-old Chato had a pistol tucked inside his belt. Don Juan was the only one who was unarmed. [intoxicated: This word is within Mari's thinking. She may have the concept if she's seen drunk people, but not a big word like that. It's important to stay with the person's language, because it induces the reader to identify with the character. For example, her story of Christ was excellent like that.]

They hoped to get rifles and ammunition after the march to the Ministry of War, because the government had already begun distributing guns to the civilian population. The rebel army could not and would not be allowed to enter Madrid. Enough time had been wasted by the government's attempts to repeal the uprising by constitutional methods and making the fatal mistake of denying arms to the civilian population. Now, Moors from Franco's Foreign Legion, free from any armed opposition and allowed passage through the Strait of Gibraltar without penalties by the British government, poured battalions of Moroccan troops into southern Spain, leaving behind a cloud of death and violence as they rapidly approached Madrid.

The men did not notice Mari as she turned away from the kitchen door and watched her grandfather get his feet into heavy boots. Her grandfather had never worn boots before or coveralls; something really serious must be happening. Mari was used seeing her father dressed in coveralls when fixing something or when he played with his rifle, which he often took out of the closet and cleaned when he had nothing else to do. With the gun tucked in his pants, Uncle Chato looked like a movie gangster or a cowboy. Mari did not recognize the ugly things that looked like metal balls that hung from the belts of her other two uncles; she had never seen anything like them before. Much later, she learned that they were grenades and that grenades killed people. Mari watched for a time before taking a few steps toward her grandfather, who was now tying his bootlaces. Noticing a pair of small bare feet in front of him, don Juan looked up, only to find himself face-to-face with his granddaughter, who pointed her chin toward the balconies and the sounds that came from them.

"Abuelo, are the Visigoths trying to steal the land from the Iberians?"

Taken by surprise, don Juan bent down and put his arms around the child. He hugged and kissed her. "Yes, little one, you could say that is what is happening. No one wants to share anything anymore."

Alfonso looked at his father and rebuked him. "Father, why are you always filling her head with fairy tales?"

Shrugging, don Juan let go of his granddaughter and walked to the kitchen. He took the package wrapped in newspapers and made his way to the front door, muttering under his breath, "They are not fairy tales, my son. It is history—your history, my history, and now your daughter's history."

The four men followed their father and closed the door without saying good-bye to anyone. Mari ran toward the door after them, a door to which she now unconsciously projected all that was hateful, painful, and frightening. The abrupt closing of the door made a harsh sound that rooted Mari to the floor, and she felt unable to move. That same door had opened and closed many times before, but it had never continued to open and close over and over again as it was opening and closing now, without making a sound and in slow motion. Every time the door opened, the figure of the woman with black curly hair and large brown eyes appeared, blowing kisses at her. It was the same woman she sometimes called "Mommy," the same woman who held her when she was afraid or could not sleep, but this time, the woman was crying.

Time passed, and the door stopped opening and closing. The woman with the dark hair and large, tearful brown eyes disappeared. Feeling a long-ago familiar twisting pain inside her chest, Mari crumbled to the floor, shaking with uncontrollable rage. She stood up and threw herself against the door, crying out over and over again, "Mommy!" She waited for the door to open, but it remained closed. She thought that her father was angry and had left without saying good-bye because she believed her grandfather's stories, or maybe he had heard that Mari had broken Pilar's eyeglasses. Mari must have been very bad to make the woman with the dark hair and large brown eyes cry. Mari sat on the floor and thought that the voices from the radio were directing curses at her and that something terrible was happening and that it was all her fault. Everything was her fault.

Mari's grandmother lifted her screaming, crying grandchild from the floor and carried her to an empty room with only a small bed and a dresser, a room away from the front of the building and balconies from where the noises were coming, a place less menacing. Pushing the bed against a corner of the room, the grandmother gave the child a blanket and asked her to cover her head if the noises bothered her. She asked, "Are you hungry?"

"Yes."

Mari soaked a slice of the same crusty bread her grandmother had used for the sandwiches earlier that morning in a cup of hot coffee half mixed with milk, and her grandmother watched her, feeling immense sadness. It seemed as if time had never passed, and it was still three years ago when Mari's mother, ill and needing medical attention, had returned to America. She had been diagnosed with an anemia newly discovered by a Dr. Cooley, an anemia that affected some people from the Mediterranean, an illness too new for Spain to have available treatment, which made Rosa decide to go back to New York. The day that Rosa left, she had walked through the same front door the men used that day, and Mari had watched her go. Mari had waited for her mother to come back, and when Rosa did not return, Mari had cried "Mommy!" over and over again, lying behind the door for hours. It took days before the child ate solid food or stopped getting up at all hours of the night, silently sitting by the door, sucking her thumb and wetting her clothes. Her grandmother could not remember how many times she had carried the child to bed or how many times she had to change and clean her while she sat on the floor behind the front door, waiting for her mother. Would it be better for the child to live in New York, watching her mother die, or stay in Spain, watching everyone else die?

My first and only grandchild, thought the grandmother. *So strong, yet so fragile.* This was a child she had dearly loved but had not wanted at first, fearful that the child might have been born with physical characteristics of another race. This pensive grandmother was Maria de Avila, a proud peasant woman of pure Castilian stock born and raised in a small village hidden behind the hills near the walled medieval city of Avila, where foreigners were rare and not to be trusted. Her family descended from pure European northern tribes, so it was hard to accept her son's marriage to a woman of Italian parents—not only Italians but also Sicilians. As far as Maria knew, Sicilians were first cousins to the black Abyssinians, and to make matters worse, this woman had carried her son's child before they were married. Maria could neither read nor write. All her knowledge about the world had been the things learned from the gossipy women washing clothes by the river until she met her husband, Juan .

Juan was a "citizen of the world," as he liked to call himself. He tried to convince her that blood other than Spanish blood was just as honorable and that all men were the same, just born and raised in different places, with different ways of thinking and doing things—that was all. Well, she tried, but she still believed that Sicilians were descended from black Ethiopians, and all black people were uncivilized barbarians. Even the doctor said that Rosa's type of anemia was believed to affect Mediterranean people long ago descended from Abyssinia. As far as Maria knew, the only people that had mixed with the Abyssinians were the Italians. All this thinking was giving her a headache, so she stopped her bitter thoughts, rearranged the pillows on the bed, and asked her granddaughter to take a nap.

Thinking back to what had happened that morning by the door, Maria was now afraid that the child might still remember her mother. It was all very sad. Maria regretted the angry times when she had told Mari that her mother was a black Abyssinian with kinky hair who lived in Africa. How could she have been so cruel? She made the sign of the cross and whispered, "Oh, God. Please forgive me."

Mari closed her eyes, and her grandmother kissed her on the cheek and talked to her softly as she gently stroked her hair. "I have to leave for a couple of hours. Pilar will be here if you need anything. Try to sleep."

"Please, Abuela. Don't leave me here. Take me with you. I'll be good; I promise!"

"I know you will be good, but that is not why you can't come with me; there are problems in the streets, and I want to be sure that you are safe at home with Pilar."

Mari stared at the wall for a long time after her grandmother left the room. After a while, Mari got up from the bed, leaned on the windowsill, and looked out, waiting to hear or see something familiar. She had forgotten that the usual everyday noises had been gone from the courtyard for two days; there was no yelling of mothers at their children, no flapping noises from clothes hanging out to dry, just silence. Fear and anxiety of something unknown happening overwhelmed her again, so she looked under the bed for the dragons and snakes that her aunt had told her would get her someday. Finding no dragons or snakes, Mari curled her body on top of the bed. Wrapping the blanket around her head, she cried herself to sleep.

After leaving her granddaughter, Maria went to the kitchen to talk to her daughter, who was washing dishes with her back to the door. Maria tapped Pilar on the shoulder to get her attention and said, "I am going to see what is happening; they told us yesterday that the sandbags would get here today, but no time was mentioned, so I need to check on that and maybe take a walk to the Plaza Mayor. Mari is going to sleep, but if she wakes up, try spending some time with her until I get back. I don't know when your father and the boys will be back, so you and Mari will probably have to eat something by yourselves."

Pilar picked up a kitchen towel and dried her hands. She asked her mother, "What is going on? I can still feel the vibrations of the radio under my feet. How come the radio is still on?"

"We yet have to learn what is happening. Now I can hear bullets popping from time to time. I hope these crazy fanatics are not shooting at each other in the streets." Maria kissed her daughter on both cheeks, took off her apron, and stepped out of the apartment carefully, closing the door behind her. After reaching the first floor, she walked through the glass double doors to the sidewalk and paused for a moment before crossing the street to look into the front windows of the neighborhood bakery. The sun was sliding down the sides and front of the building, beginning to squeeze between the slits of the blinds drawn across the front window. Maria attempted to turn the door handle, but the door to the bakery was locked. She looked between the blind slits into empty bread bins behind the counter.

Everything was quiet. The only sounds came from voices of women farther down the street as they unloaded sandbags from a truck. Maria looked at them sadly, remembering that these were the same women who only three days earlier had laughed as they shared stories with each other as they stood in line waiting to take home freshly baked bread. Today, these same women were unloading sandbags from a truck, preparing to use them to build barricades in an attempt to stop an unseen enemy. She walked down a few doors from the bakery to the coal shop that had supplied Maria's stove every day and found the front doors wide open. Huge metal bins, dark and empty, almost resembling the mouths of legendary dragons, stared at her. She walked inside the shop and looked for signs of activity, but there were none.

She stood outside the shop with tear-filled eyes, remembering the day in New York City only four years earlier when her husband had shown her a letter from the editor of a newspaper in Madrid offering him a daily column in their publication. Juan was elated. "Just think, Maria. Just think! The opportunity to get back home and be able to enrich and be enriched by a democracy Spain has never known before!" The dream of don Juan's utopia had been short lived. He and his sons now carried guns and were ready to kill or be killed. Fighting an almost paralyzing sadness, Maria walked to the end of the street. Without saying a word, she joined in the unloading of the sandbags from the truck.

A plump woman remarked, "That was fast work, Maria. Your group sure got these sandbags here in plenty of time. Let us hope that we don't have to use them." The group continued to work, talking and joking with each other in an obvious attempt to make light of the situation, but it was evident that they were fearful and worried. After the truck was emptied and all the sandbags were neatly stacked, ready to become barricades, the women hugged each other and took their separate ways home.

Maria did not want to go home just yet. She walked from one street to another, overwhelmed by what she was seeing. The streets had once been filled with vendors and women arguing prices and children playing games, but were now almost empty. Neighborhood cafés at this time usually were filled with older men playing dominos. Now they were closed. She greeted the few people who passed her in the street, but they did not respond or acknowledge her presence in any way. She continued her walk toward the center of the city, looking for a friendly face on the way, but there were none. In just two days, Madrid and its people had changed.

The early afternoon was getting hotter. Maria's face started to sweat. Feeling immense thirst, she walked through the cobblestone streets and looked for a public fountain. She soon found one at the end of the street in the shape of a large sculptured iron lion's head that stuck out of a concrete wall. The lion's open mouth sprouted water to drink that could be pumped by hand. Maria drank the water she pumped, granting her great relief from her thirst. With her energy renewed, Maria thanked the Moors for introducing this form of channeling water from the mountains.

Strange, she thought. *First the Moors enrich the peninsula with five hundred years of fresh water, art, music, architecture, irrigation—and now they are allowing themselves to be used by Franco to kill us. Juan would call this comic irony.* As she continued to walk, the streets and the almost empty sidewalks gradually opened into wider, more populated streets, and Maria walked next to groups of young women and men singing "The Internationale" as they neared the historic Plaza Mayor. This was Madrid's largest square, built in 1619. It was a historic area that had witnessed many bullfights, many fiestas, and some coronations. It was the place used by the Inquisition for public executions and torture. The majestic statue of King Philip III on horseback had towered over the middle of the square since 1790 and was now being stoned, pushed, and defaced by a group of young men as people seated by the sidewalk cafés all around the square cheered them on.

Maria sat in an empty corner of one of the sidewalk cafés, happy to be among people bustling with life and activity, but she was sad as she watched the statue being destroyed because of misdirected hatred. The statue of Philip III was a work of classic Spanish art. Why give it political symbolism? The open shops and cafés around the square helped lift some of the heavy feelings Maria had felt walking through the almost deserted streets earlier that morning. Watching the people around her eat made her a little hungry, so she ordered the curled, sometimes twisted pastries called churros and a steaming cup of thick hot chocolate.

All around her, other customers talked and laughed as they dipped their churros into hot beverages, acting as if the world outside the Plaza Mayor did not exist. Others stood in the balconies of the three-story buildings that encircled the square and watched as members of the militia in blue coveralls marched with military precision toward trucks waiting to transport them to bordering townships to set up barbed wire fences and barricades. Maria finished eating and slowly walked toward one of the exits from the Plaza Mayor on her way back home. She was almost smiling, thinking about the combination of Spanish traditional temperaments that she had witnessed in the Plaza Mayor on this day, a people preparing for war, but first taking time to socialize and indulge themselves with churros dipped into hot chocolate. Spaniards had always been this way; they had suffered through invasions, persecutions, tortures, cruel monarchies, and murderous dictatorships, yet they always continued to eat the nationally loved jamon serrano and dunked churros into hot chocolate as they clapped their hands to the tunes from wailing gypsy guitars before they were killed.

It was already late afternoon, and the sound of stray bullets was becoming more frequent. On her way through the same streets she had traveled that morning, Maria was surprised to find them beginning to get busy with people gathering, young and old, walking toward major avenues, where groups listened to various speeches. Others gathered to sing songs about Spain and their pride in being Spaniards. Maria looked at the crowds and wondered whether those following Fascist ideals at the other side of Madrid were also singing songs about their pride in being from Spain. Yes, she was sure they also felt that their way of thinking was the best for the motherland.

She got home as the darkness of the night was beginning to slide through the windows of the apartment, but there were no lights lit. Her husband and sons were in a darkened dining room, talking and gesturing, unaware of the darkness around them. Maria walked into the dining area and lit the single lightbulb that hung over the table as she greeted her husband and sons.

"It's getting dark," she said. "I am glad to see you are all on one piece. How was the day? Are we really going to have a war?"

Don Juan stood and stretched. "I am afraid so, Maria. A bad war. We spent most of the day digging trenches by Casa de Campo. The good news is that we are pretty much ready for an attack. I don't think that Franco will be able to enter Madrid."

Maria began closing the balcony's blinds and asked, "What is all that shooting about?"

Alfonso looked at his mother as his facial muscles tightened. "There are fanatics out there killing each other, as well as armed groups raiding churches and killing anyone that even smells like a Fascist. There's a lot of cruelty and disorder right now, but we will soon settle into that which is important: winning the war and restoring peace to Spain."

As she walked toward the kitchen, Maria asked the men whether they were hungry.

Alfonso said, "Oh, yeah. We have had nothing to eat since we finished the sandwiches at noon."

Pilar was already in the kitchen, preparing a salad and a Spanish egg, potato, and onion omelet with chorizo *sausage*.

Maria asked about her granddaughter. "How is Mari? Did you give her something to eat?

Pilar replied, "She's alright, Mother. I gave her a sandwich and some milk a couple of hours ago. She is in one of those 'I am not here moments and spent most of the day staring into space or covers."

Maria went to the back bed room and found her granddaughter under the bed, curled up as if still in her mother's womb, covered with the smell and wetness of urine. The child kept her eyes closed as her grandmother silently washed her and changed her soiled clothing, after which she was held in her grandmother's arms.

"What a bad day this was," whispered Maria, adding, "I am so sorry that you were alone all of this time. It must have been scary listening to all those noises. Why didn't you go to the kitchen and stay with Pilar when you woke up?"

Mari's voice trailed as she answered her grandmother without looking up. "At first, I could not sleep, Abuela, and Pilar can't hear anything, so she thinks that I make things up. She has been mad at me since I broke her eyeglasses, and the voices from the radio were yelling at me, and I wet myself, and I was afraid that Pilar would find out." Mari did not tell her grandmother how at first she had been so afraid that she could not move until the lady with the dark curly hair and large brown eyes held her in her arms until she fell asleep.

Maria sat her grandchild on the edge of the bed and helped her put on her socks and rope-soled alpargatas before they walked together to the dining room.

They were all there—Mari's father, her grandfather, and her uncles. Mari looked at them, all covered with dust and grease, seated at the dining table. She was surprised that her grandmother did not make them clean up. It was unfair that she had to wash even a small dot on her face, yet they were allowed to sit at the table to eat with smelly, greasy hands and faces. Aunt Pilar would surely get at them, but Pilar came and left the room without saying a word. Things were really not right, and Mari again felt uncomfortable and afraid. She waited for her father to ask her what she did all day so that she could tell him how scared she had been, but he was busy listening to his father talking and pounding on the table with a clenched fist, holding a fork and complaining that the omelet was made with onions.

There had been guitar music and singing coming from the streets, as well as the music from radios that still played from every apartment. Suddenly, the radios stopped, and the streets became silent. A dry and powerful female voice dramatically thundered from the radios and from loudspeakers installed in small trucks that traveled through the streets.

"Shh," said don Juan. "It's La Pasionaria!"

It was Dolores Ibárruri, the strong leader of the Communist Party from the Basque regions of northern Spain, where women had until now supported their families selling sardines from huge baskets carried on top of their heads. She was don Juan's idol. Her voice was strong as she spoke via radio across the barricades, barbed wire fences, and trenches around the city. It was her first speech urging violence, asking resistance until death. It was a mother's angry lullaby to thousands of her children who were about to die.

"You must fight and resist. Women of Spain, you too must join in the fight with knives and burning oil if necessary—for it is better *to die standing up than to live kneeing down!*"

"¡*No pasarán!*" (They shall not pass!) became the cry of the Spanish people through the next three terrible years.

The following day, the Ministry of War began organizing military operations against the rebels in all provinces of Spain. All bullfights were canceled throughout Spain.

[Chapter 1: Language and imagery beautiful, very clear and evocative.

There is a preliminary part, from the author's point of view (POV), which is journalistic writing. Then, we enter little Mari's POV. This starts bringing the story to life, but makes the previous part unnecessary. Seeing it all through Mari's eyes gives us the same information in a much better way.]

2

Madrid quickly became a bloody nightmare following the first days of popular enthusiasm and patriotic fervor. The battlegrounds changed from minute to minute as thousands of young men and women dressed in blue coveralls pushed Franco's troops away from the city. The streets were barricaded. The jokes, the laughter faded from people's faces. Each neighborhood had its own pile of sandbags and stones that protected the streets from possible attacks coming from other streets. The army in overalls, with the help of the Guardia de Asalto—a corps of men and officers founded after the riots in 1931 and who were especially loyal to the defense of the Republic—stubbornly pushed the Fascist attacks away from the city as women, young and old, and their children guarded the streets and continued to build barricades. Militia groups formed and roamed the city, looking for the bourgeoisie or any suspected right-wing citizen. A fever of assassinations and destruction possessed people. Churches were set on fire. Ad hoc courts were quickly set up, and rebels were quickly tried and immediately executed. Sometimes, the executioners mistakenly placed their own comrades in front of the firing squads.

Equally in nationalist Spain, people were arrested, tortured, and shot at the least suspicion that they might have been Republican sympathizers. Spain divided and subdivided itself over and over again, becoming a growling, wounded organism infected with a malignancy, a sick organism that had lost the ability to prevent or reverse its own destruction. A people who had strongly and sometimes fanatically lived by Judeo-Christian traditions now reversed their sacred ancient practices by taking each other's lives.

Affected by the monumental and sometimes unpredictable events that threatened their daily existence, Mari's family became more focused on daily survival and less on how their survival efforts were affecting the child. Barely noticeable at first, Mari learned to find comfort in her own daily experiences without associating the experiences with any one person; she learned to live in a world nurtured by her own fantasies and imagination, a world from which her family was excluded. The sight of her father leaving the apartment in his blue coveralls, wearing the funny pointed hat with the tassel in the front and carrying a gun, was no longer an issue for which Mari manifested emotion, even though he sometimes did not return home for days. However, emotions are only the visible aspects of feelings, and Mari learned to watch her father leave the apartment without running after him, submerging her inner feelings in an abyss of silent fear and desolation. She had learned instinctively to exchange the childhood need for comfort and dependency for a life of emotional muteness, keeping her feelings a secret trust within herself, a trust that she shared at night with the woman of long ago that she secretly called "Mommy". [This is outside view. By telling me about what was happening, and Mari's reactions, you are distancing the reader from those events. It would be far more powerful to make me BE her, as you've done earlier. Necessary information is better through conversations she overhears rather than an author lecture.]

Playing with newly gathered toys—which consisted of bullets stored in the apartment, together with extra rifles—distracted Mari from the long daytime hours spent alone in the apartment with Aunt Pilar. Every day, Mari would line up the bullets and set them out in opposite lines by the color of the tips and imagine herself a great general directing the bullets into battle against each other.

Mari's grandfather turned on the radio early in the morning while preparing himself for his daily trip to meet troops entering Madrid and arranging their point of destination into areas where they were most needed. He always forgot to turn off the radio before leaving the apartment, so it continued to play long after he left, forcing Mari to spend endless hours listening to the sound of bullets coming from the street and the voice of La Pasionaria directing the people of Spain to choose death and honor rather than to surrender.

One day, Mari's daily routine was interrupted shortly after she had finished taking a nap when the war games with bullets were ended by the loud noise of sirens piercing the buildings, alerting the civilian population to the arrival of German Junker planes. Mari's grandmother screamed, abruptly lifting and carrying Mari out of the apartment into the hallway and at the same time pushing a totally unaware daughter, Pilar, who could not hear or understand what was happening, in front of her. The stairs became obstructed with shouting women and crying children, everyone running down the steps toward the shelters built underneath the apartments.

Desperate people were pushing, falling, and holding on to their own, somehow reaching the long, dark tunnels. The children whimpered as the mothers leaned against the mud walls and listened to the rush of bombs, which sounded like whistles, cutting through the air before crashing and exploding against targets loudly and systematically. Mari sat motionless on the wet floor as she watched the women and children in slow motion waiting for something to happen.

Women held children on their laps, children held other children, women covered children's ears to muffle the sound of the explosions, and children cried. The air was filled with a humanity of whispering, as if this humanity was afraid that the bombs would trace the sound of their voices. A constant humming crowded inside the damp, long tunnels as the city's buildings crumbled outside. Mothers and children huddled together, avoiding physical contact and eye contact with other mothers and other children in the shelter. Gradually, a vacant stare appeared in everyone's eyes, and the space between families widened. Elders, whose partners were long deceased, sat next to their families, and older couples sat apart from everyone, the grandfathers silent, the grandmothers holding rosaries between their fingers and whispering, "Mary, Holy Mother of Jesus, protect us." [This is much better. It's far more powerful to present information through a character's perceptions than to be told about them.]

The continuous fall of unstoppable bombs continued, and the acrid smell of danger penetrated every living cell in the shelter, arousing the primitive need for survival and creating a momentary suspension of time, allowing evolution to stop. [It'd be better to use age-appropriate words and concepts. How would a 6 year old express this?] Outside the shelters, men hunted, fighting alone and dying alone. Inside the shelters, women fiercely held on to their broods with the primordial endowment to know that in times of danger, all beings are predators.

Maria sat next to her granddaughter and held her hand, as Pilar stood with her back against the wall, hands and feet feeling the vibrations created by the airplanes and the flying missiles. After a time, Pilar whispered to her mother, "They are leaving." A few moments later, the sirens wailed the all- clear signal, and humming humanity, now laughing and suddenly acknowledging each other, returned to their homes, only to repeat the same experience the next day and the day after.

Only a few months before, the people of Spain had been totally unaware of the events to come: the misery, the destruction, and the deaths created by a social intelligence not far from that of the apes. A few months earlier, shortly before the war and the bombings began, the same women and children in the shelter, together with other men and women of all ages, had marched unafraid past the statue of Velasquez in the Paseo del Prado, cheering, laughing, and carrying banners in celebration of May Day, the day of the workers. These had been the same women in the shelter, the same determined women who only a short time after the march in the Paseo del Prado had taken turns carrying sandbags and stones to build street barricades, the same women who had held their infant children against their breasts with one hand and a bucket of sand or a rifle in the other hand.

They were the mothers and the grandmothers of the anti-Fascist militia, young women who had paraded with pride wearing the scarlet shirts of the Communist Party or the blue shirts of the Socialist Party in the May Day parade, not knowing that soon they would die wearing the blue coveralls of the Popular Front. These young women would die for the freedoms and recognition they had never known, things they would never have before being buried in mass graves.

Ignorant of the oncoming events created by selfish and corrupt world politics waiting to destroy their lives, Spaniards of all ages had gathered in the streets of Madrid to celebrate May Day with parades and enthusiastic marching bands and the singing of thousands of voices cheering for a "new free Spain." It had been a wonderful parade on that crisp but pleasant first day of May in Madrid. Mari thought that it was a parade to celebrate her birthday and not the terrible preamble to the day when she found herself alone in a room while radios blared and bullets whistled past her window. It was her birthday, with hundreds of banners. Hundreds of people cheered, saluting her with clenched fists and bent arms. Small children, four to seven years old, passed in front of Mari, the anti-Fascist pioneers, most of them trying to keep cadence but hardly able to keep up with the pace, singing marching songs and from time to time saluting with their bent arms and clenched fists.

Mari cheered and tried to join them, but her grandfather gripped her hand and pulled her back. She frowned, but she soon laughed when the tiny pioneers passed and one of them stumbled and fell. Mandolins played "The Internationale," and Mari hummed and moved to the tune. Her grandfather bought her custard from a street vendor. She stopped humming to savor the rare treat. It was a good day, one filled with music and excitement for Mari. It was a good day for the people of Spain, filled with patriotic fervor as they chanted their hopes for the future. *"No land without crops! No farmers without food!"* [Why is this in italics?]

The parade went on most of the day and ended in the late afternoon. After the parade, the family walked to Casa de Campo, part of the old royal palace, now a public area for the picnic-loving people of Madrid. Mari's grandmother prepared sandwiches from a basket she had carried with her all through the parade. There was ham, sausages, fruit, wine, delicious crusty bread with thick slices, and onions, garlic, and thinly sliced potatoes slowly fried in generous amounts of Spanish olive oil and bathed in beaten eggs to make the traditional Spanish omelet. Maria spread the white tablecloth on the grass and began preparing the food while cautioning her husband, "Juan, you may want to skip the omelet. It has onions."

"*Cojones*, woman. You know I hate onions!" the grandfather grumbled.

"There are other things to eat. It's the kid's birthday. Don't start one of your tantrums."

Mari closed her eyes and waited. Onions were always what started the loud fighting between her grandparents with the throwing of the food on the floor by the grandfather, but when she opened her eyes, don Juan was quietly eating a piece of the omelet.

"I eat this," he said to his granddaughter, sounding very much like Christ talking to his disciples, "in honor of your birthday. I want you to remember that on your sixth birthday, your grandfather ate onions, and the republic of Spain had a new beginning." [Oh, I like this man! ☺]

It was a good day, with cool, bright skies. Families everywhere sat on the grass, ate, and rested, bathing in the simplicity of each other's company. From a short distance away, the sound of a guitar wrapped itself around lively conversations. The family passed a *bota*—a leather wine bag— around, lifting it, pointing the black opening high above their mouths, and squeezing a thin stream of red wine directly into their throats without the lips ever touching the tip of the bag.

Mari drank from a small glass *porrón*, similar to the leather bota, which was filled with a mixture of water and a little wine. She too lifted the porrón above her mouth, and thirsty from the long hours of standing and watching the parade, she eagerly let a stream of the liquid travel down her throat without touching the glass tip. She felt happy. Three of her uncles were there, along with her deaf aunt and her grandparents. Missing was the redheaded lively Aunt Cristina, who had married a house painter and moved to Alicante. Street vendors everywhere sold custards and roasted chestnuts.

Her father arrived late and told his daughter, "Happy birthday, *niña*!" The leather wine bag got passed around once more.

"¡Salud!" Mari said to her father as she drank from her porrón as the wine and water mixture slopped down her chin.

Mari's grandfather looked at his wife sadly. He told her, "I wish Hortensia and Fernando could see this. A new Spain. They would never believe it!" He was referring to his oldest daughter, married to an immigrant farmer who owned his own home and land in California, and his second son, who ran a meat business in New York City. Both children chose to remain in America when the family returned to the Iberian Peninsula.

Yes, it had been a happy birthday; a birthday Mari did not remember some months later as she stood in the same place, looking at the dead bodies of men strung on the barbed wire fences built to protect the city.

The air raids continued every afternoon and soon extended to any time during the night as incendiary bombs lit the city, making the targets easier to find in the dark. It was three o'clock in the morning when the wailing sirens woke up the family. Don Juan shouted, "Let's go! Let's go!"

The family gathered, cold and sleepy, but the youngest of Mari's uncles, Chato, was missing.

"Where is Chato?" Maria shouted. She ran to the bedroom and shook her son, who was still asleep under heavy blankets. "Chato, get up!" she shouted. "The planes are here!"

"Ah, Mother. Leave me alone! If I am going to be killed by bombs, I'd rather die comfortably in my bed!"

The grandfather growled, "Let him be! If we waste any more time, we will all be killed. Let's go! Let's go."

Mari's father carried Mari to the shelter and placed her on the ground, wrapped in a wool blanket.

With or without her father, Mari was used to the nightly routine and was half-asleep and half-awake when a little girl next to her asked, "Can we share your blanket? We are cold." Two identical girls stood beside Mari. They were about Mari's age and dressed in clean but worn skirts and sweaters with torn sleeves. They had no shoes, and their toes stuck out from holes in their socks. The girls looked at Mari, shivering, obviously dressed under the frenzy of the air raid warning, not prepared for the cold, damp shelter. "We are the Justin twins. We just moved into the apartment under yours. Can we share your blanket?"

Mari extended the blanket toward the twins, and the three children bundled together until the all-clear signal. The next day, the twins knocked on Mari's door and asked the grandmother whether Mari could go out and play with them.

One told Mari, "I am Conchita."

The other said, "I am Rosa Maria."

From that day on, Mari replaced her solitary war games with the bullets for the company of the twins. Eventually, a four-year-old, the twins' cousin, Manolito, joined them. Because Manolito was smaller than the girls, he usually followed behind the group, skipping as fast as his short legs allowed, a dark, timid little boy always dressed in short pants that showed his knees, skinned from frequent falls. The heavy cut-up tires made into shoes wrapped around his feet further impaired his ability to maintain balance when attempting to run, and each day added another scratch to his knees and legs. Because he was small, because his nose was always running, because he was clumsy, but mainly because he was a boy, Manolito held the lowest rank in this army of four and was constantly kidded by the girls, given orders, and made to follow after them as they roamed the streets pretending to be soldiers defending their apartment building.

The words of La Pasionaria were a constant echo in Mari's head. *Fight. Resist. Fight. Resist.* She commissioned the small group of playmates into an army of three, giving herself the title of general, and marched the small group up and down streets and into alleys as she bellowed commands that she had learned from her father and her uncles. During these trips, the small troop sometimes came upon the putrid remains of a dead dog or a skinned cat that had been used for food. Sometimes they encountered the remains of human parts left behind following the firing of artillery shells upon the civilian population by the German Condor Legion.

Manolito, who ran home shaken, always met these findings with panic and tears, leaving the twins behind and huddled together, waiting for orders from their leader. At these times, Mari would cross her arms, stand straight, look at the girls, and slowly unfold her arms, pointing at the remains. She would clip her words as she uttered blasphemies reminiscent of her father's language and mannerisms. "Fuck! Look at that poor bastard! Some poor son of a bitch left his fingers behind." She did not know the meaning of some of the words she used, but they seemed powerful when used at the appropriate time to give her troops courage. This tactic seemed to work. The twins always snapped back from their trances and regained courage after each of these flagrant discourses. It seemed as if the greater the blasphemy, the greater the courage and the greater the power of their leader.

The days passed. The neighborhood residents became accustomed to and amused by the seriousness and marching precision of the group as they circled the neighborhood looking for "Moors." One morning, while roaming in and out of bombed buildings looking for the enemy, the troops uncovered the remains of old chipped and rusted porcelain enema can that still had the rubber tube attached. They all looked at it, but only Mari seemed to know of its uses, which she gladly demonstrated by filling the can with water and ordering Manolito to lower his pants.

The little boy looked at her with apprehension, his lower lip quivering. "It's cold! I don't wanna—"

"Lower your pants, soldier. It's an order!"

They were behind the steps of their apartment building, unseen by the pedestrians who walked in the street. A timid and scared Manolito lowered his pants as the fearless leader inserted the tube between his legs with great pomp to assure her followers that she knew what to do.

The water from the enema can drenched Manolito's clothing, his pants, his socks, and his feet. As the tube snapped upward, it drenched his coat and face. The little boy ran home screaming and taking off his pants as he stumbled up the steps to his apartment. The twins found all of this very amusing, so they covered their mouths to stop the giggles. Mari, whose clothing had also been drenched as the tube from the enema can snapped backward, stood silent with a slight smile to hide her confusion. Her grandmother had given her an enema once when she got sick, but she did not remember the tube snapping—or getting wet.

It was not very long before Manolito's mother came out of the apartment, loudly engaging the powers of the Blessed Virgin and her son, Jesus, against the girls. She gathered the twins' mother and Mari's grandmother in the hallway. Amid much yelling and waving of the hands, Manolito's mother demanded that the girls be punished.

The enema can was immediately confiscated, and promising her grandchild eternal damnation in the hot coals of hell, Mari's grandmother dragged her up the stairs, waving the empty enema can in the air for all to see. More painful for Mari than the prospect of burning in the hot coals of hell was having to confess the day's activities to her father in front of the rest of the family. She heard them laughing after she went to sleep and felt deep shame and humiliation at the thought of facing her followers in the morning. She knew that this incident would surely damage and lessen her social standing, as well as her authority over the army of three. Feeling anger and defiance, she made up her mind to win back the respect of her troops by doing something daring and heroic for her country.

Mari stayed in hiding. She did not leave the apartment for the next three days. Although she longed for and missed the company of the twins and Manolito, she was too embarrassed by the enema events to face her troops. She ruminated on the incident in her head over and over again. She paced back and forth, clasping her hands behind her back, emulating the strides of a person trying to resolve great and serious problems. After a time, she finally created a conspiracy story to explain and give the enema can secret meanings that would mend her shattered image. She stood in front of the mirror and glanced at her reflection as she practiced a speech. "There was a secret message inside the enema rubber tube, a message from La Pasionaria. There was a message inside the rubber tube, a message from La Pasionaria. There was a message."

"A message?" asked the twins.

"A message?" mumbled Manolito. "What kind of a message?"

"It's a secret."

"What kind of a secret?"

"Never mind, dumb ass! A secret means that I can't tell you; that's why it's a secret. Just follow me."

The troops followed as Mari walked up and down the street, mysteriously peeping into doorways and corners.

"What are you doing?"

"I am looking for a new message."

"A message in an enema can?"

Mari felt chagrin at the mention of the enema can by the twins but quickly recovered and continued her air of authority and importance. "No, stupid, just a message." She kept walking and looking around doors and under stairs and lifting rocks, debris, rubble, and any remains of bomb- shattered buildings, when suddenly, she let out a loud "Aha!" followed by "Mary, Jesus, and the Holy Spirit, here it is!" It was always good to evoke the name of the Holy Family in vain. It gave a person a certain aura of valor, but Manolito wasn't sure.

"You gonna go to hell, Mari," he whispered.

Mari paid no attention. She knew that the priests and nuns had made up the story of Jesus and His Mother to scare the workers of Spain to part with their hard-earned money. Her grandfather said so. She picked up a small piece of newspaper stuck unnoticed in the inside corner door of what had once been the neighborhood bakery shop. Torn by bombs, the rear ovens where the daily bread had once been baked now stood open and empty, gaping at the children like dark, hungry mouths. "Here it is!"

"What is?"

"A secret message from La Pasionaria."

The small army of three listened to their leader with the bright eyes and open mouths of young sparrows to be fed.

"What does it say?"

Mari could not read. The war had aborted any system of education for the young. She held the piece of newspaper in her hand, pretending to be reading the directives from La Pasionaria that she had memorized from listening to Madrid Radio: "'Women of Spain, fight and resist!' We must go to the front to fight the Fascists. La Pasionaria said so."

"But…but…" mumbled the twins.

"Are we women of Spain?"

"Of course we are!"

Manolito said nothing, embarrassed to be a little boy, not a woman of Spain.

Mari turned toward him and said that they would let him go with them as a matter of honor to the men of Spain.

He looked down at his feet and kicked the sand. His bottom lip quivered.

Mari crossed her arms and stood in front of him. "You can stay behind, if you are afraid to go."

The little boy did not look up; his eyes filled with tears, and his nose ran. He muttered, "My mama told me not to go too far from the house."

"*Bueno*," replied the leader with cold, clipped words. "Stay behind. We don't need any cowards in this war!" She walked away. The twins followed. Soon they noticed that Manolito was behind at a short distance, his unstable little body struggling to keep up with them.

He cried out, "Wait! I am coming with you."

On that day, the rebel army had launched a bloody attack against Madrid, and as thousands of men marched to defend the city, women and children could be seen everywhere building trenches and barricades. The rebel army, composed mostly of Moroccans and legionaries, was quickly opposed in a desperate struggle by the urban population. Men fell, and reinforcements did not arrive. Not to retreat or give the enemy one more inch into Madrid was the popular cry of "¡No pasarán!" This could be heard everywhere as the last words of those who were killed and by those who took their places in the trenches.

It was a cold day in November, and the poorly dressed Republicans huddled together against a far superior army supported by Italian and German aircraft and tanks. Inside the city, the voice of La Pasionaria was constantly heard from loudspeakers, urging all women to fight, to pour boiling oil on the enemy, if necessary, to defend their homes. Men young and old abandoned their jobs and, without arms with which to fight, went to the battlefields, picking up the rifles of those who had been killed and taking their places in the trenches.

The bombing of homes with incendiary explosives had created a desperate mood among the masses to defend Madrid until death. In all this chaos and bloodshed, four children walking the streets were of little consequence and went unnoticed. Mari and her little troop reached Calle de la Princesa by noon. The battle trenches were at the other side of the park. Stumbling and falling, Manolito had further skinned his knees and legs. He was limping and sobbing. The sound of gunfire was overwhelmingly loud. The air was heavy with the metallic taste of gunpowder in the children's mouth.

The twins also cried. Holding hands, they refused to go any farther. They had reached the edge of Casa de Campo.

Mari stood electrified at the sight of dead soldiers and at other soldiers still alive in torn coveralls drenched with blood, some missing hands and legs, their body parts hanging from barbed wire fences, skin torched black from explosives. She looked at Manolito for support.

He had wet his pants and was standing as if frozen, rigidly looking into space in a trance.

The twins embraced each other, hiding their faces on each other's shoulders.

Mari's ears began a clicking sound inside her head, while at the same time, a silent stillness engulfed around her. Nothing moved. She heard a cry, a secret voice coming from inside her throat. "Mommy!"

The shell exploded right in front of the children. The force of the explosion threw the twins up in the air. They landed, unconscious, against the trunk of a tree. Mari's right leg hung bleeding, pieces of shrapnel having torn into her knee. She looked up as Manolito's severed head rolled past her and crashed against the barbed wire fence, his eyes filled with tears, his nose still running. Mari's pain was unbearable. It ran up from her knee to her right thigh and hip. Blood flowed from her knee wound, from her mouth, and from her nose. The trees whirled as a dark shadow settled over her eyelids, and a woman with dark hair, olive skin, and large brown eyes held her in her arms.

It was dark when Mari opened her eyes, and the woman with the dark hair, olive skin, and large brown eyes was gone. Floating high above the ground, she could see her own body strung over the left shoulder of a man who wore coveralls, a funny pointed hat with a tassel in the front, his right hand holding a burlap bag from which Manolito's blood-soaked hair stuck out. [This is very well written. I was THERE.]

Manolito's body was never found, just his head. The twins never regained consciousness. Next to the dead twins behind the Republican barricades, Mari lay, covered with dust and metal fragments. She held Manolito's head in her arms amid dead soldiers awaiting mass burial. There was no time, there was no space, and there were too many to individually bury the mutilated dead bodies of Spain's youth. Their comrades gathered their remains in a hurry. Crouching to avoid enemy fire, they dragged the bodies into a large pit.

Mari was discovered by a young Andalusian soldier, a native of Seville who was barely seventeen years old and had been visiting relatives in Madrid to attend his cousin Marcelo's wedding when the war began. It had been Marcelo who convinced him to stay in Madrid and join the Republican Army, which he did, unaware that his father and brothers in Seville had joined the rebels and would eventually fight against him across the trenches. Tired and dirty from a whole day of breathing gunfire and smoke, the young soldier had taken a cigarette break and sat on the ground near the open grave, trying not to look at the faces of bodies lying inert against each other at the bottom of the pit. Some of those faces belonged to his friends, and one of those faces was the face of Cousin Marcelo, for whose wedding this young man had come to Madrid.

He was tired. Tears were clouding his eyes. The ground was humid and uncomfortable. Taking a deep breath, the young soldier lit a cigarette and exhaled the smoke as he rested his head on his arms and knees. He covered his face and allowed the tears from his eyes to slide onto the ground. In his attempt to block the sounds of guns, the soldier also became unaware and inattentive to the sounds around him, but gradually, as his own muffled cries died down to silent, deep sobs, he imagined that the wind was whispering. He looked up, but there was no wind. The sound persisted, shaping itself into human sobs and moans.

He looked down into the opening where the bodies had been placed, and to his horror, his eyes merged directly into the face of a very small girl who was holding in her arms the head of a small child with eyes wide open and a runny nose. The soldier stood up, unaware of the searing pain on his lower lip from a still-burning cigarette that he was clenching between his teeth as the contents of his stomach surged from his nose and mouth as he tried to yell for assistance. "Oh, dear God! Oh, God, dear God, there is a child here —alive and holding a head. Dear God, she is holding a head, just a head! Oh, dear God—"

Others arrived as the soldier leaned on his rifle, weakened by stomach spasms and nausea. Two soldiers climbed into the pit. Trying not to step on the dead bodies, one soldier lifted the child into his arms as his comrade struggled to take the head from the girl's arms.

"She won't let go!"

"Never mind, son of a bitch! Just let Raul get her up here!" yelled his sergeant.

"With the head?"

"You fucking dumb Gallego. Yes! With the head!"

The two soldiers climbed out of the grave with the child as a group of their comrades looked at them with wide, unbelieving eyes.

"Who puts children in the grave?"

"Fuck, man. Who looks at anything when the bullets are flying past your head?"

Two other soldiers climbed into the pit and began looking among the dead for the body of the decapitated head in the girl's arms.

"Hey, Sergeant, there are two dead girls here. They both have heads. No bodies without a head."

"Shit! This war is nothing but shit."

Mari opened her eyes in a wide stare past the man who was holding her as another took the head from her arms.

"Can you hear me, niña? Can you tell me your name?"

"Mommy," whispered Mari.

"Sergeant, her name is Mommy."

"I don't think so, Pablo. *Mommy* is the word for *mamá* in English. I learned that from an English girlfriend I had before the war when I was stationed in Morocco."

"The kid is English? I thought that all foreigners had left Spain when the war started."

"Maybe not. Let me talk to headquarters. Maybe somebody knows something. A foreign family in Madrid at this time should not be hard to find."

The child's knee was torn apart, bone and flesh shredded together. Her eyes were wide open. Her lips were moving, and she was whispering inaudible words.

The young soldier carried her back behind the barbed wire fences, away from the gunfire, to a truck that carried the wounded back to the field hospitals in the city.

Mari was transported home by ambulance in a stretcher, wet and dirty from the loss of bladder control and covered with green stains from the regurgitated gastric contents in her stomach.

Surprised and devastated, her grandmother took the child from the arms of the medic and gently laid the limp body on a bed. Maria looked at her grandchild with disbelief and could not quite understand how this horrendous act of violence could have happened. True, Maria had not been home for two days, as she had been taking food and water to the women and children building sand barricades in the streets, and in the anxiety and confusion created by the Fascist attack, she had assumed and trusted that the child was safe at home with Pilar. Pilar was the only one left at home that day; her husband had been gone for a week to direct the arrival of troops in Madrid, and her sons went back and forth from the front lines and rarely came home, but she had not worried about the child, because Pilar was home to take care of her.

After two days working in the streets and taking naps in trucks that delivered sand, Maria was tired and hungry and headed home to rest. She arrived at the apartment in the early evening, just in time to greet the two men from the militia who were looking for her husband. It was from them that she learned what had happened to Manolito and the twins and the incredible news that her granddaughter had survived the shell explosion and was still alive.

After undressing her grandchild and washing away all traces of vomit and waste with a wet cloth and soapy water, Maria wrapped a blanket around the inert body and cleaned and dressed the injured knee; when she was finished and holding her granddaughter tightly against her chest, Maria de Avila—the warrior, the mother, grandmother, daughter, and wife— screamed into the darkness of the night.

No one heard her.

The only other person in the apartment was Pilar, and she was deaf. The echoes of Maria de Avila's wrath funneled upward into the heavens without disturbing the sleep of uncaring gods.

Outside Madrid, men and women continued to fight and die; men and women who in life had been joined together by blood and national origin were now strewn upon the ground in opposite battlefields, joined together by death. Brothers and sisters, fathers and sons, mothers and daughters, cousins and uncles, all buried in a common grave at the very edge of the city they had all loved but would never see again.

But Madrid did not surrender. The First International Brigade, made of brave and angry civilians from other countries, arrived and helped the battered Republican militia defend their city, a city whose casualties and wounded almost outnumbered the living.

It was a good day when the brigade marched through the streets of Madrid on its way to the Popular Front, cheered and blessed by a city that came alive as the people chanted, "¡No pasarán! ¡No pasarán! ¡No pasarán!"

Almost at the same time of the arrival of the International Brigade in Spain, Russia sent tanks and aircraft that were used to stop the Fascist attack on Madrid, but not before hundreds of men and women from both sides had died and not before the Fascist army crossed the Manzanares River. Madrid was left without the food supplies from the north and west of Spain, and a people who had always indulged themselves with robust, flavorful meals and good wine now learned to stand in long lines every day just to receive a handful of lentils from the storage bins in the municipal cellars. Yet these half-starved people were strong and stubborn. They cooked and ate the lentils boiled in water without oil, without any meat or condiments, and they flavored them with rancid old bones cooked over and over again. Weeds were used as vegetables, and when available, people used the flesh of cats that people jokingly called "rabbits" to disguise their repugnance.

Sometimes, and on very rare occasions, small amounts of flour and medical supplies trickled in from the east of Spain, carried in slow, old trains that managed to reach the city after multiple breakdowns and gunfire. This permitted the deprived population the luxury of a slice of real bread from time to time. Never had a people been submerged in such desperate resistance as they lived from hour to hour waiting for France and the United States to send food and help. But those countries never sent aid, and Madrid waited as the wounded lay on hard, cold floors inside overcrowded field hospitals and the militia went from house to house asking for mattresses and blankets.

Every day, people's legs and arms were amputated to control the gangrene in untreated wounds; every day, bodies were found dead and unnoticed by the overwhelmed and tired volunteer hospital aides. The stench of putrid flesh forced those attending the wounded to wear handkerchiefs tied around their noses to avoid the smells coming from the bodies for which they cared.

On every wall, on every fence, on every park bench, every day, new big, black slogans appeared: "*¡No pasarán*"

Mari had been in bed for almost three weeks, unable to walk because of the wound in her knee and unaware of anything around her because of the wounds in her mind.

Her grandmother bathed and fed her every day.

Pilar helped and recited stories that she had learned as a child, hoping to arouse some interest from her niece.

Alfonso held his daughter's hands every night until his eyes blurred, and he would fall asleep sitting on a chair next to the bed.

All through this time, the bombing intensified, especially at night, when incendiary bombs set the city on fire, neighborhood by neighborhood. At these times, Mari's grandmother wrapped Mari in blankets and carried her to the underground shelters while the child was totally unaware of the sights and the sounds around her. At these times, Mari's mind was filled with the buzzing of whispers and the giggles from ghosts traveling through shadows in space, shadows from which Manolito's head danced, suspended in midair, his eyes never closing as tiny, sparkling tears slid down his chin.

The twins laughed and giggled, asking, "Are we dead yet? Are you dead, Mari?"

"We are dead," said Manolito. "Now is your turn, Mari. There was no secret message. You lied."

Mari said, "I am sorry, Manolito. I am sorry, Rosa Maria. I am sorry, Conchita."

Late one evening, Mari opened her eyes for the first time and looked around. She saw the walls, the dresser, and the window. It all felt familiar, as if she had gone back into the past. She heard voices coming from another room, voices she knew but that offered no sense of comfort. The dark- haired woman with the olive skin and sad eyes who had held her in her arms for a long time—days, maybe weeks—was now gone, and Mari wanted her back. Mari closed her eyes and silently mouthed the magic word, "Mommy," hoping that the woman would appear, but this time, the dark-haired woman with the olive skin and sad eyes was gone and did not return.

Mari twisted herself out of bed and limped toward the sound of the voices and recognized the voices of her grandmother and grandfather. Mari felt afraid and embarrassed because she had lied; there had been no message from La Pasionaria, and her lie had killed her friends. Her grandmother was right: she had bad blood. These feelings of guilt and humiliation made her afraid to face the family as she leaned against the hallway wall and held her breath.

Her grandfather was in the dining room, silently waiting for his wife and daughter to finish preparing their evening food. Tonight they were eating a salad made from weeds carefully selected by Maria from a rarely traveled empty lot across town, along with potato skins and sardines fried in lard. The bread was yellow, made from corn; the beverage was chicory, the closest drink to coffee.

Not too excited about dinner and the room getting dark, don Juan looked around and lit the one single solitary lightbulb that hung from the ceiling and sat watching the silvery reflections on the balconies. Madrid was quiet; only the sound of the women preparing food in the kitchen could be heard in the apartment. As Maria moved about, she whispered prayers under her breath, asking the Blessed Virgin to bring her sons home safely.

Don Juan heard the whispering and growled, "Woman, what are you saying? I can't hear you."

"Oh, nothing. I was just wondering when the boys will get home tonight. I know that what we have to eat is no reason for which to come home, but it is not safe out there tonight with the moon so bright."

It was impossible for Maria to admit to her husband that she had been praying, as her husband did not believe in a God, particularly a Catholic God. She didn't, either, but prayers were a soothing mantra in times of apprehension. The radio had been silent, preparing the city for the sound of sirens alerting its citizens to turn off all lights in preparation for possible air raids. Maria was not the only one who felt apprehensive; fear was everywhere as the full moon lit up the streets and made every building, every home, and every moving creature a visible target for incendiary bombs and machine guns.

Mari stood in the darkened hallway as her grandfather draped blankets over the balcony doors to block the light in preparation for the blasting sirens, after which he would turn off the ceiling bulb and light a candle, something hard to detect from an airplane in search of a target. Busy making these preparations, the grandfather was totally unaware that his granddaughter was watching him from behind the door.

In the kitchen, Aunt Pilar was removing her shoes to better feel the vibrations of oncoming airplanes through the soles of her feet when the front door opened, and Mari's father came into the apartment, followed by two of his brothers.

The men went straight into the kitchen, laughing and failing to notice Mari as Alfonso hugged his mother and placed a bottle of red wine on the table. Alfonso smiled and said, "Look, Mother. I got us a bottle of wine for dinner! I traded it for my boots. Not bad, uh?"

His mother said solemnly, "Not bad until we finish the wine, and you need to run across the bushes on your bare feet. Where is Chato?"

"It was his turn to stand guard tonight. He'll be home in the morning."

Maria's face relaxed. It was a strange war. Both sides of the trenches stopped the fire at night because of the darkness and resumed the fight at sunrise. During the full moon, it was hard to guess whether the fighting would stop, and Maria had worried that her sons might have been forced to stay in the trenches all night without rest or food, the light of the moon making them easy targets. But Alfonso, Fernando, and Max were home safe, and Chato was just standing guard, not dodging bullets.

The family gathered in the dining room and ate, unaware of the small figure flattened against the hallway wall, shaking and listening to the voices in her head.

"Are we dead yet?"

"I am sorry, Manolito. I am sorry, Rosa Maria. I am sorry, Conchita."

A noise of something falling made everyone sit up and run to the hallway, where Mari lay slumped against the wall, unconscious.

Mari's grandmother held Mari in her arms all night, and her father, Alfonso, dozed in a chair next to the bed until early morning; the sirens had been silent all through the night. Don Juan stayed awake all night. Only the clicking of his typewriter keys could be heard throughout the apartment as he typed words of hope, words of anger, and absurd recipes for a utopia in Spain and in the world. Opposed to the stubbornly rooted "Spain for the Spaniards" fervor of Iberian natives, he was trying to convince his countrymen to become open to change and support Spain's movement toward international involvement and world peace. But he was slowly losing hope. For each act of violence labeled "patriotism," thousands of common folk died without improving anyone else's life; only the powerful survived and prospered. Nations lusted after power, and to attain and maintain this power, they killed, tortured, and destroyed each other, using false gods and patriotism as an excuse. This son of Old Castile—the modern Marxist who had inherited the Semitic lust for knowledge and languages along with the Arabic love of beauty and the written word, the dreamer of days when workers would control their own destiny, this Iberian shepherd whose total energy had been directed to the survival of his family and of his country, the Celtic warrior who had fought to enlighten workers from one continent to another—was beginning to question the reality of his dreams.

Early in the morning, Mari opened her eyes, startled to find herself in her grandmother's arms. At first, Mari thought that her grandmother was the woman with the olive skin and the dark curly hair, but somehow it did not matter that she was not. Mari loved her grandmother and wished that she did not have the bad blood that sometimes angered her. Mari looked at her grandmother.

The grandmother looked back and held Mari tighter against her breast. Through the child's behavior and emotional fragility, the grandmother felt her own fears and emotional fragility. It was hard to be vulnerable; it set a feeling of uncomfortable weakness traveling through her body, and her eyes filled with tears as she remembered her own childhood in the isolated mountains of Old Castile, where she had been born and reared in a typical village where people followed strict, ancient Christian-Judeo laws of conduct—laws that dictated the power of fear to be greater than the power of love.

In Maria's village, children were serious and expected to be strong. They were taught that self-esteem was egotistical and that self-satisfaction was selfishness. The most fearful of all beliefs that Maria was taught was that love, a nondescript phrase, was something that God demanded from all his subjects in exchange for safety and survival from divine wrath. Maria's mother, the only person Maria had ever trusted and perhaps loved, had died from childbirth before Maria completed her first communion, after telling her, "Child, Jesus is calling me, and I must go. Don't be afraid, and don't be sad. You will be safe and have a good life if you listen to and follow the voice of God. He will protect you."

Maria believed her mother, and after her death, Maria made frequent visits to her grave, holding pictures of saints, angels, and religious symbols in her hands to help her hear the voice of God.

Maria listened for the voice of God each time she gave birth, each time one of her children died, each time she felt small and alone. But as the years passed, God never spoke to her.

Now, holding her grandchild's body against hers, Maria heard a strange voice—her voice but not her voice; a powerful, strong voice; a gentle, loving voice; a voice she had never heard before. This voice came surging from the depths of her heart. She stroked and kissed Mari's head, and the voice said, "I love you, my child. Please forgive me."

Maria had given birth to ten children of her own, having lost an infant son in France from pneumonia as the family was getting ready to embark on a ship to America as well as a six-year-old daughter who died in the desert of California. She now had eight living adult children, but the child she held in her arms was her only grandchild. She was a small six-year-old girl born to a fifteen-year-old child-woman her son had impregnated when the family was living in New York, the person at whom Maria had directed all her rancor and anger. It was her son Alfonso to whom she should have directed all criticisms, not Rosa, her grandchild's mother.

Maria remembered the day she had been told of the pregnancy. Rosa stood with her head lowered with tear-filled eyes and asked to stay in the apartment after having been thrown out of her parents' home. A sullen, frightened Rosa, who, aware that Maria did not speak English, struggled to communicate with her in Italian, which perhaps was a language closer to Spanish than English. It was the best Rosa could do.

Rosa looked so frail, the youngest daughter of Sicilian immigrants. Rosa had left school to help her parents by working in a factory. She was one of three children and had a sister who had entered a cloistered nunnery as well as a brother who was in a seminary with hopes of becoming a Catholic priest. None of her siblings had been able to contribute to their father's limited income. Rosa's father was a part-time street cleaner, and Rosa had spent her adolescence in a factory sewing sequins on to dresses.

Maria remembered reacting to the pregnancy with anger and unforgiving feelings toward the young mother. She was sad when she remembered how she tried to persuade Rosa that an abortion was the best solution to her problems. Maria remembered how she attempted to have the young mother abort by giving her large amounts of castor oil to drink, followed by hot baths, using herbs recommended by the women in her village with the hope of facilitating the expulsion of the fetus. When everything failed and Rosa's body began to show the presence of her unborn child, don Juan ordered Alfonso to marry her. Alfonso had always been his mother's pampered and a spoiled first child, but he had never failed to obey his father, so Alfonso married Rosa in spite of his mother's negative opinions. Rosa and Alfonso had a full wedding in a Catholic church in New York City, exchanging their vows of fidelity in the presence of both families, except Rosa's sister, the cloistered nun.

Now, a little over six years later, Maria held their child in her arms, while remembering her own past cruel and unforgiving attitudes and behavior toward Rosa, all because she was unlike their family in physical appearance and temperament. Rosa was a sullen young woman with dark-olive skin and hair with such tight, dark curls that it could almost be the hair of a Negro.

"The Abyssinian." That's what Maria had nicknamed Rosa. "The Abyssinian." How could she have been so unkind? Rosa was quiet and reserved, unlike the loud, self-expressive members of Maria's family. Maria had interpreted Rosa's personality as cold and lacking a sense of duty to her husband and to the family when she preferred spending most of her time with her child, avoiding socializing with others or helping with the household chores.

But now Maria questioned the motivation for all her continued superficial prejudices against his son's wife and realized that this prejudice may have been an attempt to avoid addressing more serious realities. Rosa became ill shortly after arriving in Spain with a then one-year-old daughter to join her husband, a husband who had abandoned a pregnant wife and his first child months earlier in New York. Rosa never complained, but after giving birth to a supposedly dead son, she became ill. Robbed of the strength necessary to exist in a strange country or to survive her husband's repeated infidelities, Rosa returned home to seek treatment for a then little-known anemia that could be fatal in young adults and for which no treatment was available in Spain. At first, Rosa had refused to leave without her child, choosing death in Spain if necessary, but Alfonso promised to join her with the baby as soon as money was available.

Maria's eyes filled with tears as she remembered how she had encouraged her son to stop all contacts with Rosa and how glad she was when Alfonso continued his involvement with another woman, making no efforts to join his wife in New York.

Mari grew up without a mother, and when she asked why she did not have a mamá like the other children, Maria told Mari that her mother was a "black Abyssinian somewhere in Africa." At times when Maria became angry, she accused the child of having bad blood like her Abyssinian mother.

All these thoughts now became intolerable to Maria, piercing her chest and making it hard for her to breathe. She placed the child in the bed, kneeled on the floor, and made the sign of the cross. "Dear Blessed

Virgin, if indeed you exist, please allow Rosa to be safe and forgiving of me." Thinking that her grandchild was sleeping, Maria kissed the child on the cheek and whispered, "I love you." Maria left the room sobbing.

Halfway down the hallway, Maria realized that Mari was following her. Maria turned back, took the child's hand, and went to the kitchen, where she found her husband resting his arms and head on the table next to a cup of cold, coffee-like chicory. He looked pale and tired, and instead of a three- piece suit and bow tie, he was dressed in wrinkled coveralls. Up all night, he had waited until his sons drove back to the front lines at dawn in the truck-ambulance Alfonso used to transport wounded soldiers to the hospitals in Madrid. Don Juan got up and removed the blankets from the balcony doors, allowing the pale rays of the morning to enter the dining room before going into the kitchen to wait for his wife.

He was feeling guilty and responsible for what had happened to his granddaughter and was deeply disturbed by Mari's emotional breakdown and knee injury; after thinking about it all night, he needed to discuss with Maria some plans that he was considering. The child was an innocent victim, and he had to make a decision, follow it with a plan, and implement a resolution. He just needed to convince his wife and Alfonso to agree with him.

Maria sat next to her husband, placing the child on her lap. She asked, "Where are the boys?"

Don Juan looked at her and raised his eyebrows. "They went back to the front before sunup. As far as I know, the war is still going on, even for your sons." His voice was tinted with sarcasm, but Maria did not take the bait; she was used to his lack of softness at times of sadness.

Their life had been filled with turbulence since they had gotten married. There were hard times but also exciting times, and don Juan had always responded to difficulties with sarcasm and distance. A long time ago, Maria had questioned his moods and wondered whether she could live with someone who was at times so distant, but she had really loved him since the day they met at a village dance. They later married and moved to Madrid, and it had been a peaceful life at first. She cooked for a wealthy family, and don Juan ran a printing shop, and there was sufficient money to maintain a comfortable apartment and a comfortable life. Things changed when the children arrived. Don Juan began his obsessive crossing of the Atlantic in search of utopia in the New World, first alone and then with the family. They never found utopia. America had been a nightmare for Maria, but her husband had been a good and faithful husband and father. He was a handsome, arrogant husband and father whose love and emotions he kept hidden and private in times of distress, but Maria learned his moods and felt safe with him.

They sat in silence for a few minutes until don Juan reached and transferred Mari to his lap and tried to smile. He asked his granddaughter, "Are you hungry?" He placed a piece of the yellow bread in front of her.

Maria got up and warmed the chicory, filling and placing a cup of the make-believe coffee next to the child.

Mari looked at her grandparents for a moment with a gaze resembling that of a wounded animal from inside a cage. Mari whispered, "Yes, I am hungry." She ate the bread after she soaked it in the chicory from time to time.

Don Juan cleared his throat and asked his wife to sit next to him. He was no longer trying to smile, and with his drawn, unshaved face and unkempt mustache, he almost looked like a tired Don Quixote after battling windmills.

"Maria," he began, "I have been thinking. You and I must make a decision with which I hope Alfonso will agree. Madrid is becoming a living nightmare, and this is becoming traumatic, especially for the children. I see no end to this war in time to avoid permanent damage to the innocent. It would be total emotional torture to keep Mari here for the rest of the war. The roads to your pueblo are still open. Do you think that we might be able to persuade Alfonso to take Mari to the pueblo and stay with your cousin Miaja and his family?"

Maria looked away into space without answering. It would be hard to let go of her granddaughter just when her granddaughter was beginning to make a difference in her life. She thought, *Oh, dear God. Not now.* She looked at her husband and agreed to join him and speak to Alfonso that night. [Wonderful chapter.]

Mari sat in the front seat and silently watched her father steer the old truck through the bumpy cobblestone streets of old Madrid, sometimes having to look for alternate routes because of the street barricades that obstructed the main arteries that led in and out of the city. The truck he was driving was an old model Ford with torn seats and dangerously bald tires that squeaked with each turn of the steering wheel. The broken front-seat springs bounced and rocked up and down and from side to side every time the truck made a turn. It was not a comfortable way to travel, but it was the only transportation Alfonso had been able to find after agreeing to take his daughter away from Madrid to the safety of his mother's village.

As the truck squeaked and bounced from one street to another, Alfonso had repeatedly attempted to break the silence between his daughter and himself by asking her to sing with him. When this failed, he told her jokes. When that also failed, he encouraged her to return the waves from the women standing on the sidewalks.

All of Alfonso's efforts to break his daughter's silence failed; Mari remained sullen and silent. She stared at the road ahead without looking at her father when he talked to her. Alfonso could not think of anything else to reach his daughter; he had seldom been alone with her and had never learned how to talk to her without the distraction of other people and other conversations. Actually, he had never been alone with her long enough to engage in a one-on-one conversation, not long enough to give her a chance to display the usual chatter of children her age.

These thoughts and his limited insight into her made him grumpy and uncomfortable, but the thought of not having his daughter's trust and confidence made him sad. He could not understand the child's aloofness, how she avoided physical contact with him, the way she failed to bring him into her confidence during the rare times when they had been alone. Mari always reached out to other members of the family for her physical and emotional needs, and this had given him the opportunity to avoid taking the responsibility for parenting a child who decided to be born against his wishes, a child he learned to ignore because she never seemed to need his attention—not even on this day, far away from home in a run-down, uncomfortable truck traveling on cold and dangerous roads.

Alfonso drove on. Busy with his thoughts and excuses, he took no time to feel, observe, or interpret the child's behavior at a time when she needed his love and attention the most. There were many things about his daughter that Alfonso did not know, but his lack of insight into his own and others' emotional needs made it impossible for him to understand his daughter's defensive behavior after her mother left. It was impossible for Alfonso to imagine the human brain's ability to supply safety zones for those needing support when feeling abandoned by others. [This is an author lecture. We're not in his point of view, but are analysing him from the outside. That's something to be avoided.]

Mari's brain had opened safety zones for her to use and find comfort when she felt lonely and unsafe. During the day, she defended herself by hiding behind a wall of distance and silence that she created while waiting for someone to penetrate her heart with love and understanding and remove the guilt that she felt for her friends' death. She yearned to feel less guilty for what had happened, and she needed love to endure the traumatic memory of waking up holding Manolito's head in her arms as she lay on top of—and next to—many dead bodies. At night, after Mari fell asleep, her brain tapped into leftover dangling threads of the past to create a fantasy world in which it was easy for her to neutralize her guilt—as well as her father's inattention—by curling herself into the soft arms of a woman with olive skin and sorrowful eyes who whispered loving words in her ear, whispers of long ago, whispers that she could remember but not understand, whispers that made her feel loved, whispers that made her feel safe and forgiven.

The truck passed through the outskirts of Madrid. As it entered a poorly maintained open road, a group of young man wearing coveralls and holding rifles behind machine guns blocked the road. One of the men, a little older than the others, the only one wearing a red-and-black armband, walked toward the truck and saluted Alfonso with a bent arm and clenched fist. "Salud, comrade. Do you have your credentials and permission to leave Madrid?"

Alfonso looked out the window, turned off the of the truck's engine, dug into his pockets, and produced a small card with his picture and credential as a Republican soldier, as well as a paper signed and dated by his commander giving him leave from the front lines to attend "urgent family matters for three days." After reading Alfonso's credentials, the militiaman stepped aside and waved Alfonso on. "Be careful, comrade. There are Fascist sympathizers hiding behind every bush from here to Avila."

Alfonso smiled and returned the soldier's clenched-fist salute as he started the truck. He told the soldier, "Thank you. I will be careful. Keep Madrid safe until I come back, comrades."

After driving in silence for a time, Alfonso tried once again to ease the discomfort between himself and Mari. He said to his daughter, "Tell me when you get hungry. Grandma made us a wonderful omelet, and we have real bread and real wine!"

Mari turned her head and looked at him for only a moment and then leaned toward the window and pretended to be absorbed looking at the landscape to avoid having to talk to him. The truck passed several empty one-story buildings on each side of the road. Alfonso forgot about his silent daughter and food for a moment as he recognized a building that had once been a gasoline station and souvenir store with a small restaurant next it. The gasoline station was now standing derelict, with empty gasoline pumps and broken windows. As the truck traveled past it, the scenery became more and more deserted, with only occasional abandoned houses in the middle of empty fields.

"Tell me when you have to go to the bathroom," Alfonso said.

Mari's silence continued. She closed her eyes and pretended to be asleep.

The truck left the outskirts of Madrid on an empty two-way road, heading toward the mountains far away. Suddenly, a few miles ahead on the other side of the road, small groups of people appeared, walking toward Madrid. The number of pedestrians on the road grew, forcing Alfonso to slow down to avoid hitting anyone. Men, women, and children filled the road ahead. They carried sacks of personal belongings on their backs. Carts pulled by oxen carried household items. Pigs, goats, and sheep strolled ahead of the carts. Mothers carried children, children carried other children, men drove carts, and older folks sat next to the furniture on the carts, holding more young children on their laps.

Someone waved at Alfonso from the road. A middle-aged man wearing a black beret and missing his front teeth spoke to Alfonso. His voice was strong, and his speech was Castilian, pure and clear, without any provincial accent. "Young man," he said. "My name is Andrés, and it is a pleasure to see you and your child. I thank you for stopping. We have been on the road since yesterday, and if you would be so kind, can you tell me how far are we from Madrid?"

Alfonso smiled at the traveler and answered him, while wondering where in Madrid all these refugees and animals would be housed. "It is my pleasure to meet you, Andrés. I am Alfonso, and this is my daughter, Mari. You are very near the city, but because of the way you are traveling, I think it will still take you about four hours to get there, maybe less. You should be there before dark, that is for sure."

"Thank you, Alfonso. May you arrive safely to wherever it is that you are going."

"Good-bye, Andrés. May you, your family, and your friends also have a safe trip."

After having been on the road for a time and after the number of refugees finally dwindled and the road was once again clear, the truck began passing one deserted village after another that showed no signs of life other than occasional dogs, walking skeletons roaming the streets looking for something to eat, too weak even to bark at the passing truck. Signs of destruction were everywhere. There were houses torn down and walls pitted by bullets, and half-eaten, rotting carcasses of animals filled the air with foul smells. The long, wide fields that once grew wheat were now stripped and full of weeds. Dried arroyos lacked the usual sounds of birds or frogs. No signs showed any kind any life moving. Nothing acknowledged the passing truck.

Alfonso's chest tightened and his breathing became rapid and shallow as he looked at the long row of empty houses resembling ghostly landscapes from a world that seemed to be dying. He had been born in Spain, but he had spent more than half of his life traveling through France and the New World, watching his father preach equality without success to politically dumb and numb workers. Now he was in a country, his country, where workers were politically alert and fighting for their right to a life of freedom, a life of progress and equality. These workers were willing to fight and die for rights they truly believed belonged to all human beings. Alfonso passed the ruins of homes that factory workers and farmers had sacrificed to the cause of equality, and he no longer questioned his role in the war. He was glad to be fighting for his native country. Maybe the young factory workers and farmers who were fighting in the trenches could save Spain from the grasp of greedy landlords and the greedy church that stole the workers' earnings through a self-serving Vatican. Alfonso realized how much he sounded like his father, and he smiled. Maybe not all of the old man's preaching had been wasted.

Alfonso looked at his map and estimated that he could reach the foothills of his mother's village the same day—that is, if nothing happened to hinder his efforts. There was enough gasoline stored in the back of the truck to get there, and he hoped to fill the cans again in the village for his return to Madrid. He felt a sense of relief at the thought of returning to Madrid without the distress caused by his daughter's behavior. Her silence was damned uncomfortable, and he felt lost and somewhat angry. Yes, she was his child, but he had never felt what a father was supposed to feel for his children, and now he was beginning to regret not having sent Mari to New York with her mother. Maybe he should have tried loving her more. He did not know whether he loved his daughter or whether the feelings in his chest were just feelings of responsibility for a child he had never wanted, a child born against his wishes who had messed up his life.

Alfonso remembered the day Mari was born, how hard it had been for him to get to the hospital, a long ride in the subway followed by standing in a bus full of smelly people, and then a long wait for the ferry to Welfare Island, where the hospital was located. It was a free hospital, where free treatment allowed no complaints from the well-known, unsafe, and rough treatment of patients whose economic status in a country undergoing a depression was poor. His daughter was almost a day old when he arrived at the hospital, convinced that he would find a dark child with black hair whose physical characteristics would make it impossible for it be his child but instead the bastardly product of her mother's affair with some dark Italian man. Alfonso looked and looked again to the row of babies in the nursery. The baby in the cradle bearing his name was the smallest fair- skinned child with yellow hair in all of the nursery's cradles. There was no question that the little piece of humanity in front of him was his child, and he tried to feel something for the little sparrow bundled in a baby blanket in front of him, a sparrow that later on grew to be a happy little girl who sometimes called him Daddy. The next three years were filled with stress and hardship for Alfonso and his wife. Rosa became seriously ill, but no treatment was available in Spain. At the same time, Alfonso was becoming emotionally attached to another woman, a lively, strong Spanish woman he had met when first returning to Spain before his wife and child arrived. It had been hard for Alfonso to be what a father and husband were supposed to be. He tried to feel something special for his happy, active child, who, without warning, after days of screaming and crying, retreated to a world of her own when her mother returned to New York. After that, Mari changed from talkative to sullen. Alfonso never learned how to deal with his child's frequent silences.

The truck's engine sputtered and stopped, interrupting Alfonso's thoughts. The gas gauge indicated that the tank was empty. He turned off the engine and sat for a moment, looking at the landscape ahead of him. Hills and more hills appeared, with the silhouette of somber olive trees against the horizon. The land was beginning to show some signs of fertility in the meadows and hills. Sprouts of green things pushed upward from the earth and through the melting snow, announcing that spring was near. Had Alfonso been a different kind of man, he might have felt the passing shadows of his ancestors on the very same meadows where he was and be amazed by those ancient, peaceful men who had always lived within clans and tribes in the dawn of Spain, men who did not know how to use weapons for anything other than to secure food. This peaceful way of life had existed until the "river men," the Iberians, appeared and taught them the art of killing each other, one century after another. Peace in the peninsula never returned. The wind swept across the mesa, carrying the smells of blood and history, but Alfonso could smell only dust. Stepping out of the truck and opening the door to the passenger's side, Alfonso asked his daughter to jump into his arms.

Hesitating, Mari looked at her father's face, but he was smiling, so she felt safe. She jumped and held on to him. She pointed at something and shouted with excitement, "Look, look, Daddy, look!"

Stunned by the sudden sound of the child's voice, Alfonso stood still, staring into space while recovering from the impact of hearing his daughter call him Daddy, the only word in English that she seemed to remember from a language she had forgotten after her mother left. His throat tingled, and the muscles of his face expanded into a wide, happy smile. He turned to look. At some distance ahead, he spotted a shepherd with a large herd of sheep scattered between rocks and small islands of green.

"Daddy, look! Goats!"

"No, niña. They are sheep—first cousins to goats."

Mari had never before seen goats or sheep. She jumped up and down with excitement after her father let go of her and asked, "Can we go see them?" [So, has her knee injury resolved? I'd have expected her to have been crippled for life.]

Alfonso took the child's hand. He was still smiling as he said, "Yes. We sure can. We are going that way, but first I have to put some gas in the truck, and we need to eat something." He filled the truck's tank with gasoline from one of the cans he was carrying in the back.

As they ate, Mari's face seemed to come alive with her first bite of omelet. She puckered her lips as her mouth savored the taste of potatoes, garlic, and onions that had been slowly cooked in olive oil with freshly beaten eggs, the traditional Spanish omelet eaten by shepherds for centuries, which now seemed to fit the scene and mood of the area. Mari had not eaten a Spanish omelet for a long time, and every bite was now a delight as she smiled at her father. "Umm, good," she said.

Alfonso pulled a leather bota from behind the truck's front seat, and they took turns trickling the wine-and-water mixture down their throats.

Mari chattered about wanting a baby sheep and being able to roam the hills with her sheep.

Alfonso listened, filled with bewilderment and strange new feelings of tenderness. It was an unforgettable moment for him as he listened uncomfortably. He was afraid to feel. As the firstborn, he had been his father's extended arm, carrying the older man's arbitrary and uncontested decisions, which included not only actions but also feelings. Alfonso had grown with little awareness of himself as a person who had choices. Today, he was experiencing feelings without consent or criticism from anyone; today, he was himself, and this scared him.

Alfonso started the truck, smiling at himself for all his thoughts and feelings. Stuff like that, he thought, is a luxury better practiced sipping a glass of cognac when there is nothing else to do. He was once again his father's son. The truck reached the plateau where the sheep ate, ignoring the new arrivals, but the shepherd standing next to his herd looked at them with suspicion. Early human history was again curiously open as the two men stared at each other. The shepherd was a short, dark man with a remarkable likeness to the ancient Iberian river men, and Alfonso was slightly taller, blond, resembling the northern Celts who had followed the river men into the Iberian Peninsula shortly afterward. They inspected each other carefully.

After a short silence, both men seemed to relax. Alfonso spoke first. "Good afternoon. I am Alfonso, and this is my daughter, Mari. We come from Madrid."

The shepherd rearranged a wool mantle that hung over his shoulders. Shifting a tall wooden cane to his left hand, he extended his free hand toward Alfonso and said, "Good afternoon. I am Pablo. I have never been to Madrid, but my brother Ernesto was just killed there, fighting with the Republicans."

Alfonso took a deep breath, and his face muscles tightened. "I am sorry, Pablo. I too am in the Republican Army and have lost many comrades and —"

The shepherd interrupted angrily. "Are you a deserter? What are you doing here?"

"Oh no, I am no deserter!" exclaimed Alfonso. "I am here to take my daughter to my mother's village and stay with a cousin until things get better in Madrid. I only have three days off from duty. I can show you my papers, if you like, and will return to the front lines after that. I would never desert my comrades."

The shepherd looked at Alfonso carefully and seemed to relax as he took a leather bota filled with wine that hung across his chest and handed it to Alfonso, saying, "Salud, comrade!"

"Salud!" answered Alfonso, lifting the bota above his head and allowing a stream of wine to travel down his throat.

The shepherd did the same, and the two Celtiberian men smiled. The shepherd asked, "What's your mother's name?"

"Maria. Maria de Avila."

"I know your mother. We are from the same pueblo." The shepherd's sentences were short, typical of the enduring Castilian folk living in remote areas. He added, "Going by truck, you are almost there. About ten kilometers from here up in the mesa and then down a bit, you will enter the pueblo from the rear. I wish you good luck, comrade."

Alfonso took the shepherd's hand with gratitude. As Alfonso was about to turn away, he asked, "How long have you been out here, Pablo?"

The shepherd nodded his head from side to side and squinted. "Um, must be over three days, because I am running out of food and wine. Guess it's time to go back—maybe tomorrow."

"It's quiet out here," said Alfonso. "Have you noticed any activity, maybe from someone pretending to be a shepherd that could have been a Fascist scout? Avila is awfully close."

The shepherd again shook his head from side to side. "No. Your truck is the only thing that has been here, and anyway, I know all of the shepherds that use this land."

"Pablo, stay alert. Those sons of bitches have no hearts when they enter the villages," Alfonso said.

The shepherd looked down while tapping his long wooden cane on the ground. In an almost half whisper, he addressed Alfonso's concern. "The news travels fast, my friend. Franco and his Moors have been doing terrible things, especially to the women. I know that in my pueblo, we will fight to the end, and as long as one of us is alive, my pueblo will never yield to the rebels." While talking, the shepherd reached to his back. From the wide woolen wrap around his waist, he pulled an Albacete knife with a twelve- inch sheath and a foot-long crackling blade that could be snapped into action rapidly. His voice was loud and strong as he announced, "I have killed many a pig with this blade, comrade, and I will do the same to any Fascist pig who comes near my village."

Alfonso was amazed by the fervor in the humble shepherd's voice and waved good-bye while walking toward the truck, holding Mari's hand.

Mari was so excited about being able to touch the sheep that she had been totally unaware or disturbed by her father's conversation with the shepherd. "They have curly hair, Daddy!" she exclaimed as she looked back at the sheep.

Alfonso did not answer. After lifting his daughter into the truck, he sat behind the steering wheel and started the engine.

The shepherd watched in silence as the truck headed for the village, not knowing for certain whether Alfonso's had stated his true reason for being on the mesa. Pablo was one of many shepherds in the area who watched out for strangers and was ready to alert the town of any suspicious activity coming from the hills between Avila and the village by setting bonfires that could be seen from the village and that would alert the people of a possible attack. The shepherd decided that Alfonso did not look as if he was a threat to the town, but if he returned the same way that night, there was no doubt that he was on his way to Avila with whatever terrain information the rebel army needed. Child or no child present, he would die. Pablo placed his Albacete knife inside the front of his woolen wrap for easy reach in case he spotted Alfonso going back toward Avila later that night.

Unaware of the shepherd's plans, Alfonso drove on, leaving behind a stretch of dotted poplar on either side of the narrow dirt road and steering the truck toward the sierra outlined on the horizon. The landscape changed, with the intermittent appearance of twisted dark olive trees and sumac that grew between rocks capped with melting snow. The truck was leaving the treeless Castilian planes, ancient witness to the constant destruction of Spain by its people, and entering the windswept, rocky slopes. The air was becoming drier and colder as the distant sun descended behind the mountains. The same sun that helped the plains survive the winter now shone obliquely on the lone Celtiberian and his child. The sky darkened. As the chill of winter asserted itself, Alfonso leaned toward his daughter and covered her with a woolen blanket. "Better?" he asked.

"Yes, Daddy," Mari said, sounding tired. She was beginning to fall asleep.

Alfonso smiled and pointed to the blanket. "You know, niña, the curly hair of the sheep you touched today is really wool. About once a year, the shepherds cut the sheep's hair, and after they wash and stretch it in a special way, they knit blankets like this one out of the wool."

"Does it hurt the sheep when the shepherds cut their hair?"

"No. It's the same as getting a haircut."

Mari was silent for a moment. "Do they ever cut their heads?"

"No," replied Alfonso. "They do not cut their heads." He stopped the truck to hold his daughter in his arms until she fell asleep. Battling his own exhaustion, Alfonso continued traveling the narrow road in what had become a dangerously dark night. Out of fear of being detected by advanced enemy scouts, he used only his dim lights, so it was hard for him to see the road. This forced him to slow down. As the truck crawled down the side of the mountain to avoid the fallen rocks, the truck shook, hissed, and creaked with occasional louder sounds, disturbing the profound silence of the night and increasing Alfonso's anxiety. Despite the advent of spring, the northern wind remained cold.

Mari, covered with the woolen blanket, rested her head on her father's lap. She dreamed that she slept undisturbed in the arms of the dark woman with olive skin and sad eyes as her father drove in a state of melancholic surprise at his feelings of tenderness and love for the child who slept next to him.

Shortly before reaching the village, Alfonso left the narrow, unpaved road they had been traveling and joined a wider road, the only thoroughfare to and from Avila. He tasted the air and smelled the comfortable aroma of burning wood. He knew that they were nearing the village. Hungry as well as tired, he looked for Tio Miaja's house as he passed a medium-sized slaughterhouse to the left of the road, followed by quiet, small, dark, two- story brick and adobe houses on the right. The truck made loud resonating sounds as it bumped its tires on the cobblestones on its way into the town, but no lights came on, and no doors opened. Horses tied inside the small stables that adjoined each house made snorting sounds as the truck passed.

Alfonso stopped in front of Tio Miaja's house. Leaving the lights of the truck on, he turned off the engine. Lights came on from inside the house, and the front door opened.

A tall, strong-looking man stood in the doorway, holding a rifle. He had obviously been awakened by the noises and had quickly stepped into his black flannel pants, still unbuttoned at the waist, which covered the long legs of his white cotton winter underwear. Suspenders hung from his shoulders over the top of long-sleeved underwear. He wore no shirt or shoes. The voice of the man who pointed the rifle at Alfonso was intimidating. "Don't move another step. Tell who you are."

Alfonso obeyed. He said, "I am Alfonso, the oldest son of your cousin Maria de Avila from Madrid."

The man seemed to relax, but he kept his rifle pointed at Alfonso. "Has something happened to Maria?"

"No. I have a letter from my father, Juan, which explains everything. My little daughter is in the truck, and it is cold out here. Please let me bring her inside. We have been traveling all day long, and she is very tired. She's not quite seven years old. It was a hard trip for her."

The man walked past Alfonso. After looking into the front seat of the truck, he leaned his rifle against the front bumper of the truck and lifted the sleeping child into his arms. He walked toward the house. He said, "Turn the trucks lights off, Alfonso, and bring my rifle into the house. You are all grown up, and I did not recognize you. The last time you were here, you were still in short pants."

Alfonso followed the man. Alfonso did not recognize the man but assumed that he was Tio Miaja. Alfonso stepped into a large kitchen warmed by logs burning inside a huge fireplace, from which hams and sausages were hung to be cured. The smell of garlic and olive oil made Alfonso keenly aware of his hunger. His mouth watered, and his stomach growled. He leaned the rifle against the wall and looked around the room for a door to other rooms, but there were no other doors, just a handmade wooden ladder propped against the wall. This ladder led to an upper level in the house.

Tio Miaja carried the sleeping Mari up the wooden ladder into a loft. The loft was divided into two large sleeping areas and separated by a wall with a small door. He placed the child on a large feather bed next to his two sleeping daughters and covered Mari with a woolen blanket. On the other side of the room, Tio Miaja's two adopted sons were also soundly asleep; none of the children woke up when the door separating the loft opened and Tio Miaja's wife came out in her nightgown, yawning and looking confused. Tio Miaja looked at his wife and climbed down the ladder. He held on with one hand and used his other hand to make a gesture of silence with his index finger across the lips. He whispered, "Pilar, nothing is wrong. Come down to the kitchen. Don't wake the children."

Once in the kitchen, Tio Miaja and his wife sat with Alfonso around a big, round wooden table as Alfonso explained his reasons for bringing his daughter and gave his father's letter to Tio Miaja.

After reading the letter, Tio Miaja handed it to his wife and sat in silence for a moment as if trying to find words. When he finally spoke, his voice sounded distant. "*Aiii Dios*, Alfonso." He sighed. "I am sorry for what happened to your child, but do you realize that this town is but a couple of hours from Franco's army? We go to sleep every night with one eye open. Our shepherds are out in the hills, taking turns listening and watching. They hardly sleep. If Franco attacks us, we have no defenses. All our young men are in Madrid, defending the republic, but the republic has sent no one to defend us. We have maybe two hundred hunting rifles and not too many fit men, just lots of old people and children to protect."

"I know, Tio Miaja," answered Alfonso. "I discussed the situation with my father when he and my mother decided that I should bring Mari here. My father thought that a handful of farmers in adobe houses and an old church would not be worth the effort for bringing troops."

"My town has no value in terms of money or power, Alfonso," interrupted Tio Miaja, "but it would be a valuable military outpost for Franco to prevent the Republicans from trying to take Avila and valuable to the Republicans if they decide to advance and take Avila, which would immediately make the town the scene of a bloody confrontation."

Alfonso looked down and tapped his fingers on the table. "It's bad everywhere, and I know there is no safe place, but at this moment, your village is still a safe place, and my daughter needs a little time to recover and find some peace. If anything happens here, I'll come to get her. She cannot survive in Madrid at this time."

Tio Miaja stoked the fire and brought Alfonso a cup of hot coffee. The host placed a large piece of bread and chorizo in front of his guest. "Eat, and get some sleep before going back. Wait for daylight. It will be safer to travel without headlights. We will wake you up in time to eat some breakfast and for Pilar to make you some sandwiches to eat on the way back." He climbed the ladder again and returned with pillows and blankets, which he gave to Alfonso. "You'll have to sleep on the floor down here, but I think these are enough to make you comfortable." Tio Miaja waved as he and his wife climbed up the ladder. "Good night, son."

Pilar looked down and made the sign of the cross. "May God keep you safe, Alfonso."

The sun was blinking across the sierra when Alfonso filled the truck with gasoline from small cans that Tio Miaja stored in the shed next to the house. Alfonso made sure that the radiator had enough water and put air in the tires with a hand pump he carried in the truck. He went back to the house, climbing the stairs to the loft and kneeling on the floor next to the bed where Mari was sleeping. He kissed her on the cheek as she opened her eyes. He told his daughter, "We have been in Tio Miaja's house all night. You were asleep when we got here, and I did not want to wake you." Alfonso added, "It's time for me to go back. Remember what Grandma told you about staying here with Tio Miaja and the family until things get better at home. It won't be long. I'll come to get you. You will like it here. They have sheep, goats, and pigs—and children your own age with whom you can play; you will like it. I will come to get you when the bullets stop in Madrid. I promise. I love you, niña."

Mari listened to her father and slowly recoiled into herself, her recent trust in him rapidly slipping away. He was leaving! Of course he was leaving. He was always leaving. She was used to being abandoned. It hardly mattered anymore. She stared at the ceiling as her father stepped down the ladder. "Grown-ups are but transient, migratory birds that cannot be trusted," someone had once said to her. She did not know exactly what that saying meant, but she closed her eyes and envisioned her father flying back to Madrid over the hills, across the sierra, far, far away from her.

Every night, after a day of toiling in the fields, gathering the animals, and bringing enough wood into the kitchen to heat the house all through the night, the family gathered around the fireplace, and Tio Miaja would read a chapter from a history book. After he finished reading, Tio Miaja usually closed the book to expand the content of what he had just read with additional stories that had been passed down from one generation to another. Pilar, Tio Miaja's wife, poured thick hot chocolate into large handmade clay bowls for everyone to drink as the children were transported back to Spain's ancient days of chivalry, honor, and glory.

The present civil war was seldom mentioned by anyone, and when it was, it was always addressed by Tio Miaja as a dispute between brothers soon to be resolved and finished. As a simple farmer, Tio Miaja had no specific political beliefs. To him, there were no villains in this war, just Spaniards with different ideas, but they all loved their country. The war had disrupted his love for life as it had always been and as he had hoped it would always be. His lifelong serenity had yielded to fear and apprehension as he thought of Spanish blood spilled upon Spanish soil by Spanish brothers fighting brothers. Although painful for Tio Miaja, to his children he taught uncomplicated faith and solidarity among those who had been so blessed as to be the fruit of Iberia.

Mari listened to every word of Tio Miaja's stories, filled with excitement. At night, before falling asleep, she expanded the content of Tio Miaja's stories by adding to them the stories her grandfather had told her. Her eyes closed as she imagined that she was galloping on top of a white stallion behind the shield of Castile and Leon. Sometimes she was alone, but most times, she galloped next to the horse of the blonde, blue-eyed Queen Isabella. When he was not busy, King Ferdinand joined them. This was very exciting, but the most exciting time for Mari was when she felt the wind on her face as she galloped across the plains chasing Moors, next to hundreds of Spanish warriors chasing infidels in the name of the Holy Crusades. She was proud to have Iberian blood in her veins. Iberian blood was good, strong blood, and she was sure it purified the bad Ethiopian blood her grandmother accused Mari of having.

Her father was right. Mari loved this village of adobe-brick homes at each side of the narrow cobblestone streets where pigs, chickens, and dogs roamed freely without attacking each other. Women dressed in long, wide skirts and shawls and covered their heads with black bandanas tied in a knot under the chin. Men wore worn baggy black pants with wide woolen girdles wrapped around the waist. They walked in homemade footwear of cloth alpargatas with soles made of hemp or cut-up car tires. In the streets, the smell of freshly baked bread in the communal ovens impregnated the air with good feelings. Everyone greeted each other by their first name.

Mari was fascinated by the aroma of baking bread in the streets, as well as the smell of sausages and hams hanging from fireplaces in the homes. People traveled everywhere on horseback, some on mules or donkeys. There were no cars, no tanks, no gunfire, and no barricades. The village was nestled in a valley surrounded by huge rocks with dozens of hiding places, out of which snakes and lizards came to sunbathe. It was a wonderland full of exciting living things for Mari. The people were strong, the men were handsome, and the women's faces were a classic mixture of Celtic beauty and Iberian strength. Men and women shared a rich sense of humor, sprinkled with superstitious beliefs and unmovable rules of behavior and morality. There were no toilets or running water in the homes, but everyone managed to appear clean in their worn homespun clothing. The women washed clothing at the edge of the small river flowing at the end of town where they could be seen talking and laughing every day. A small stream of fresh, clean water ran behind the slaughterhouse across from Tio Miaja's house, and it became Mari's source for keeping clean and neatly groomed without having to go to the river.

Tio Miaja's nightly tales developed in Mari a strong identity with the spirit of her father's ancestors, the blood of Celtic warriors, the Phoenicians, and the Carthaginians. Hers was the blood of Roman glory mingled with Moorish splendor. Her veins contained the flowing life of Castile and Aragón. She was the ultimate of Iberian purity. She loved this land of rocks, twisted olive trees, and contradictory landscapes filled with grapevines, fruit trees, and tall, lush grass. It was exciting to share the people's passion for the land with a deeply rooted addiction to Spain that tolerated no criticism of Spanish heritage. She became part of Tio Miaja's family and shared all aspects of their life. This filled her with a sense of belonging that she had never experienced before. Every night after her imaginary adventures and before falling asleep on a warm feather mattress, she felt the softness of familiar lips lightly brushing against her eyelids, and she knew that the woman with the olive skin and sad, smiling eyes was with her.

This was a dry land, and every year, with the advent of spring and the planting of new crops, each family was allocated specific times for irrigation. Three times a week before sunup, Mari and Tio Miaja's youngest daughter, Mari Carmen, together with Felipe and David, his two adopted sons, were awoken early in the morning and sent to open the irrigation ditches to supply water and life to the newly seeded fields. Mari had developed a special relationship with Mari Carmen, an active little girl the same age as she, and the two girls ran and jumped in the company of Tio Miaja's sons, Felipe and David, who were a little older than the girls but who enjoyed chasing and teasing the girls with stories of sea serpents that lived beneath the irrigation ditches and waited to eat small girls.

Tio Miaja's oldest daughter, named Pilar, like her mother, stayed home and helped prepare breakfast for Tio Miaja before he left to tend the stock and newly planted fields. The sun was but a nascent glow coming from the east at this time of the morning, shining against one side of the encircling hills and mountains on the horizon, while on the other side, long shadows were cast flat against the earth. The children went to the irrigation ditches, running and skipping over the dewy grass and small streams as their teeth chattered from the cold. They blew on numb fingertips to keep them warm while thinking of big bowls of hot coffee and the crispy pieces of freshly baked bread waiting for them at home by the warm fireplace.

For a long time, the opening of the ditches had been a daily task for Mari until, one day, Pilar asked Mari to stay home and have breakfast with her and Tio Miaja. Mari felt anxious, not knowing why she had to stay home. Mari stood in front of Tio Miaja and his wife and looked down at the ground, ignoring the aroma of hot coffee and freshly made toast. She squeezed and cracked her fingers to stop her hands from shaking. Finally, she asked, "Are you sending me back to Madrid?"

Tio Miaja cleared his throat and smiled. "Back to Madrid? No. Do you want to go back to Madrid?"

Mari looked up. "No. I don't want to go, but I thought that's why I am not going to the ditches today."

Tio Miaja sipped his coffee and placed the cup down in front of him. "I see. No. That's not why I wanted you to have breakfast with us. I have a special favor to ask of you. Sit down, little one. As you know, I bought more sheep and goats the other day, and now there are too many sheep and too many goats to graze by the house, so they need to be taken up to the hills. I thought maybe you could be in charge of this. What do you think?"

Mari could not hold back her excitement. She sat on the chair in front of her, rocked, and waved her hands in the air. "You really, *really* mean it?"

"Yes, I mean it. But there is a condition—you *must* promise me to return home from the hills two hours before sundown. The wolves get hungry after dark, and they particularly like the tender flesh of little girls from Madrid. Do I have your promise?"

Even though Tio Miaja was smiling, Mari knew that he was serious about the wolves. More than once, they had attacked animals left in barns at the edge of town, leaving behind torn, bloody legs and hooves of the cows and horses that had tried to kick back at their attackers. But Mari was not afraid. She felt proud of having been given the most profound of assignments, indeed, an assignment to which only the older children had been entrusted in the past.

After breakfast, Tio Miaja took Mari to the field where the sheep and goats roamed. As Mari watched with excitement, she was shown how to round up the herd and keep them together, as well as how to walk them up and down the hills.

This was a magical time. Mari's heart pounded with anticipation and pride knowing that Tio Miaja was going to trust his sheep and goats to her! Shortly after the lessons were completed and after Mari showed that she could manage the sheep and goats without problems, Pilar hung a leather bota filled with diluted wine on Mari's shoulders and gave her a small basket filled with brown bread; a potato, onion, and garlic omelet; and several pieces of fruit.

Mari left the village feeling strong kinship with the shepherds in the mountains of Spain and with all the shepherds in the mountains of the whole world. The hills across the meadows were beautiful, and just as beautiful standing behind the hills were the twisted, aged olive trees and rocky slopes that silently held the history of Spain inside them. Mari passed several women on their way to the river that carried large baskets of laundry on their heads.

The women laughed and yelled after her, "*Anda, muchachita!* Tio Miaja found a good shepherd! Be careful of the wolves and snakes."

Mari smiled at them and kept walking, swinging a stick and holding her head up behind the sheep and the goats. The sky was intensely blue, and the sun, radiantly bright, was beginning to melt the snow from the nearby mountaintops. Mari remembered that this type of weather usually appeared shortly before her birthday every year, but she did not know her birth date, and she did not know how old she was; no one had asked her for a long time, and she had forgotten. The memory of a parade on her birthday was distant and almost nonexistent, but in trying to remember it, her throat felt tight, and her eyes watered. Struggling to ignore these feelings, Mari walked faster until she found a grassy meadow with a small stream of water on the other side of the hills. She settled there as the goats and sheep grazed and looked for the tender new weeds and grasses that were beginning to grow.

Mari left the wine bota in the stream to keep cool and placed the basket with food and fruit under a tree. She spent the next couple of hours chasing lizards and rabbits. Hot, thirsty, and hungry by midafternoon, she returned to the stream for lunch, but as she was reaching for the wine bota, her hands touched something that moved. A green snake lay floating in the water. The snake was not easy to see, as it was partly submerged in the vegetation, so it blended with the bottom of the stream, but after sensing movement in the water, the snake's squinty, dark eyes without lids stared directly into Mari's eyes. She pulled her arm out of the water, but it was too late. Mari's arms and legs were rigid, heavy, and unable to move. The village women had been right! Snakes were capable of paralyzing people before attacking.

Overwhelmed with fear, Mari stood transfixed, unable to move a muscle in her body. The sun was reaching down to the mountaintops from the west when the snake moved. Swimming away, it released Mari from its hypnotic powers, allowing Mari to move again.

Looking at the sun, Mari started to realize that it was very late. There was no time to eat, and there was no time to waste. Almost in a frenzy, she gathered the sheep and goats and grabbed the wine bota. In desperate haste, she left her lunch on top of a small rock, hoping that the wolves would eat it and be too full to come after her. She chased the small herd of goats and sheep, running as fast as she could down the hills toward the village. The sun was setting when she reached the valley. When she looked back, she was horrified to see packs of wolves standing on the edge of the rocks at the top of the hills she had just left.

There was nothing said that night about her late return or the still-full wine bota. When she was asked about her first day with the sheep and the goats, Mari shrugged, unable to tell them about having been kept in a spell by a snake for hours. She said, "Oh, it was nothing. I had fun, and the omelet was very good." She did not know that her late return from the hills with the sheep and the goats had been cause for concern, and Tio Miaja went looking for her with two men from the village. When they spotted the sheep and goats racing down with Mari behind, the men decided not to let Mari see them or to let her know how much her late return had made them worry.

The next morning, after breakfast, Tio Miaja told Mari that he wanted to show her something. Holding her hand, he walked her to the bottom of a hill next to a dirt road rarely used by anyone. As they neared the end of the road, neatly folded in the middle of the path was a small dress, and a small pair of cloth alpargatas with soles made out of rope was neatly placed on top of it with a pair of white socks. Tio Miaja let go of Mari's hand and pointed at the clothing and footwear.

"Do you see that dress? Those are the clothes of a small girl who was watching sheep and goats and did not come back from the hills before sundown. There was nothing else left of her! The wolves ate her right up." His eyes were smiling, but the rest of the face was serious.

Mari looked at the dress and the alpargatas. They were very clean. The dress was intact, ironed and neatly folded. She was amazed at the cleverness of wolves to be able to devour a little girl without damaging her dress and to be able to fold it after they were finished! From that day on, Mari was put in charge of pigs that grazed on a field not far from the village. The wolf incident was never mentioned by anyone, and Mari was grateful for that.

The days grew warmer and longer. Summer came, and Mari became totally engrossed in the early trips to the irrigation ditches, in roaming the fields next to the village in charge of Tio Miaja's pigs, and in afternoon, games with the other children. They would run, tease, and chase each other through the narrow streets of the village. Sometimes, they made fun by exchanging embarrassing nicknames, but there was always laughter and mutual feelings of joy after it was all over. At other times, they sat on the ground together playing marbles or took turns swinging a string tied to a rock to see who could throw it the farthest. Sometimes, the boys and the girls played separately, the boys playing ball while the girls jumped rope. There were other games that tested each other's courage and skill, such as climbing steep rocks or hanging from tall tree branches.

Mari loved to be admired and tried to appear fearless as she climbed the tallest rocks or jumped from the highest trees. David, Tio Miaja's oldest son, was also competitive and hard to beat, but Mari did win many times, making David the target of much laughter and teasing from the other children. David tolerated the kidding from "the little ones," as he called them, and he laughed with them.

Mari had been at peace with her life since she had come to her grandmother's village, where people did not yell and argue during mealtimes and where the nights were long, peaceful, and silent without the noise of air-raid sirens or bombs exploding. Sometimes, the strange feelings of long ago persisted, making Mari quiet and sorrowful. At such times, she entered into the fantasy world of softness, warmth, and safety from the dark-haired woman of long ago holding her tightly in her arms and whispering the same familiar song in the language Mari could not understand. She loved the evenings in front of the fireplace, smelling the enticing aroma of sausages hanging as she nibbled on ham and cheese, drank hot chocolate, and listened to Tio Miaja's stories of ages past. When the warmer, longer days began, the gift of longer daylight hours was used by the townspeople to spend more time working in the fields. This made the evenings around the fireplace shorter, but they were still the core and strength of family unity.

One night after dinner, Tio Miaja seemed worried and distracted. His voice was distant and lacked its usual dramatization of the events in his stories. As he stared into space, his face was somber and unsmiling. He did not seem to be enjoying his storytelling.

Mari became fearful and apprehensive, remembering the way her grandfather looked and acted at times when he was angry. "Are you mad at me?" she asked Tio Miaja.

Tio Miaja moved closer to the child and gently kissed her on the cheek. He smiled at her and said, "Oh no, *mi hijita!*" He had looked anxious since returning from a meeting with the town's council that morning. It was Sunday, and Father Rafael had called the meeting after the church's services, which was unusual. He had been the town's priest and religious advisor, a protector and loyal friend to everyone for twenty years, but he had never before called a meeting or interfered with the town's council. Father Rafael had remained faithful to the people and to the republic. He had taken off his religious robes at the beginning of the war, breaking all connections with the Catholic Church and with the Vatican. From that day on, he dressed as one of the men in the village and toiled the land with the other farmers, and on Sundays, the village people became accustomed to a priest dressed in a plain black business suit and a church without incense or altar boys, a church where Latin was no longer used.

On that Sunday morning, Father Rafael spoke to the councilmen slowly and carefully, using words that would not hurt or alarm anyone in the room. "As you well know, this war is not about gain or conquest. Is not even about changing the way anyone thinks. We are a peaceful democratic republic by the choice of a people forced to defend themselves against those who are killing and torturing our women and children, those who are destroying our land. We are not warriors, and we are not killers. We are farmers who want to remain farmers with the privilege of owning our land. Since the war began, we have been blessed with no need to defend ourselves."

The priest took a deep breath. He did not quite know how to tell these simple, unsophisticated men that the progressively more savage tactics of Franco's army and his German and Italian allies threatened the peace and safety of their village. The ruthless destruction of a small town without defenses in the Basque province of Vizcaya indicated that the Fascists would now target anyone and anything, even peaceful civilians without defense in small towns. German Heinkels and German Junkers used by Franco's army had machine-gunned women and children in the streets, while at the same time, incendiary bombs and high explosives were dropped on houses and on farmers living in that area who brought their produce for sale into town every Monday. This massacre made the world hold its breath with shame and disbelief, but nothing was done to prevent Franco from repeating this horror in other towns and on other innocent civilians.

It had taken a week for the news of the latest Fascist massacre to travel by word of mouth to reach Father Rafael. The news made it clear that the rebel army would not respect defenseless civilians in unprotected villages. Father Rafael kept his head lowered, unable to look directly at the men in front of him. Slowly and softly, he then told these simple farmers what had happened in the province of Vizcaya.

"We need to be realistic," he continued. "We must decide whether we will surrender before the same happens to us—or if we will prepare ourselves to fight."

"We are about two hundred men in this village," muttered a pale young man.

"Yes, Father. Let us be realistic," said the mayor. "Some of those two hundred men are too old to fight. We may have altogether about three hundred hunting rifles and probably no more than a hundred cans of gasoline between all of us."

All the men talked at the same time, loudly and anxiously. One said, "We could build trenches around the town. The women and children could help; they helped in Madrid."

Another commented, "That would slow them only a little, if they came by foot, but it seems that they like to use bombs from airplanes, so trenches would be useless."

"We could abandon the town and move up high into the mountains until the war is over."

"If we did that, we might as well all be dead!"

One of the men shouted, "I am not going to abandon my home or my land!"

The talk went on until it was time for the men to go home for the midday Sunday meal with their families. Missing this meal would panic the women. The men decided to do nothing until a safe plan could be formulated.

The farmers continued plowing the land and seeding the fields. Mari's life became totally engrossed in the early trips to the irrigation ditches. As the person in charge of Tio Miaja's pigs, she roamed the fields, full of the awakening energy of spring as she listened to the magical sounds of birds, chased lizards, and watched the movement of all kinds of wild crawling creatures she had never seen before. She spent late afternoons in games with the other children.

In the evenings, Mari continued to listen to Tio Miaja's magical stories of Spain's beginnings, which were filled with the heroes of long ago. After each story, Mari entered into her own world of fantasy. Mounted on a white stallion, she galloped over the plains of Castile, sometimes with El Cid Campeador—Spain's hero and noble warrior who bravely fought and defeated the Moors—and at other times with Queen Isabella. At these times, they together chased Moors on horseback through the streets of Granada.

"There were also other noble persons who were not warriors or men," said Tio Miaja. "Nevertheless, they contributed to the greatness of Spain. One of them was Doña Juana, the daughter of Queen Isabella and King Ferdinand, who was also called 'La Loca,' the Crazy One, by the people because she was always yelling. They did not know that her husband, Felipe of Austria, was always entertaining other women behind her back and that he had loud and vulgar drunken parties with these women. Doña Juana was jealous, and every time her husband had a party with other women, she would go into violent rages that could be heard all over the castle. The people working in the castle did not know why she was yelling, and they thought that she was crazy. When Felipe died at a young age, supposedly from a fever after having drunk a glass of water when he was overheated from playing ball, Doña Juana further encouraged her reputation of being unstable when she insisted in traveling for weeks across Spain at night with her husband's dead body to bury him in the south of the peninsula. Only much later was it understood that Felipe of Austria, when alive, had asked Doña Juana to bury him in Granada, south of Spain, should he die before her. The entourage carrying the body traveled at night to avoid decomposition of the body under the hot sun during the day. The people felt sad and ashamed when they found out that Doña Juana had been double- crossed by her husband when he was alive and that the way she had traveled with the body at night was justified. Time passed, and like everything, the people forgot about their name-calling and their shame, and they went on to pick on someone else. With a few ups and downs, Doña Juana reigned for many years after her husband's death. She left many documents and letters that she could not have written if she had been crazy. Indeed, if she had been crazy, she had sure lived through many intervals of sound and profound sanity."

After listening to the story, Mari felt sorry for poor Doña Juana and wondered whether her grandfather was crazy. He too had many rages, and he too wrote sound and profound documents. It did not really matter. She admired Doña Juana, and she loved her grandfather. These tales and fantasies always excited Mari, and after her imaginary adventures at night in her bed, the fantasy that really helped her sleep was the one in which she envisioned being held by the olive-skinned woman with the sad eyes who kept humming the same familiar tune in a language Mari could no longer remember.

With summer, the mornings were brighter; the sun seemed to wake up earlier and seemed to stretch itself taller behind the mountains from the east. It was one of these mornings when, after the children finished eating breakfast and gathered to get ready for the day's chores, Tio Miaja's wife, Pilar, asked Mari to wait before she left with the pigs to go to the grazing fields.

"*Hija*, before going out with the pigs today, see if you can first take Chata to Andrés's house. Chata is going to mate with El Gordito."

Mari had no idea what the pigs were about to do. The word *mate* was not in her vocabulary. Nevertheless, Mari accepted Pilar's request as if she understood. Singling out Chata from the other pigs, she led her through the small village streets, waving a small stick with concentrated pride and seriousness.

"Good morning, Mari!" called out a group of women on their way to the bread ovens. "Where are you going with that pig so early in the morning?"

Mari continued her pace without looking at the women. She lifted her chin, and throwing back her shoulders and looking ahead, she answered with a voice and tone of authority, "This pig's name is Chata, and she is going to mate with El Gordito. I am taking her to Andrés's house." Mari did not understand why the women laughed, but she was not going to be distracted from her journey by the giggles of "gossipy women" (which was what Pilar sometimes called them). She reached the house where Andrés lived, feeling tingly with anticipation of the unknown.

What occurred was not what Mari had expected. El Gordito mounted Chata, standing on his hind legs, and after some grunts, it was all over. She looked at the pigs, expecting something else to happen. Nothing did. Her eyes filled with tears.

Andrés walked toward the child. Kneeling down in front of Mari, he smiled at her. "Chata and El Gordito made some babies."

Mari did not see any baby pigs. Her eyes let go of the tears they had been holding back, and the salty liquid flooded her cheeks.

"What's wrong, little one?"

"I don't see any baby pigs."

Andrés wiped her face with a large handkerchief. "Chata has the babies in her belly. They are too small to eat by themselves, and she needs to feed them in her tummy until they are a little bigger."

Mari could not trust Andrés. She was sure that pigs were made the same as people babies: by the beautiful and loving goddesses with long, flowing hair and the soft, shiny white wings who lived above the clouds in the never-ending spaces of love and light. When a baby, any kind of baby, was wanted and needed down on the earth by a sad and lonely mother, the beautiful goddesses stayed up all night, lovingly transforming pieces of heaven into a baby. When the baby was finished, they flew down to the earth and placed the baby in the mother's arms, early in the morning before she woke up. Mari's grandmother said so.

Andrés kissed Mari on the cheek. "The little piglets will be born in a couple of months. Chata is a very good mother, and the babies will be really cute. You'll see!" He looked as if he was telling her the truth.

Mari pondered this. Maybe pigs were different from people. Could she trust him? She looked at his large, smiling eyes. "Is El Gordito the *papá* of the babies?"

"Yes."

"Will he live with us and help Chata take care of the babies?"

"No, niña. El Gordito has to stay here."

Mari was angered by this answer. Why did fathers always have to be somewhere else? She picked up the stick and went back into the street with Chata. She again passed the women who had been laughing and talking in the street before, but now they were busy making bread in the ovens. No one noticed Mari, and she did not want to be noticed. Apparently untouched and unconcerned by the day's events, Chata skipped ahead, grunting and waving her short tail from time to time. Mari, still too young to be able to use reason to explain troubling new experiences but old enough to feel the pain of unresolved feelings, ran behind the pig, sobbing. The noon sun was not yet over the mountains. It was too early for the afternoon meal, and no one was in the house. She gathered the pigs and walked them to a field at the edge of town. The pigs grazed happily on the new grass. Mari perched herself on top of a flat rock. Sitting cross-legged, she looked at Chata, envisioning a little piglet next to her without a father.

Chata suddenly disappeared, and the little piglet stood alone without a mother or father.

They had been in the mountains for five days looking for stranded cows and their calves after Mari had pleaded and begged to go with Tio Miaja, excited by the idea of climbing the sierra on the back of a powerful white stallion, one just like the stallion she rode with Queen Isabella in her daydreams of glory and conquest. Her mood did not change when, instead of a horse, she was lifted in the air by Tio Miaja and straddled on top of a rather cranky old donkey that shook and complained about everything. The donkey placed itself behind the mule that carried Tio Miaja and the supplies for the trip, and there was nothing Mari could do to change its mind. There was no galloping into the clouds for the glory of God and Spain, just a cranky old donkey staring at the rear end of a mule for hours.

They had slept on soft piles of straw inside a stone shepherd's shelter after they ate in front of a big fire. Tio Miaja had put the child to sleep every night with his tales of knights and queens. It had been a wonderful trip, but now, as they descended from the hills, guiding a few cows and their calves to the valley below, Tio Miaja felt uneasy. The irrigation ditches were closed. There were no women by the river washing clothes. No one attended the sheep. Down in the meadows, pigs roamed freely without any sign of human activity.

Tio Miaja was a man in close contact with the invisible essence of nature. He could predict the weather and the presence of wolves by the smell of the wind. Danger always had the same acrid smell that made his nostrils dry and painful. It was barely noon, yet the sun was hot. The sky was clear, but the acrid smell was strong. Instead of descending straight into the village, man and child traveled along the side of the mountain, bypassing the town until they reached the orchards along the main road to Madrid. Tio Miaja's heart was pounding with apprehension as he led the cows into a grassy field and proceeded to unsaddle his mule.

After leaving mule and gear behind, Tio Miaja trailed the donkey and child behind him as he walked toward the village, squinting against the sun. He looked for the usual movements of women carrying water or women walking together on their way back from baking bread in the public ovens, men returning home from the fields to rest before the early afternoon meal, or older men playing checkers in front of their houses. No one. The streets were empty. He pulled on the reins of the donkey in a desperate effort to move faster.

The donkey pulled back with the characteristic stubbornness of his breed.

Tio Miaja pleaded with the donkey, *"¡Jo, burro, vamos, vamos!"* Tio Mia's home was one of the first houses in the back of the village on a small street that led into a secondary road at the edge of town that ran up into the hills toward Avila. He could almost see his house. Dampness from his armpits soaked his shirt. *"¡Jo, burro, vamos, vamos!"*

The child said nothing. She stared ahead, feeling the man's desperation and wishing that she could again be safe up in the high mountains in front of an open fire, sharing food, stories, and laughter with Tio Miaja.

Not very far ahead of them, a young man, almost still a boy, slept while leaning on his rifle against a heavy rock. He was dressed in a military uniform and had dark skin and thick, curly black hair covered by a soiled and torn white turban. As Tio Miaja and Mari approached, the young man moved, and his rifle slipped from his hands and fell by his side on the ground.

The realization of the turban's meaning sent numbing shocks through Tio Miaja's body—the Moroccan army had arrived in his village. Slowly, Tio Miaja traced the handle of the hunting knife tucked inside the sash around his waist. Tears filled his eyes as the pounding of his heart choked him. He was a farmer, a husband, and a father. He knew nothing about the killing of men. He let go of the knife, dropping his hands. Unarmed, he walked closer to the sleeping youth.

The boy jumped up from his sleep and grabbed the rifle, ready to shoot as the silhouette of a man and a donkey appeared before him. Straddling the donkey was a small girl.

After centuries of history passing between them, Christian and Moor once again faced each other under the hot Castilian sun. Each one was a unique and divine creation, creations that had been constrained and deprived of mutual brotherhood with each other by fourteen kilometers of water separating the lands of their birth. Yet, unknown to either Muslim or Christian, there had always been an obsession with each other after having shared five hundred years of history and brotherhood under the Spanish sun. Their common humanity was severed after the defeat of the Moorish rule in Spain by the Spanish monarchs Ferdinand and Isabella, but those five hundred years of brotherhood left them harboring inexplicable feelings about each other across the Strait of Gibraltar. And now, facing the feelings created by centuries of history, a Muslim boy and a Christian man faced each other.

The spell of silent, secret memories nestled in each other's genetic unconsciousness was aborted by the conscious awareness of danger. Man and boy each experienced a brief melancholic nostalgia of familiarity and affection for the other, but they also felt uncomfortable by their inability to identify these feelings. Long years of messages had echoed across back and forth over the Mediterranean, a sea of living, breathing water that, as if directed by mischievous forces, had carried the voices of long-ago spirits, voices that had resonated across Spanish soil, whispering, "Allah is the only God, Mohammed His only prophet!" These voices returned, enfolding the currents across the sea to the coast of Morocco with a message proclaiming the divinity of the Father, the Son, and the Holy Spirit. Soul opened a small door in infinity and united boy and man. Only self-consciousness, with its morbid products of awareness of fear and death, separated the son of Allah from the son of the Father, the Son, and the Holy Spirit.

Still straddling the donkey, Mari remained unchanged through the brief spiritual journey experienced by both Christian and Muslim. She stared at the young man's eyes. They reminded her of the eyes of the woman with the olive skin and dark curly hair. She jumped down from the donkey and stood between him and Tio Miaja. She asked the turbaned youth, "Are you an Abyssinian?"

Ignoring the child, the Moor moved closer to Tio Miaja and pointed his rifle at the Spaniard's chest. "Halt! Stop! Identify yourself!"

"Are you an Abyssinian?" repeated Mari.

"I am called Antonio Redondo," said Tio Miaja. "This is my cousin's granddaughter, Mari. She is visiting from Madrid."

Mari looked up at the Muslim as she pulled and tugged at his uniform, asking yet again, "Are you an Abyssinian?"

Tio Miaja stood motionless with fear and disbelief, not understanding the child's actions but too preoccupied to silence her.

Mari continued to question the Moorish youth, placing herself in front of him with her hands on her waist, the chin tilted forward, and her small body erect with arrogance and authority, only a breath away from the pointed rifle. She said imperiously, "I said, 'Are you from Abyssinia?'"

The young soldier continued to ignore the child, directing his question to Tio Miaja instead. "Do you live in this village?"

"Yes," replied Tio Miaja. "Mine is one of the first houses to the right, across the street from the slaughterhouse. We have been in the mountains attending to the cattle for a few days."

The Muslim looked toward the buildings, still pointing his rifle at Tio Miaja. The street was deserted. Houses were silent. There was no sign of human movement. His orders were to shoot anyone trying to leave the village; nothing was said about anyone entering. He could hold the man and the child prisoners until the change of his watch and turn them to his sergeant. The man would surely be shot, the child probably raped and left to die. Remembering the atrocities committed against the villagers on the other side of town created tightness in his chest, making it hard for him to breathe. He did not want to be responsible for any harm to this man or to this child. Lowering his eyes to the ground, he silently pleaded with his God, "Forgive me, Allah, if what I am doing is wrong." He took a deep breath as he looked at Tio Miaja and said in an almost inaudible whisper, "Leave your donkey tied in the barn. Go into your house, and don't come out. Don't burn any fires; don't light any lights. Stay quiet, and above all, don't make yourself known to anyone after I am relieved of my watch. Our troops will be leaving for Avila in the morning."

Tio Miaja's eyes shone with tears. "My family. What has happened to the women and children? I have two daughters—and two sons—my wife."

The young Moor looked down at the ground and muttered, "Sometime tomorrow, those who are still alive will be released to their homes." He paused. The words choked him. How could he tell this simple farmer that his wife and daughters had probably been beaten and raped and his sons maybe tortured and killed? He said aloud, "I pray to Allah that your family will be among those released tomorrow."

They faced each other and shook hands. "Your name?" asked Tio Miaja.

"Boabdil. I am called Boabdil." The Muslim smiled at the child. "Boabdil, from Tetuán. I have never been to Abyssinia."

"Thank you, Boabdil," said Tio Miaja. "I also pray that Allah will keep you safe."

Tears of sadness continued to blur Tio Miaja's eyes. He walked toward the house. The girl followed. *What strange people, these Moors,* thought Tio Miaja. *Some are bloody savages, others noble and caring souls.*

The Muslim youth had similar thoughts about the Iberians. *What a strange breed, these Castilians: arrogant, brave, and proud little men who cry like women.*

Tio Miaja went into the barn next to his home and led the donkey into an empty stall. He felt a heavy choking sadness in his chest; he knew that neither he nor the young Muslim had guaranteed safety from any god. They were both victims of national greed, a type of greed that would never allow changes in their lives except perhaps suffering and probable death. Tio Miaja tied the donkey to a large metal ring that hung from the wall and carefully closed the double doors of the barn. He went into the house while he held Mari's hand. Once inside the house, he secured all the shutters on the windows that faced the street. He climbed the wooden ladder used to reach the opening in the kitchen ceiling that led to the second-floor bedrooms.

The rooms had been left in a state of chaos. The big feather beds were unmade, and clothing was scattered on the floor. He sat on the edge of his bed, held his face in his hands, and cried. After a time, Tio Miaja's tears stopped. He stepped down to the kitchen and sliced pieces of sausage and bread, which he offered to Mari.

She ate silently.

Tio Miaja kept the front door slightly ajar as he took a jug of water and a large piece of cheese and bread to the Muslim youth who stood guard outside of his home. "I thought you might be hungry," he said to the youth.

The young Muslim soldier looked at him and smiled. Taking the food offering in his hands, he admitted, "Yes. I am. Thank you. May Allah always be with you and yours."

Tio Miaja returned to his home. He cleaned, oiled, and loaded his hunting rifle and sharpened two large knives that he used to slaughter pigs. When he was finished, he placed his arms around Mari, held her in his lap, and said to her, "All of this will soon be over. Are you all right?"

Mari leaned her head on the man's chest and whispered, "Yes, I am all right, but I am a little afraid. Do you think the Moors are going to kill Boabdil for helping us?"

"Oh, no. He is a good soldier, almost a friend. I would never let anything happen to him because of us, even if I have to die. I feel sorry that he is out there all by himself, so young, so far from his family."

Mari let out a sigh of relief. "I hope he will be safe. I like him. That's a funny name, Boabdil."

"Well, it's really not that funny," replied Tio Miaja. "He is named after the last emir of Granada, who was only seventeen years old when he came into power. His real name was Abu-Abadala, but because he was so young, the people gave him the nickname of Boabdil, which means *El Rey Chico*, the Boy King."

"Was he a good king?" asked Mari.

Tio Miaja sat back on his chair and relaxed his body without letting go of Mari. "Well, he did not get to do much of anything. The Moors had lost most of their holdings, and Granada was about all that was left. Boabdil loved Granada, but he could not hold on to it. The Catholic kings were ruthless in their quest to free Spain from the Moors, and Boabdil had to surrender the city to them. It was a very sad day for Boabdil. Mounted on a magnificent black stallion, he stood high above a hill facing Granada and surrendered the keys to the city to the Catholic monarchs Queen Isabella and King Ferdinand. They say that Boabdil was crying when he gave the keys to the city to Queen Isabella, saying, 'These are the keys to this paradise. Receive the city as is the will of God.'

"After that, when Boabdil's had barely finished these words to the queen, high in the sierra, echoing down to the gardens of the Alhambra, Christian trumpets together with the voices of Spain's happy people heralded the end of the Moorish empire in the Iberian Peninsula. It is written that the smell of lilac and mint was everywhere and that Boabdil turned his horse away from the Christians and from Granada, shaking with sadness, and his eyes blinded with tears. Oh, yes. He dearly loved Granada. I don't know if it is true, but someone told me that Queen Isabella told Boabdil he could live in Granada, if he wanted, but Boabdil said that he could not do that because Granada had been his mother, and he had failed to protect her, so shame was with him."

Mari had listened to Tio Miaja feeling love and loneliness. Her grandmother had told her many times that people with dark skin, such as her mother, came from a country called Abyssinia. Now she was puzzled, because obviously they also came from Tetuán. Maybe she was a Moor. She sat on Tio Miaja's lap for a long time, half-awake and half-dreaming. Legends, stories, and visions crowded her mind until she finally fell asleep.

Tio Miaja climbed the ladder to the bedrooms and placed the child on one of the feather beds. He carefully covered her with a light blanket and kissed her on the forehead before returning to the kitchen. He sat in the dark and thought about his life. He pondered over and over again what he could do to save his family. This was not about politics. This was not about patriotism. This was about those for whom he cared more than his own life.

He had always been a farmer with no specific political direction. Adopted from an orphanage when he was six years old, he grew up with a family of farmers in a village of nothing but farmers, and with the exception of a short tour of military duty in Madrid, he had always lived in this village. He was a simple man. Madrid had suffocated him, and the pace of life in the city had overwhelmed him. He had no formal education, but while stationed in Madrid, he had taught himself to read and write. When the news of the war reached his village, he worried about the valley, about the land, and about his family. Married since he was eighteen years old to a young woman from the village, he had fathered two daughters. When his youngest child was five years old, it was accepted that his wife could bear no more children, and Tio Miaja convinced her that there had to be a good in God's decision when they adopted two brothers from the same orphanage from which Tio Miaja had been adopted.

The boys, six and ten years old, called him Tio Miaja, and the people from the village soon used this nickname for him too. He loved his life as it had always been and as he had hoped it would always be. The war had disrupted his serenity. The thought of Spanish blood spilled on Spanish soil by brothers against brothers had disrupted his uncomplicated faith in the solidarity among those who had been so blessed as to be the fruit of Iberia. He was in pain, as well as ashamed by the war, and the nightly cries and sobbing of his cousin Maria's granddaughter as a result of her encounters with the war in Madrid had him experiencing a form of anger he had never known before. Through the child's words, he understood the meaning of war as she described her fear of incendiary bombs and the sight of machine- gunned bodies on the streets. Spanish blood. Spanish bodies killed with Spanish bullets on Spanish soil. Now the terror of war was really threatening his life and the lives of those he loved. A surge of primitive, pack-animal instinct clouded all the years of civilized thinking. He was ready to kill his own brothers. He was the leader of his pack, ready to kill anyone and anything that threatened his woman or his young ones.

By nightfall, Tio Miaja had carefully tucked the butcher knives inside the sash around his waist. He checked the rifle and slid out of the house through a window.

Boabdil, a short distance from the house, totally exhausted from his lack of sleep, did not notice Tio Miaja leaving his house silently.

Tio Miaja headed toward a hill that led to the town's plaza and to the church.

Boabdil heard nothing. He had kept himself awake by ruminating about his life and the unbearable nightmares of his present situation. Yes, he had been named after the last Moorish king of Granada, but he lacked any resemblance to the warriors of long ago. He was a shy, quiet, and unassuming boy, fifteen years old when he signed into the Moorish army newly formed by a Spanish army colonel named Francisco Franco Bahamonde. Boabdil was very thin and of small stature. He had angular facial structures, high cheekbones, and a well-rounded chin. His hair was black and thick, his skin the color of honey, and his large, deep, dark eyes had a veil of sadness that clouded the brightness of his pupils. There was no arrogance or defiance in his appearance. He was just a melancholic young boy taken away from his mother and his land much too early. He had crossed the Strait of Gibraltar from his native Tetuán and landed in Algeciras with his platoon, which moved on into southern Spain.

For a short time, life in the army had been exciting, but as time passed, Boabdil missed his mother and his two sisters. He grew sad, always tired and homesick in a strange, unfriendly land. His life as a Moroccan soldier was no longer exciting. The news from Tetuán was always about the hunger and sickness, and it kept him in a perpetual state of anger and depression as he worried about his mother and sisters.

Boabdil was in the midst of infidels. What did Allah want from him? It had been two days since they had arrived in the village. There was no battle, no resistance, and just a few shots. He received a small wound on his leg. Because of the pain in his leg, his depression, and his lack of interest, the details of his arrival in the village were obscure in his mind. He remembered the shooting of the city officials in the town square. Bodies had been left where they fell, exposed, covered with blood, and infested with flies.

Some of the men had been forced to dig their own graves, and some had been buried alive. Wives were made to dance on top of their husbands' graves. Women were forced to drink large amounts of castor oil, and their heads had been shaved. Some of the women had been raped in public as the townspeople were forced to watch. The worst was the sight of a tiny infant impaled upon a bayonet and carried high around the square for all to see. That made Boabdil gag and run behind one of the houses to empty the contents of his stomach. After that, each woman who was raped was his mother, and each child who was killed was one of his sisters.

It became impossible for Boabdil to watch any further killings or rapes without feelings of nausea and tightness in his chest making him unable to breathe. At these times, he forced his eyes to close tightly until a cloud of darkness covered his eyes, mercifully preventing any further watching. Because of the wounded leg, Boabdil was allowed to stay in the temporary barracks set up at the edge of town, which blocked the road to Madrid for a day. He spent most of the day and night unable to sleep due to hearing the voices and the cries of the villagers. Boabdil asked Allah to make the voices stop, but Allah did not answer, and the voices continued all through the night. By the second day, Boabdil was ordered to stand watch on the other side of the town on a road that led toward Avila. No military action was expected from that road, since Avila was still secured by the rebels. Boabdil was instructed to kill anyone who attempted to leave the town.

After almost twenty-four hours without sleep, Boabdil fell to his knees, confused, hallucinating, and hearing voices of the dead. He bowed to the east and said, "Allah is the only God, Mohammed His only prophet." Boabdil had saved the lives of two infidels, and Allah was angry.

A soft voice above all other voices whispered from the very depths of Boabdil's heart. "I am the God of all Gods. My children have given me different names at different times, but I have no name. There are no infidels. You are all my children, such as you are, my child. I am not angry. I want you to come to Me and find peace." Allah had spoken.

Still bowing to the east, Boabdil ate the last piece of cheese that Tio Miaja had given him. Sitting up, he held the rifle in his hands with straight arms. Placing the barrel in his mouth, he pulled the trigger.

The sound of the single bullet resonated through the night. Tio Miaja stopped running for a second to look back toward his house. A shiver went through his body as he thought he heard the trees whisper, "There is no Allah. There is no Holy Trinity. There is only Me, and I am Nameless."

It was a dark and moonless night. Mild, soft breezes coming from the mountains impregnated the air with the odors of wildflowers and mixed with the sounds and scents of wolves that howled on the peaks of a nearby sierra. An all-white church stood bright against the dark skies with all its lights on, illuminating the plaza and exaggerating the grotesque shadows behind nearby homes.

Tio Miaja approached the first of the houses away from the church. Slowly and silently, he took advantage of the shadows to hide his presence as he looked for his wife and children among the people outside the church. They were not there. Instead, a few soldiers sat in front of wood fires, talking and laughing as they waited for large pots of coffee to finish brewing. Other soldiers, stretched out on blankets, slept. Sitting on the ground huddled together, small groups of women and children trembled with fear under the watchful eyes of armed Moorish soldiers.

At a short distance from the women and children, a few girls still in their teens had been forced to drink large quantities of castor oil and had been denied bathroom access. These girls hid their faces, unable to prevent the painful and wrenching emptying of their bowels and soiling themselves in public view. The girls' heads had been shaved. Wrapped in dirty clothing, reliving the vivid experience of rape, they tried to hide from the lights as they sobbed quietly, feeling unbearable self-loathing.

A young Moorish soldier walked out of the church, armed with a rifle and a bayonet, which he pointed at the town's mayor as he yelled at his prisoner to keep moving down the steps. Disoriented and half-naked, the mayor shuffled in pain, blinded from the rifle beatings across his face. His eyes were swollen shut, and drops of his blood slid to the ground. The Moor cursed and pushed the point of his bayonet against the mayor's back. He ordered the mayor to stop at the bottom of the steps and fall to his knees in front of a rebel Spanish officer who was dressed in an immaculate uniform and shiny boots.

The crisply dressed rebel officer crossed his arms, adopting a defiant and arrogant posture as he looked at the mayor with total indifference. Behind the officer, Father Rafael, wearing a crown made from barbed wire tightly pushed down on his head, slumped forward, his arms extending backward, tied to a wooden cross.

The officer stared at the mayor for a moment and slowly forced a smile as he annunciated his words slowly and with great care. "Where is the town's money kept?"

The mayor looked at the officer through his swollen eyelids, taking a moment before declaring loudly, "The town has no money. We collect donations, as needed, for street repairs, electricity, or whatever needs come up."

The officer frowned and pointed his finger at the mayor. "Who pays your salary, Señor Mayor?"

"I raise cattle," the wounded man said. "I have no salary. I volunteer my services for the keeping of the town's civil records, and once a month, I preside over a meeting of the town's elders to discuss any problems having to do with the municipality. You are wasting your time! This town has no money."

The officer scowled and squinted as he kicked the mayor and threw him across the steps. "You useless son of a bitch! At dawn, we will shoot out the arrogance from your balls, as well as the arrogance from the balls of this fairy tied to the cross who calls himself a priest. Who knows? Maybe God will make some money appear from your testicles!"

Crawling on the ground from house to house until he reached the plaza in front of the church, unnoticed by the soldiers, Tio Miaja looked everywhere for his family, but his wife and children were not there. He feared that they were dead and had been thrown into the newly dug common grave behind the houses. He frantically crawled on the ground toward a back entrance to the building. Just as he neared the rear door, he felt a faint tremor under his feet, followed by the distant humming of an airplane engine.

At first unnoticed by everyone else, the humming grew closer and louder until the Moorish soldiers stopped all activity and looked at each quizzically. This was not expected; there had been no messages about airplane aid or supply deliveries. The officers shouted orders for all prisoners to be placed inside the church and for every soldier to prepare for battle. Within five minutes, a small plane appeared from the direction of the mountains, throwing flares and illuminating the skies above the town.

The howling of the wolves stopped. The rebel soldiers let all prisoners go and hid behind the houses as unshaved, tired young men in ragged uniforms appeared from the shadows and circled the plaza and yelled at the civilians to take shelter. The townspeople hid inside the church, crawled under benches, and crouched behind the altar and inside utility closets. They slid under the organ and under any other hollow place that had room for a body. They did not know whether the approaching men were Republican soldiers or volunteer members of unofficial guerrilla troops roaming the mountains in search of any rebel activity. Nevertheless, the townspeople were grateful for their appearance.

Pandemonium broke out among the nationalist rebels as they clumsily defended themselves. The strangers attacked from everywhere with gunfire. As they moved closer to the rebel soldiers, they thrust bayonets into their bodies. Soon, the safety of the townspeople was secured. Grenades and mortar shells blew up the rebels' ammunition supply trucks and headquarter tents.

Thrown into trancelike behavior, Tio Miaja joined the fight. Without hesitating, he used his butcher knives to stab as many of the enemy as possible. He became one with the splash of blood and flesh against his face and clothing.

In less than an hour, it was clear to the rebels that to fight on would be useless, and the officers in charge of the defense waved dirty pieces of cloth attached to their bayonets to signal their surrender.

The fight stopped. No one cheered.

Using a manual loudspeaker, a bearded young man with a husky voice announced that he and his men were Republican soldiers under the command of Colonel Mangada who had been on their way to cut Avila from Palo de Alto Pass when they realized that this town had fallen into enemy hands.

After a brief silence, a different voice came to the loudspeaker, offering emergency help to those who had been hurt by the enemy. Almost immediately, the wailing of women and the crying of children echoed through the night as the Republican soldiers rushed to attend those with the most pressing needs. Standing in a remote corner of the plaza, hands by their sides and staring at the ground, a group of young girls stood in clothing soiled by human waste. They had been raped and then robbed of their femininity by having had their heads shaved. For a moment, the older townswomen looked at the young girls, not knowing what to do. Then, all at once, as if directed by invisible hands, the women ran over to embrace each girl. The women removed some of their own clothing to cover the girls' shorn heads and soiled garments.

Inside the church, Tio Miaja found his wife sitting on the floor. Her head was shaven. She held the bodies of her young daughters. He looked around for his sons, but they were not there. He sat next to his wife and daughters. He leaned over to embrace them. The young girls were dead. Tio Miaja kissed his wife's face and removed the scarf from his neck and covered her head. They said nothing. What could they say?

Two of the Republican soldiers took the dead girls from the arms of their mother and placed them on blankets in front of the church, along the bodies of numerous other victims.

Tio Miaja lifted his wife from the ground. Placing his arm around her shoulders, they walked toward their home. The first lights of dawn rose from the mountains as Pilar and Tio Miaja reached their house. The door was open. They called Mari's name, but no one answered.

Tio Miaja ran into the street. He found the sleeping child on the ground, curled up next to Boabdil's body. She did not wake up when Tio Miaja carried her back to the house, climbed up to the bedrooms, and placed her on one of the empty feather beds. Tio Miaja silently returned to the kitchen and sat next to his wife. He placed his elbows on the kitchen table and held his head between his hands. Silent tears filled his eyes.

Pilar moved closer to him and wiped her tears with her apron. She asked her husband, "Antonio, who was lying out there with the girl? One of our boys?"

"No, Pilar. He was Boabdil, a Muslim who saved my life yesterday." Tio Miaja rose from his chair and looked at the face of the woman who was his life's partner, his friend, the mother of his dead daughters. He marveled at her quiet bravery. He helped her up to the bedrooms and asked his exhausted wife to rest. He told her he would prepare the two-wheeled cart to transport Boabdil up the hill to the cemetery. "Later on," he whispered, "we will bury him in the family plot with our daughters."

Pilar lay down next to Mari, careful not to wake her, and closed her eyes without asking her husband any more questions. She was very tired, numb with the grief of watching her daughters raped and then die in her arms. She had attempted to rally herself through anger, but these attempts had failed. Her anguish made it impossible to feel any other emotion.

Tio Miaja pulled the cart out of the barn and prepared the donkey. Once everything was ready, he placed Boabdil's body in the cart and covered it with a white sheet. After returning from his grim errand in silence, he stood by the cart and looked up at the sky. He was sad, he was angry, and he was tired and dirty. Blood stained his face and clothing as the new day began. His eyes followed the movements of soft white clouds suspended from the blue sky, and he imagined angels dancing for the amusement of the gods, as if nothing unspeakable had happened on earth. How could God be so indifferent? He looked at the undisturbed sky. He fell to his knees and yelled, "Allah, you son of a whore! This young boy really believed in you! Why did you abandon him?"

Hearing her husband's cries, Pilar looked out from the bedroom window. "Antonio?" she called out. "Who is there? Is someone with you?"

"No one. There's just me." He ripped off the gold crucifix that he'd worn around his neck since his childhood in the orphanage and threw it in the air. The gold chain and crucifix sparkled for a moment, and then, without a sound, the chain and crucifix fell to the ground on top of animal waste. "There is no one," he repeated to himself as he looked at the chain and the crucifix. "There has never been anyone. All the God stuff. Lies feeding superstitious weakness and ignorance. There are no gods, no virgin whores, no bastard sons of divinities, only scared men trying to find excuses to avoid responsibility for their own thoughts and actions!" Surprised and scared by these thoughts, Tio Miaja walked inside the house. After making coffee, he sat in the kitchen, sobbing.

Pilar came down from the bedrooms and sat next to her husband. She held him in her arms.

The following day, trucks came with supplies and left the village as the Republican soldiers established bunkers and built trenches around all points of entry into the town. Scout trucks roamed the hills, looking for runaway rebels. Republican soldiers came upon several young boys who, naked and tied together, were unable to move. They had been beaten and sodomized and then left to die on the side of the road. They bled from cuts and wounds all over their bodies. They had been without food or water. Even the strongest and the toughest of soldiers in the scout truck could not hold back a rush of tears. Here were frail children, covered with dried blood and massive purple marks from the blows inflicted upon them before they were sexually violated. As the soldiers approached, and unable to distinguish one army from another, the boys trembled and lost control of their bladders.

As the soldiers struggled to untie them from each other, an older, tough veteran from the Spanish Foreign Legion walked toward the boys, muttering, "Tell me, God of gods, protector of the innocent and the helpless, you fucking son of a bitch, where were You when all of this happened?" Struggling to hide his tears and twitching face muscles, the sergeant pulled a handkerchief from his pocket and began blowing his nose as he slowly moved from one youth to another, saying, "Shh, *muchacho*. Don't be afraid. We are the good guys. We are not going to hurt you. I swear it on my mother's grave." He untied the boys.

Soon the soiled, bloodstained boys were carried to the truck as each soldier donated a piece of his clothing to cover the naked boys who sat in the truck staring into space. After the truck returned to the village and was parked in front of the church, the boys remained still and silent, showing no acknowledgment or reaction when the village people ran toward them to look for their own missing sons.

At first, there were screams of joy, but soon the joy was followed by muffled groans as the boys remained frozen and unresponsive when their families hugged and kissed them.

Tio Miaja and Pilar, unaware of the boys' return, arrived in the plaza to claim their daughters' bodies and were surprised and overjoyed to see Felipe and David, their two adopted sons, alive in a passing truck. Tio Miaja jumped in the vehicle while it was still running, and among the other boys in the truck, he found his sons staring into space with no expression in their eyes. He called after them, "Felipe! David! It's me, Tio Miaja, your father."

The truck stopped. While Tio Miaja tried to get some sign of recognition from his sons, an ambulance stopped in front of his cart. Tio Miaja stepped down from the truck as Alfonso jumped out of the ambulance's driver's seat and embraced him.

Alfonso cried out, "I am sorry, so very sorry! I heard what happened. Two daughters lost at the same time must feel like an enormous painful void in your heart."

"No, *mi hijo*," responded Tio Miaja. "It is not just one pain. There are two enormous painful voids in my heart."

Alfonso looked at the bodies of the two girls on the ground. They were covered with blankets that did not quite reach their feet.

"Yes, you are right, Tio Miaja. I am sorry. It must feel like being stabbed in the heart twice. Please let me help you take them home and bury them."

"The boys," Tio Miaja said. "I have to get them home first. They were taken away yesterday and left stranded in the hills. I do not know what has happened to them. They are not responding."

Alfonso had not met the boys on the night he left Mari in Tio Miaja's home. He looked in the truck and tried to guess who among the young men were Tio Miaja's sons. It was impossible for him to tell. Every child's bruised face and swollen eyes were covered with dried blood and dirt. Each boy stared sullenly at the bottom of the truck. Alfonso placed his hand on Tio Miaja's shoulder and said, "Take your sons home in the cart. I will bring the girls right after I drop off some medical supplies."

Tio Miaja led his sons to the cart. Wrapping them with the blankets with which he had intended to cover his daughters, he waved back as Alfonso started up his ambulance.

Just as they were preparing to leave, Father Rafael appeared in front of the church's steps. Everyone in the plaza kneeled as the priest, his head bandaged but otherwise immaculately groomed and showing no signs of the torture and hardship he had endured, began praying and blessing the dead bodies in front of him. After Father Rafael was finished, a strong "Amen" resonated throughout the plaza. Tearful families began to gather the bodies of their dead.

Tio Miaja did not have enough time to make caskets before the bodies decomposed in the summer heat, so he wrapped the bodies of the three dead youths in white sheets and gently lowered them into three separately dug holes in his family plots and covered them with dirt.

Alfonso and Tio Miaja's sons, David and Felipe, watched in silence as Pilar, wearing a black veil that covered her face, whispered good-bye to her daughters before they disappeared under the dirt. When it was all done, Pilar handed her husband three small, roughly made wooden crosses.

Tio Miaja hesitated before placing two of the wooden crosses on top of his daughters' graves. He said, "Mari Carmen and Pilar, forgive your father for not being there to protect you. You will live inside my heart all of my life, and I hope we shall meet again in eternity, whatever eternity is. These crosses are from your mother, who still believes in a God." Taking a deep breath, Tio Miaja placed the last of the crosses on Boabdil's grave and said, "My gentle Muslim friend, thank you for saving my life. Please forgive me for not being there to save yours. This is a wooden cross my wife made for you. It is a symbol of love and faith for a God in which I no longer believe, but if God does exist, it is the same God for Christians as it is for Muslims, the one and only God, as Mohammed preached. Please accept this cross as the symbol our love and appreciation for your short time in our life. Rest in peace, my children; rest in peace, Boabdil."

Returning to the house, Alfonso found Mari by the door, where Tio Miaja had asked her to wait while he buried the three youths. Alfonso tried to connect with his daughter, but Mari turned her head away to resist her father's kiss.

Mari had not thought about him during all the time she had spent with Tio Miaja's family, and she felt fearful and uncomfortable with his sudden presence. Tio Miaja had been her father and her teacher, but most importantly, he had been her friend. He had shown her love and had protected her. He had made her feel proud of herself and glad to be an Iberian of good blood, not Abyssinian with bad blood. She cried when she thought of having to leave the place that had given her countless happy moments, a place where she felt useful, a place where Manolito's head had never been severed, a place where Conchita and Rosa Maria still giggled. She feared that her father was here to take her away and of having to return to the smells of bullets, back to hunger pains and long days without friends. She shrank from her father and sought comfort behind Tio Miaja's legs.

For a moment, Mari envisioned hearing her grandfather at mealtimes, waving a fork with a clenched fist, his face twisted with a mouthful of food, shouting at anyone or anything about Roosevelt's hypocrisy and France's cowardice. She remembered the horrifying moments that followed the sound of air-raid sirens as the bombs whistled through the air, when everyone in the shelter stopped breathing. She remembered the loud crashes when the bombs exploded, when people started to breathe again, safe for now. "They did not hit us—not this time." Mari lost control of her bladder and ran into the house, crying. This time was awkward and painful time for Tio Miaja as well as for Alfonso.

Trying to reassure Alfonso, Tio Miaja placed a hand on his shoulder and said, "Give her a little time, Alfonso. It has been a while since she last saw you."

It was hard for Alfonso to sit eating dinner with Tio Miaja's family that night. The death of their daughters, along with the death of their neighbors and the total devastation of their town, had changed their laughter into silence. These were uncomplicated people without harsh political views to whom every Spaniard was a brother, so they were devastated when the war actually became a reality, shattering their simple way of life. It was hard for them to connect with this reality, not here, not in their town where the most serious disagreements between its people had been the shared hours for irrigation and the changing prices of sheep. Alfonso ate slowly as Tio Miaja, unaware of the complete horrible experience of sexual abuse and humiliation suffered by his sons, attempted to make some form of conversation by asking the boys about their experience as prisoners of the rebel soldiers.

"They were Moors," whispered one of the boys.

Pilar stopped eating. She rose and ran out of the kitchen in tears. She knew what had happened by looking at her sons.

Tio Miaja went after her, and Pilar shared her suspicions with her husband before returning to the table. Tio Miaja was pale. Every muscle of his face and neck was taut as he hugged his sons. He told them, "I am sorry, so sorry. I love you, and your mother loves you. You have been brave, and we are proud of both of you."

Alfonso continued eating, feeling the pain around him. Having experienced the horrors of the war in Madrid and in the front lines, he was no longer able to find words of comfort. He felt that everyone was a victim, including himself. He knew what had happened to Tio Miaja's sons, but the rape and humiliation suffered by the boys were not much different from the pain and humiliation suffered by women in the war, and he was used to it.

After dinner, the two men sat outside the house. They sipped red wine and discussed Mari's possible return home. Having received orders to transport soldiers in his ambulance that most urgently needed care to the hospitals in Madrid, Alfonso had his commanders' approval to bring back his daughter.

Tio Miaja sat, silently nodding his head. He had lost his God, and he had lost his daughters. Now he was about to lose the little child whose curiosity and admiration of all living things had awakened a sleeping world of magic inside him. "Yes," he said with a slow and distant voice. "Your daughter needs to reestablish her bonds with you and with your family in Madrid. For now, this town is yet another war zone that can only reinforce her fears and destroy the memories of the good times spent here." Tio Miaja closed his eyes and tried to hide the pain in his voice. In less than a week, life had changed. A voice from within told him, *Life has changed, not ended. Changes bring new beginnings and responsibilities with infinite choices.* The voice was his voice. He had lost his flesh and blood; he had lost his God of rewards and punishments, but he still had the energy that connected him to all things. He had to believe in that energy and use it to find peace.

Taking a deep breath, Tio Miaja placed his wineglass on the ground. Yes, life had changed, but it had not ended. He went into the house. A moment later, he returned, holding Mari by the hand and smiling. He told her, "Sit down here on my knees, little one. You know we all love having you here with us. You have been a great help to my family, and we love you. Nothing can change the way we feel about you, but your father has missed you very much, and now the three of us need to talk about the possibility of maybe you going home."

The child tried to listen, but she could not hear the sound of Tio Miaja's voice through the sound of thunder coming from her heartbeats. Her eyes filled with tears. She slid from his lap. What did he mean by "a help to his family"? Wasn't she family? She said, "I want to be here to see Chata's baby."

The two men looked at each other. Tio Miaja smiled and told her, "When Chata has her baby, I will send you a picture, I promise. Later on, when things get better, you can come back to see Chata and the baby."

Alfonso knelt in front of his daughter. Holding her face in his hands, he kissed her forehead. He said softly, "Mi hija, Chata will always be your friend, and I promise to bring you back to visit with her, but you will also have friends in Madrid. There are many children your age in the city, and you will make friends in no time. Chata can be your friend in your grandmother's pueblo; it is fun to have friends in many places."

Her father was an idiot. Mari said, "Chata is a pig, not my friend. I take care of her; she is going to have a baby."

Alfonso blushed to hide his embarrassment and told his daughter, "Sometimes animals make the best of friends." He kept on talking, but his daughter was not listening.

Conchita, Rosa Maria, and Manolito, the only friends she had ever had, stood a few steps from the corner of the house, looking at her and listening to everything she had said. They said to her, "Tell your father. Tell your father how you lied. Tell him what happened to us, your friends, because of your lies about the La Pasionaria leaving you a message." Mari turned toward her father, who was still talking to her.

Alfonso said to her, "I love you. I will always take care of you. I promise."

Mari bit her lips, trying not to cry. She ran into the house as her father continued to talk about how the family had missed her and about the new friends she was going to make back in Madrid. Mari did not believe anything that her father said. Once in the house, she glanced out the window to the corner of the house to look for her friends, but Conchita, Rosa Maria, and Manolito were gone.

The next morning, Pilar gathered the clothing Mari had after a year of wear and tear without replacements and added some of her youngest daughter's things into Mari's bag. Noticing Mari's questioning glance, Pilar held Mari's hand and asked her to sit by the bed with her. "You were like family to all of us and a special friend to Mari Carmen, who thought of you as another sister. She would have wanted you to have her things."

Mari understood; it was done. She was leaving. She was going back to Madrid. She was not family.

8

Clouds opened in the sky briefly, allowing rain to cool the hot Castilian landscape and washing a hint of sweetness into the air from scattered wildflowers. Alfonso and his daughter had been traveling for three hours, and Alfonso took advantage of the momentary relief from the heat to check and assist the wounded soldiers he was transporting to a hospital in Madrid. It had been a bumpy ride, made worse by the hot sun beating down on the vehicle's metal roof, creating heat unbearable if not for the slight breeze from the front windows when the ambulance was in motion. His daughter and a young soldier who carried a rifle sat in the front of the ambulance with him. Struggling with the heat in undershirts, two other soldiers sat in the back, scanning the road they left behind for enemy scouts through the open doors.

The soldiers were all very young men, boys hardly out of school who had been working on the family's farm when the war started. Now they were armed with rifles, mortar guns, and hand grenades, ready to use them to kill other young boys and men as necessary. Tormented by the shadows of dead villagers left behind and still hearing the cries of violated women who could have well been their mothers or sisters, the young men held their rifles close to their chests, caressing the triggers and wishing for the enemy to appear. These young soldiers wanted to be able to blow their enemies' bodies into pieces. Afraid of their thoughts, the young soldiers limited their conversation to an occasional complaint about heat or thirst, but each one knew what the other was thinking, even when they spoke to put a brave front on things. "*¡Hijo de puta, que calor!*" (Son of a bitch, what heat!) or "*Hombre,* drink some water!"

That command was likely to be met with "Shut up, idiot. Water just makes me sweat more!" Back to silence. Back to remembering the violated women in the village—the dismembered bodies. Sweat poured down their faces.

Mari had been sitting motionless until the ambulance stopped. Her father helped her down and offered her water. She had been silent all through the trip. She had ignored her father's attempts to bring a smile to her face with silly jokes and inane conversation. She accepted the water, but her face remained expressionless until the soldier who had been sitting next to her placed his tasseled cap on her head. She touched the cap. A hint of a smile appeared on her face. She asked, "Can I keep it?"

Holding his chin and scratching his head as if in deep concentration, the soldier bent down and offered Mari his cheek as he answered her with the melodious accent of someone from southern Spain. "I'll trade you the hat for a kiss."

Mari, who had never heard any speech other than the crisp, serious tones of Castilian, was startled by the soldier's southern accent. She asked the soldier, "Are you a Spaniard?"

He answered, "Hey, pretty one," and placed his right hand over his heart, pretending to be offended. "I am really a good-looking gypsy from the heart of Seville when I have had a shave and a bath!"

Mari looked at the soldier. For a moment, she heard the same laughter and saw the same smile on the soldier's face as that of Tio Miaja. She kissed his cheek and whispered, "Thank you for the hat."

"Oh, that's nothing, little one. Now you are a real Republican soldier. Salud."

They hugged each other, and the soldier walked away to join his comrades, keeping watch on the road while drinking water from a metal container and smoking a cigarette.

Mari shook her head to make the tassel in front of the cap jump from one side to another as she turned toward her father. Careful not to be heard by the soldiers, she addressed him in a low voice, saying, "I have to go to the bathroom."

Alfonso took Mari's hand and walked her to the front of the ambulance, where the soldiers in the back could not see them. "Do you need help?"

Rolling her eyes and curling her upper lip, Mari let out a sigh of impatience and exasperation. Her father was really dumb. She had been going to the bathroom without help for a long time, a very long time. For a moment, she remembered feeling a pair of hands placing her on a round, white urinal as dark eyes looked down at her and soft lips made a smacking sound on the tip of her nose. Was that the last time she had been helped to go to the bathroom? Remembering nothing else and feeling a familiar emptiness inside her chest, Mari walked away from her father and hid behind bushes to relieve herself. She yelled, "I am all grown up now! I don't need your help!"

Alfonso stood still for a moment after listening to his daughter before he walked toward the back of the ambulance to make sure that the wounded were hydrated and clean. He offered water to wounded soldiers and emptied the almost full containers on the side of the road. He lit a cigarette and blew the smoke in the air with a sigh of relief.

Mari was walking toward him with a frown on her face and complaining of having been left alone in the bushes.

Alfonso decided not to dwell on their relationship at a time when he was on the way to the hospital with six critically injured soldiers who could die at any moment. He felt tired and depressed for taking his daughter from a village turned into the coals of hell to a yet another existence of anxiety and fear of bombs and mortar shells that was part of the daily life in Madrid. If only he had known! His daughter could now be safe in her mother's arms in New York. He felt guilty for having cut off all contact with his wife, Rosa. He felt guilty for allowing his ego to place his child in harm's way, guilty for not furnishing her with the love and affection she desperately needed. He was just guilty and disgusted with himself. He stepped on his cigarette butt, trying not to show his feelings to his daughter standing next to him.

The soldiers finished filling the ambulance with gasoline and signaled to Alfonso that all was clear.

The afternoon heat was beginning to cool down when the ambulance passed small, empty towns that signaled the approach to

Madrid. They reached the edge of the city a short time later and passed one block after another of apartment buildings in total destruction. Missing walls revealed mattresses, beds, and all kinds of broken furniture hanging from the remains of crushed buildings. The once busy streets filled with families walking and children playing now were empty as the sun descended toward earth. Death silently moved in the shadows of the war-torn homes.

It was still daylight when the ambulance arrived at a temporary hospital inside an abandoned school building. Medics, alerted of the approaching ambulance, were waiting at the entrance. Alfonso backed the ambulance to the door and handed his official papers to them. "We are with Colonel Mangada. Our platoon was on the way to Alto de Leon when the Fascists attacked a village. We had a few casualties getting rid of the sons of bitches."

"How many wounded you got?" asked one of the medics.

"Six. I got six men wounded; they are the worst, and my captain thought we should take the chance of bringing them here before they died in the village from lack of medical attention and medical supplies."

Two medics jumped into the ambulance and came out carrying one of the wounded soldiers on a stretcher. "Two are dead, muchacho. Sorry," said one of the medics.

Alfonso said nothing, but he clenched his jaw with enough force to chip one of his teeth. He went into the hospital, spitting blood-tinted sputum, unable to understand the rage erupting from his stomach. *What the hell?* he thought. *Dead now or dead later, there is no way back from war but death. Death now, or death later, it's all the same. So what the hell? They died in the back of the ambulance. I will probably be killed in the front of the same ambulance. Maybe not today, but someday.*

A nurse asked Alfonso, "Are you all right, soldier?"

Alfonso was sitting on the floor, holding his head, and crying when the same voice asked him whether he wanted a cup of coffee. He nodded without looking up as a young woman in a nurse's uniform placed a cup of coffee on the floor next to him.

She said, "The coffee is next to you, soldier. Drink it. When you are finished, come to the office at the end of the hall to sign off the paperwork and be on your way home."

Alfonso got up from the floor. He sipped the coffee and followed the nurse to the office. He signed the papers and finished the coffee. Alfonso returned to the ambulance, where Mari still slept in the front seat. He hugged and thanked the soldiers for escorting him to Madrid safely and then drove toward his father's home in the empty ambulance without waking his daughter. It had been a couple of weeks since he had been in the city, and at that time, the Republican Army had been able to resist the siege against the city by pushing back the Fascist troops, offering a brief rest to the civilian population. But since that time, Alfonso knew that Franco had intensified the aerial bombardments, swearing to reduce Madrid to ashes rather than to let the "Marxists" have the city.

Alfonso worried about his daughter's safety, returning home under such dangerous conditions. When Alfonso reached his father's apartment house, laughter and loud voices mixed with the melancholic chords of a guitar stopped him at the door. His father was having one of his gatherings with friends, and Alfonso was not ready for a night of long political discussions and arguments about the future of Spain. He went back to the ambulance, where Mari was still sleeping, and he looked up at the sky. The night was quiet. It was too early for the bombardments, and Alfonso dozed, sitting next to his daughter. He was beginning to drift off into a dark, dreamless sleep when a strong, feminine voice harmoniously flirting with the sounds of a guitar came from the apartment and crawled into Alfonso's sleep, awakening him. He listened to the guitar as it trailed the seductive chords of a woman's voice into the exciting rhythm and flair of a *Malagueña*: "*Lleno de lunares negros tiene el traje de esa gitana que se parece al lucero que sale por la mañana*" (Full of black spots is the dress of that gypsy who looks like the star rising in the morning).

Alfonso smiled, recognizing the deep, resonant voice. It was Dolores singing, the woman with whom he had formed a deep emotional bond since arriving from New York almost five years earlier. He had planned to marry her when divorce became legal in Spain and his wife was back with her family in the United States. Feeling renewed excitement, Alfonso carried his sleeping daughter to the apartment, where his father and his father's guests received him with much glee. He was also met with tearful kisses from his mother and Dolores.

Mari pretended to be asleep when she was carefully placed back on her old bed inside the same room that had witnessed her terror and nightmares a year earlier. She peeked through squinted eyelids as she watched her father kiss Dolores, the woman she remembered visiting her grandparents in the past, a woman she had never liked.

From the other rooms, the men and women laughed. Raspy, lusty voices exchanged folk tunes from various regions of the country until the sound of air-raid sirens snapped everyone back into a reality that had become commonplace. Maria and don Juan spread blankets across the windows and balconies. They turned off the lights and lit small candles. Everyone listened to the sirens, but only for a moment; they soon returned to the music and conversations.

Most of the men had gathered in the kitchen with don Juan, where they sipped black-market wine and argued passionately about politics— Communists, Socialists, anarchists, Liberals. All watched don Juan gesture wildly. He argued, "The enemy is not outside Madrid, my friends. The enemy is everywhere that men persist in the aberration of believing that his ideas alone are the ideas worth having—primarily, the belief in nationalism. Ah, there is one of the best ideas invented for men to kill each other."

A tired-looking, middle-aged man who wore a Basque beret interrupted don Juan. "*Mierda*, don Juan! It is more than an idea when foreign powers try to take control of our motherland. Spain is for Spaniards. Spain does not belong to any political party, especially the political concepts of other countries that do not take into consideration our traditional values. We are not political entities; we are the living, breathing extension of Iberian soil, and I am one of those who will kill for my country. It is called patriotism!"

Don Juan replied, "You are speaking, I suppose, of the Russian intervention?"

"Bah, hombre. I am talking about any intervention! Every party that claims to be acting for the good of the people has accepted foreign ideas. What has this accomplished? Time and time again, when Spaniards have embraced foreign beliefs, it has only led them to the grave."

"It has nothing to do with foreign interference," said a man who held a toothpick between his teeth. "The problems of Spain are the result of its inability to tolerate impermanence. We keep resurrecting the bones and the dead flesh of the past to justify our present. It is our way of retaining national immortality. All new ideas in this country are merely the projection of old ideas. Authoritarian control is our oldest and most sacred approach." He did not finish his speech, because a young man jumped into the conversation.

"Fuck you, Andrés. The authoritarian approach has killed this country!"

The older man removed the toothpick from his mouth and said, "Hombre, there is not a chance in hell that Spaniards will ever shed their need for authority. It is a tradition like ham and wine; it is the same tradition that has perpetuated the Spanish addiction to death, sometimes ignoring life itself."

The young man declared, "I propose a toast! Here it is to our manly *cojones*, while they are still intact, before Franco feeds them to the hogs!"

The men grew silent. The defeat of the Second Spanish Republic was more of a certainty as every day passed. Most of them knew that the defeat and the end of the war would also bring an end to their lives. Lifting their glasses, they toasted to Spain.

From somewhere inside the apartment bedrooms, the wailing echo of the *canto jondo* pierced the walls. Dolores's deep and powerful voice dominated all other sounds as the mournful chords of a guitar trailed her voice. The women and most of the men circled around her, keeping rhythm by clapping. She was sitting next to the guitar player, her torso erect, her smooth, dark throat straining to bring forth the sounds of Spain. The audience was spellbound as it watched her mouth caress words before releasing them to the room with explosive resonance. "*Tengo el cuerpo empapado de mi patria. Soy de España. Soy de España. Soy de tierra caliente. Tengo rabia defendiendo mi gente. El que no esté contento, que se valla.*" (My body is saturated with my country. I am of Spain. I am of Spain. I am of a fiery land. I will furiously defend my people. Those not happy here, let them go.)

Mari had watched as she hid behind the corner of the door. The excitement in the room seemed contagious, but she felt isolated from the group of people whose eyes shone from don Juan's black-market wine, song, and patriotism. She was the only one whose veins were contaminated with "bad" foreign blood, yet too she was of Spain. The woman with the big white teeth was singing that those not happy with Spain should go. Mari was not happy there. But go where? After a time, she walked to the kitchen, where the men were talking with great animation and did not notice her drinking the clear, sweet liquid from a bottle of anisette saved from better days by don Juan. The world seemed kinder to her after a few swallows. Barely able to walk from the effects of the liquor, she returned to her bed. She did not want to be there. Squeezing her eyes closed, she drifted toward a white light that led to a field of wildflowers. The sky was pure blue, and at a distance, she could see Chata, her beloved pig, walking toward her with a tiny piglet next to her. Mari ran to embrace them, laughing.

Soon planes arrived and threw flares into the sky, illuminating their targets. Bombs exploded, buildings crumbled, humans were crushed, babies cried, women screamed, and men cursed. But in don Juan's apartment, the music, the political arguments, and the singing continued as everyone secretly reacted to the explosions with tremors and feared the next strike. The older women, unable to forget their Catholic childhood, whispered, "In the name of the Father, the Son, and the Holy Spirit."

With the help of the International Brigade, the Republicans were able to win the Battle of Guadalajara against the Italian battalions that were helping Franco's war against his own people. This Republican victory aborted the Fascist advance from the northeast toward Madrid, giving the city a brief respite from the daily horrors of constant death and mutilations. However, it did not alleviate the lack of food and supplies that plagued the population trapped inside the city. Without meat or legumes and with every available horse and donkey long since sacrificed, cats and dogs started to disappear from the streets. They had become the only flavor in the tasteless daily rations of lentils cooked without oil, vegetables, or spices, swallowed with the help of water and dried, hard balls of rice bread. During this brief period of silence from stray bullets and exploding missiles, women again talked to each other across the courtyards, children played in the streets, and some families were able to share the afternoon lentil meals together.

But this peaceful interlude was brief. Soon the German Condor Legion airplanes set the city on fire, street by street, and then aimed at the civilian population with artillery shells after each air raid. This concentrated intensity of attacks upon the citizens of Madrid only seemed to strengthen the people as they continued to resist repeating over and over again, "¡No pasarán! ¡No pasarán!"

From Rome, the pope instructed the Spanish Church to distance itself from Republican Spain. He asked all priests and nuns for continued alliance to Franco's rebellion against the government. In retaliation, the Republicans changed the religious utterance of "Adios" to "Salud," a greeting that wished good health and left God out. Armed patrols searched churches and convents for hidden weapons and punished covert acts of betrayal from priests and nuns with instant execution. Religious statues were destroyed and brutally defaced and abused by an occasional soldier mimicking sexual acts with the Virgin Mary.

Franco continued to transport hordes of Moorish troops from Morocco into Spain. Arms from the Nazi and Fascist powers were continuously and openly used on Spanish soil to kill Spaniards as Hitler tested new guns and airplanes in preparation for the events and attacks against Europe that would start World War II.

The mood of the Republican population grew darker. Death swept across every battlefield without regard to the political ideology of those killed. In an attempt to please France and England—and at the same time be able to retain Russian aid—the Republican government withdrew the International Brigade from Spain, which caused some weakness in the strength of the army and lowered the morale of both soldiers and civilians. Republican troops were beginning to weaken in northeast Spain just a few days after they had victoriously gained territory by crossing the Ebro River and pushed Franco away from Madrid.

The threat of a possible retreat initiated one of the bloodiest battles of the war for both sides, leaving thousands of dead along the riverbank. In the meantime, relentless attacks by air and ground descended upon the northwest coast of Spain from the Fascist army. Barcelona, in the midst of internal discord within her own ranks, would soon fall into the hands of the Fascists. Thousands of people from all over Catalonia took flight and crossed—or tried to cross—the border to France. The possible loss of one of their strongest areas of resistance in the northeastern coast was devastating to those who still fought in Madrid. They continued to find death a better option than surrender. They ignored the continued loss of lives. Madrid continued to resist but with little hope for any type of victory.

Only a few weeks had passed since Mari arrived back in Madrid from her grandmother's village. The time she had spent with Tio Miaja and his family felt like a dream or another lifetime. Back in the city of guns and hunger, she felt sadness mingle in her mind and heart. The first morning after her return to Madrid, Mari was surprised to wake up alone, lying on a hard mattress. She looked around the room, expecting to see Tio Miaja's daughters, Mari Carmen and Pilar, and maybe the boys Felipe and David. Instead, she was alone. Everything was different, from a hard mattress instead of a thick, soft feather bed to a square room with a low ceiling instead of a large room with high ceilings supported by big wooden *vigas*.

The anisette she had consumed the night before was making her eyes a little fuzzy, but her head was clear enough to realize that everything was indeed different; she was back in her old room. She was back in Madrid. From then on, she was alone most of the day, without other children with whom to play. She sat for hours by the kitchen window holding Teodoro, her small teddy bear, which her uncle in America had given her. It had the same lavender smell as the dark-haired woman with the sad eyes of long ago. She did not remember why her uncle had given her Teodoro, but she did remember someone rocking her to sleep when she held the stuffed bear in her arms a long time ago, such a long time ago.

Sometimes, if she closed her eyes tightly, a silent-movie screen flashed pictures of tall grass, croaking frogs, flying birds, rich brown soil on which all things grew, and always, Chata and her baby walked by her side. Mari escaped the long and lonely nights of listening to airplanes and bombs exploding by flying to the ceiling and assuming other shapes, other forms, and experiencing realities that were different from the realities of daylight. On these nights, after falling asleep, her body would gently rise and float through the room. As she reached the ceiling and looked down, a child very much like her was always in her bed occupying the space and pillow that she had just left, and a dark-haired woman with large brown eyes sat next to the child, stroking her head and smiling. When Mari began descending from the ceiling, just before reaching the bed, the little girl and the dark-haired woman always disappeared, and Mari woke up alone, but now the bed was wet.

It was a struggle for everyone just to stay alive, and the days passed without the family noticing Mari's silence. They blamed her occasional "accidents" of bed-wetting on questionable early training by her careless mother. The men seldom came home. When they did, there was no longer the excitement and constant chatter as before. The grandmother spent most of her days standing in line for food or roaming about empty fields looking for edible weeds with which she could add a little taste to her meager cooking at home.

Pilar, Mari's deaf aunt, was always too busy cleaning and scrubbing floors, doing the household laundry, and making beds to spend time with her niece.

Mari's grandfather spent the days outside the home attending to the needs of troops coming from the front. When he was home, he silently pounded on his typewriter without laughing or taking time to be with his granddaughter. He was also silent at mealtimes, without his usual endless speculation that Roosevelt would come to the aid of the republic.

Sometimes, Mari's daily stillness was interrupted by soldiers knocking on the door to ask for mattresses and blankets for the wounded. Mari made an occasional trip with her grandmother to wait in line for the distribution of rationed lentils and yellow bread. On these trips, Mari and her grandmother sometimes passed women and children in the street desperately searching for their belongings as they sorted among the bombed ruins of their homes. Mari did not know what they were doing. She did not ask, and she did not care. There did not seem to be any time for caring anymore.

There were times at night when the sound of tanks leaving for the front lines made the floors and walls of apartments vibrate as enemy planes made erratic flights over the city with unpredictable bombardments, as if they knew when tanks and troops were on the way to battle. These same planes returned in the morning, dropping bags of freshly baked bread with leaflets telling the people of Madrid how Franco "cared about" and "admired" every Spaniard, regardless of political beliefs. At the bottom of the leaflets, in large, bold, black letters, advice to surrender was printed "to begin building a better Spain."

Government officials discouraged everyone in the city from eating the bread, warning that the bread might have been poisoned—the same with the candy dropped in Barcelona some time earlier. The bags of candy were taken immediately to remote areas and buried. No one tried to eat the bread. Angered by the possibility of being poisoned, no one thought of surrendering.

Exhausted troops coming from the front into Madrid for brief periods of rest were housed in the empty convents and Catholic churches at night, but space was beginning to be a problem. Troops requiring rest and civilian refugees grew in number. Don Juan's responsibility to find space for the tired soldiers required twenty-four-hour availability. After discussing the problem with his wife, the family moved to one of the now empty Carmelite convents, making don Juan easily available to the troops at any time.

The move was quick, and Mari found herself with the unexpected entertainment of watching exhausted soldiers arrive to the convent-garrison during the day. These soldiers would vanish before sunup after a couple of days of rest and return to the front lines. Many were probably killed before it was time for another rest period. Every day, after the arrival of new troops, Mari roamed the buildings enclosed within a massive wall that encircled the convent. There was only one exit, a gigantic wrought-iron gate that led to an enclosed passageway that led to the street.

There were many strange buildings within the wall. Some buildings were used to store supplies, and others were used to store ammunition. The rest of the monastery, with the exception of the main house, was used as temporary barracks for the arriving troops that needed rest. Underneath the monastery ran a series of tunnels that connected the main house to all other buildings. It was at the beginning of these tunnels under the kitchen of the main house that wine was stored in barrels and bottles, neatly arranged inside wooden shelves that were built against the muddy walls. Every barrel and every bottle had been full when the army first arrived in the monastery, and now the wine was sparingly rationed and given to the soldiers during the main meal in the afternoon to improve morale and to suggest that normal Spanish dining persisted. The tunnels were dark and cold, maintaining the proper temperature for the stored wine. A solitary dim lightbulb illuminated the area of unfinished sand floors, which was always wet and supported a heavy wooden door that separated the wine cellar from the rest of the tunnels.

Maria and don Juan had visited the living quarters of the monastery before moving. After some differences between them, they chose six rooms in the main house from a seemingly infinite number of mostly empty rooms. The rooms were large, and the white walls had been finished with rough paint. When Mari leaned on them, small amounts of white, powdery impressions rubbed off on her clothing. Crosses and pictures had apparently once hung on these walls, leaving dark outlines when taken down. In the upper corners of the rooms, empty niches that once contained statues of saints and virgins now stood empty. Afraid to sleep alone inside these large, unfriendly rooms, Mari was allowed to take turns sleeping with each family member. Sleeping with another person was less threatening to her than sleeping alone, but it interfered with her nightly experiences of ascending to the ceiling, looking down to the bed she just left, and seeing the dark-haired woman with the large dark eyes and the little girl who looked like her.

Instead, there were nights when, as the dim light of early dawn was beginning to shine behind the mountains, Mari was awakened by the sounds of female voices crying and whispering prayers. These voices came from the courtyard behind the buildings, voices that were silenced after a single discharge of multiple, simultaneous rifle fire. She knew from her experience on prior nights that soon, intermittent pistol shots would follow the rifle shots and that these pistol shots would echo through the empty buildings just as the dim light of early dawn rose above the mountaintops. No one in the family seemed to hear these sounds. No one talked about these sounds, and Mari never asked.

Mari continued to shift bedrooms, but most nights she preferred to sleep with Uncle Chato, her father's sixteen-year-old brother, with whom she had a playful relationship that most times made her laugh and feel important. These feelings changed one night when, sleeping with her uncle, she woke up to the sound of a loud female voice penetrating through the windows, "Dear Jesus, son of God, receive our souls for all eternity; be merciful to the young men who are about to send our mortal bodies into perpetual sleep."

Mari opened her eyes and listened. A chorus of other female voices followed. "Dear Jesus, son of God, receive our souls for all eternity." The voices stopped without asking God to forgive the men who were about to send their bodies to perpetual sleep. Mari became more frightened that usual, as the voices were much louder and the words of the prayers very clear. She tried to get closer to Uncle Chato, but his side of the bed was empty. She opened her eyes and looked around the room. Her uncle was finished getting dressed and was tucking a small pistol under his belt, after which he left the room in a rush.

More curious than afraid, Mari followed him, but he vanished in the dark halls outside the bedrooms. The voices in the courtyard repeated the same prayers. Mari ran to one of the windows that faced the courtyard. A handful of women dressed in the brown robes of the Carmelite order of nuns knelt with their backs to the wall, holding the beads of a rosary between the trembling fingers of tied hands. Soldiers stood at the other side of the courtyard with rifles aimed at the kneeling women. At the sound of a simultaneous discharge of gunfire, the nuns fell to the ground. One minute later, Mari watched with horror as Uncle Chato walked from one inert body to another, discharging a single shot through the head of each woman. The universe spun.

Mari suddenly imagined her young uncle with large fangs hanging from the corners of his bloodstained mouth. She ran back to the room, leaving a trail of her stomach contents behind and waiting for the dark-haired woman to take her away from this terror. But the dark-haired woman with the sad eyes did not appear. Mari hid under the covers, shaking and losing bladder control.

Her uncle was back in the room and asked her, "Are you awake?"

But she was afraid to look at him and stayed under the covers, whispering, "I am sick, Chato. Please call my grandmother."

Chato woke up his sister Pilar, and she washed Mari after removing the stained pajamas and dressed her in daytime clothes as she tried to make light of the situation by smiling and joking about bad dreams that make people sick to their stomach. "It happens to almost everyone at one time or another. There is nothing for you to worry about."

Because of Aunt Pilar's deafness, Mari realized that Aunt Pilar did not know what had happened, and she had assumed from what her brother said that Mari had awoken sick to her stomach from bad dreams. But Chato knew better; there was no way he could have missed the trail of stomach contents from the window to the room. Mari did not tell her aunt about the shootings in the courtyard, but Mari never again slept in the same room with Uncle Chato.

Long days and nights passed. Mari spent her time alone exploring the convent's empty rooms, one room after another, looking for treasures that she could never find, always avoiding to look at or go to the side of the courtyard that made her nights a nightmare. Outside and inside the convent's walls, the horrors of war occurred every day, events that were always dismissed and accepted by the adults with a matter-of-fact attitude. The nightly shootings of the nuns were never mentioned by anyone.

Suddenly, the shootings stopped, and Mari could sleep through most of the nights. Food had been better since the family moved to the convent, and the family was able to eat together sometimes when Mari's uncles and her father came home for rest periods. On one of these days, Mari sat at the table with her three uncles, her father, and her grandfather waiting for Pilar and Mari's grandmother to serve one of the rare well-received meals. Mari noticed that there was another person at the table getting ready to eat with her family. Sitting next to her father was Dolores, the woman with the big white teeth, the woman who was always singing, the woman her father kissed the night they came back from her grandmother's village, the woman her father was now fondling as he laughed and whispered in her ear.

Oh, the hate, Mari's terrible hate, was back. Mari ran out of the dining room without saying a word, out of the building to the courtyard where the nuns had been shot. Imagining Dolores with her hands tied in front of her, holding a rosary and praying, Mari pointed her finger and mimicked shooting her in the head. She imagined the woman with the large white teeth falling to the ground. In a rage, Mari kicked and punched the imaginary body against the wall.

The grandmother came running out of the building, yelling at the child, "Stop it! Stop it!" Holding her grandchild gently in her arms, Maria rested her cheek on Mari's face, humming and kissing her eyelids over and over again until, exhausted and numb, Mari's body relaxed, and the grandmother let go of her. They walked back to the building holding hands in silence. Once back, the grandmother tried to make excuses, laughing and addressing no one in particular, "She has the family's temperament. She will be all right after some food and a siesta."

No one asked Mari what had happened. Her father was distracted and focusing all his attention on the woman with the big teeth, ignoring the angry tears in his daughter's eyes. Mari sat silently, a sagging feeling in the pit of her stomach, wanting to vomit.

After eating, the men sat around the table, unshaven in their blue coveralls, looking tired but talking and laughing as they passed a wine-filled leather bota around the table. The grandfather read from the many pages he wrote with his typewriter almost every day about politics, the war, the failure of Roosevelt to come to the aid of Republican Spain, the failure of the American president to act on the proposed resolutions to end the North American embargo of arms to Spain, and how this delay had given Catholics time to gather momentum and abort the proposition.

"This embargo," don Juan shouted, "is not legal now, and it has never been for our situation in Spain! The US Neutrality Act of 1935 was a response to the conflicts in Abyssinia and has nothing to do with our war." He was referring to the embargo that the powerful and manipulative Cordell Hull—secretary of state in the United States as well as a strong Catholic— used to deny help to the Republicans in Spain, ignoring worldwide protests all the way from workers to European liberal and conservative politicians and on to nonpolitical scientists, such as Einstein. "I am surprised and disappointed," continued don Juan. "I am aware that the pope is a powerful man, but so are millions of Americans and Europeans who are concerned about us."

Alfonso lit a cigarette and blew the smoke into the air. His voice was almost a whisper. "I was hopeful when Eleanor Roosevelt backed the Republic. Remember?"

His brother Max leaned toward him, his voice shaking. "Eleanor Roosevelt was a powerful woman, but not powerful enough to stop that bastard Hull. How could the American people vote for such a fucking Catholic Fascist?"

Alfonso looked at him and smiled. "He got his way because President Roosevelt traded his beliefs for the Catholic vote. He is another fucker, and now we are fucked. It is time to stop talking about past possibilities and give ourselves up. This war is over."

Don Juan stared at his son with an incredulous look on his face. He questioned the outcome of the conversation. He considered his son's remark cowardly. The issue of defeat had never entered his mind—not defeat by surrender, only by death. How could his son consider a life under a dictatorship and the Vatican? His own life had been a series of tumultuous defeats that did not allow him to surrender his way of thinking, and possibly his life, to Fascism. In all his adult life, his energy had been directed to the survival of his family, his country, and his ideas.

Don Juan now realized how he had sacrificed the expression of his emotions and his need for closeness to his wife and children by leaving Spain during the reign of Alfonso XIII with a head full of ideas and schemes for a Marxist democracy around the world. He had searched for political equality and fairness in the New World, allowing him the freedom of his political passions, but equality had eluded him from one continent to another. From the sweatshops in New York City to the immigrant labor camps in California, few wanted to listen to his ideas. No one read his words—not the immigrants in California, not the Mexican *peones* laboring without rest under the hot sun for pennies a day in Mexico. He had taken his family across the California desert in trucks loaded with furniture and children, very much like the shadow of a married Don Quixote on the arid plains of La Mancha.

Those had been hard times. He made his family pick fruit and stay in camps swept with poverty and disease. He watched his wife give birth to the last-born child among chairs and kitchen utensils in a truck stuck in the sand of the Mojave Desert. A daughter lost her hearing, and another lost her life in a disease-infested, fruit-picking California immigrant camp. This did not stop him, and he pushed his family on to Mexico, where he fed them by transporting whiskey across the border to the United States during Prohibition. All the while, he pounded on his typewriter and preached the benefits of a socialist reform to a population of Mexican Indians who thought him insane. He had aborted all his emotions, all his needs for closeness and love with his family by spending all his energy trying to change a world that did not want to be changed.

The Second Spanish Republic, crude as it was, had given him back all his hopes for a safe, free, and comfortable world without fear of slavery to the rich and powerful, an educated world, a world without hunger, a world where everyone was equal and free to choose his religion and political orientation. His world. His reality.

Don Juan turned his head away from his sons. He would not participate in a conversation of surrender, and he abruptly changed the topic of discussion by beginning one of his monologues about strategies to win the war that was already lost. He talked about the need to attack and recover some of the towns between Valencia and Zaragoza, mainly Teruel, to keep an open line from Madrid to Barcelona to begin working on an offensive.

Alfonso and his brothers continued to pass the wine bota around. It was obvious that don Juan was not ready to accept the imminent reality of a Republican defeat. They had been on the defensive for a very long time, and now the Republican government leaders were beginning to board planes from the Barajas Airport in Madrid to flee to other countries. Madrid and the northeastern coast were the only barely standing Republican fronts. Now the idealistic don Juan was talking about troop advances to Barcelona!

"Bah!" whispered Alfonso to his brother. "The poor son-of-a-bitch idealist. Too much wine!"

The women cleaned the table, taking all the dirty plates to the kitchen. Don Juan's wife and their daughter Pilar dipped the plates in a sink filled with hot water and soap. Mari had trailed after her grandmother into the kitchen, trying to get her attention or maybe a little more of the flan dessert.

Dolores, who was sitting at the kitchen table, called Mari's name. Mari stopped looking down at the floor, and Dolores picked her up. Ignoring the tense and grimacing child in her arms, Dolores placed Mari on her lap and attempted to initiate a conversation. "You look like your mother, Mari. The same eyes. Do you remember your mother? She was my friend."

The grandmother turned around from the sink, frowning, and looked at Dolores with an angry look in her eyes. She asked her granddaughter to get down from Dolores's lap, "Go to the dining room and see if the men want some coffee."

After the child left the room, Maria stood in front of Dolores and forced a smile as she dried her hands on her apron. Her words were clipped, but she spoke very slowly, attempting to soften her words. "Dolores, I know that you probably don't know that Mari does not remember her mother. We prefer it that way. We feel this child has suffered enough because of her mother and father's problems, so it is time for her to begin feeling that she belongs in this family without missing her mother every day."

Dolores looked down at the floor without answering. She did not want to create any discomfort between herself and the mother of the man she wanted to marry, but she was not comfortable with what his mother had just said. She believed that every child needed to know his or her mother, regardless of the situation between the parents. The air was tense in the kitchen. Dolores walked to the window and looked out to the garden and thoughts about Rosa, Mari's mother, which distracted her from the discomfort in the room.

Yes, Dolores remembered Mari's mother well: Rosa, the foreign teenage girl married to Alfonso who arrived in Spain a few months after Alfonso had settled in Madrid with his mother. Dolores had met Alfonso prior to Rosa's arrival, and Dolores and Alfonso had established a romantic relationship and had even made plans to marry. Alfonso was planning to get a divorce from his wife on the grounds of abandonment, which was not exactly true, as Alfonso had abandoned Rosa. They wanted to take advantage of Spain's Republican separation of church and state before the republic was defeated and Spain, once again under the Catholic mandates, declared divorces illegal. The plan was to have an immediate marriage before Dolores's parents learned that Alfonso had been married and divorced, which they would find unacceptable because of their Catholic beliefs.

All these plans ended when an angry don Juan contacted Alfonso from New York with the news that Rosa, Alfonso's wife, had given birth to his first child and was carrying another, conceived before he left for Spain. "She has been unable to get any help from her family," wrote don Juan, "and she has been living on the streets with your daughter." He told Alfonso how he had spotted Rosa standing on one of the long food lines common in New York in the middle of the Depression and how painful it had been to see Rosa, weak and frail, trying to get food for herself and a thin, unkempt Mari. "You lied to me," wrote don Juan, "When we discussed you going to Spain with your mother to find a job and have a place ready when the rest of us could join you, that included your wife and your child. How could you? How could you abandon your own flesh and blood?" Don Juan ordered Alfonso to prepare for his wife's arrival in Madrid and to have suitable living space for his family.

Dolores continued looking out the kitchen window as she remembered how the arrival of Rosa and the young child in Madrid had changed her life. With the presence of a pregnant wife and a little girl, it was impossible to hide from her family that Alfonso was married. Her family would never accept a divorced man as a son-in-law. Alfonso told her, and she believed him, that Rosa's expected child was not his and that he would make arrangements to place the baby in an orphanage and would send Rosa back to America.

Rosa gave birth to a boy, and in so doing, she developed serious bleeding complications that required that she remain in the hospital for a time after having given birth to the baby. The hospital stay extended indefinitely when Rosa was diagnosed with Mediterranean anemia, a newly discovered type of anemia not well known in Spain, which the doctors had a hard time managing. The new baby was named José. Alfonso took José home. Alfonso, together with Dolores, took advantage of Rosa's stay in the hospital to leave the newborn baby in the city orphanage. Rosa was told that her son had died at birth, and as she did not speak Spanish and was in the lonely isolation of a country and a people with whom she could not communicate, she pretended to accept what Alfonso had said, but she never believed him and mourned the loss of her son in silence.

Almost five years had passed since Rosa left Spain to undergo treatment for her illness in New York. With no expectation of Rosa surviving her illness, Dolores planned to tell her family that Rosa had died in the United States, and she and Alfonso would marry and take his daughter to live with them. With these thoughts in mind, Dolores had wanted to establish a relationship with Alfonso's daughter before the wedding to avoid another abrupt change in the life of the child. This was what she was trying to do when the grandmother interrupted and sent the child out of the room.

Maria's apologetic voice returned Dolores to the present. "I am sorry. I was a little sharp, but Mari went through so many changes when her mother left. Now that she does not remember her, it is better not to remind her."

Dolores looked away from the grandmother, her voice trailing. "I understand."

When Maria and her daughter finished washing the dishes, a prolonged and uncomfortable silence continued in the kitchen. Pilar tried to ignore the tension between the two women by busying herself drying the dishes and, with immaculate precision, slowly placing every plate and every cup inside the kitchen shelves. After Pilar finished putting away the last of the dishes, the uncomfortable silence between her mother and Dolores was unchanged. To break the discomfort, Pilar offered the women coffee. Both refused.

Finally, Dolores excused herself and returned to the dining room. She was about to sit at the table next to Alfonso when she noticed that Mari was not in the room. Tapping Alfonso's shoulder, Dolores asked, "Where is the *niña*?"

The men looked around the room, expecting the child to be there, but she was not.

"Did Mari come back with the wine?" Alfonso asked his father.

Don Juan paused from one of his readings and looked at Alfonso from the top of his glasses. "I don't think so. I don't see a wine bottle."

Dolores lifted her eyebrows, looking at the men in disbelief. "Don't tell me you sent that child to the wine cellar by herself."

Alfonso picked up a typewritten page his father was handing him, answering Dolores without looking up, "Why not? She has been there before."

Dolores turned away from the men and rushed toward the entrance of the tunnel. She found Mari, wide eyed and shaking, standing next to a broken wine bottle on the floor. A lifeless hand lay across her right foot, a hand that seemed almost to want to hold Mari's ankle. A large man dressed in the long tunic of a priest lay on the floor without moving. His eyes were wide open, looking at the ceiling. His right hand held a crucifix. Dolores was horrified by the scene in front of her and knelt on the floor. Taking Mari in her arms and turning the child's head away from the body on the floor, Dolores whispered, "Oh, God. Don't look, *niña*. Look at me."

Holding Mari tightly in her arms, Dolores ran back to the building, passing the dining room, where the men continued talking, paying no attention to what was happening as she passed them, heading for the bedrooms in the back. She sat on the first bed she found, and still holding

Mari in her arms, rocked back and forth as she called out to the men in the dining room, "Alfonso, there was a dead man in the cellar. A priest. Your daughter found him!"

The men ran to the tunnels as Dolores continued to hold Mari in her arms and whispered in the ears of the terrified child, "You are safe. You are safe."

The grandmother came into the room with her hands wrapped inside her apron. She kneeled in front of Dolores and stroked Mari's face, which was buried against Dolores's chest, and asked, "What happened?"

Dolores pointed her chin toward the dining room and explained, "The men sent Mari to the wine cellar to get a bottle of wine. A man was lying there. I think he was dead. Mari stumbled on his hand. He was a priest."

Patting Mari's hand, Maria stood up and made the sign of the cross against her chest. She left the room, saying to herself, "Dear God, I am sure you are telling me the reason for all of this, but I don't know why I can't I hear you."

The men returned from the tunnel. Alfonso went to the bedroom. He was surprised to see Dolores still holding his daughter. "You know that we would never have sent Mari into the tunnel if I thought there was any chance of anything being there."

As usual, Dolores kept silent to avoid expressing her opinions, which she felt were too abstract for Alfonso and his family to understand. She had a bit of an ego, and she was aware that Alfonso had not known her long enough to understand her contrary way of thinking.

The priest found in the wine tunnel had escaped from his cell after having been scheduled for the firing squad, accused of acts of treason against the Republic. There were no wounds on his body, and no one knew how he escaped, but he was dead when found and sent for burial to one of the many mass graves dug every day for executed prisoners. This holy man, as priests were called, was found guilty of obeying the pope and acting against the Second Spanish Republic by using his church to store arms for the rebels, as well as sending information to the enemy detailing weak points in the defense of the city. He was a traitor whose death was of consequence to no one except to the child who found him, a child who now lay on her bed and stared into space fully conscious but not responding to anyone or anything.

Night after night Maria held Mari in her arms, making no effort to hide the tears travelling down her cheeks, tears of sorrow and regret. Sorrow for what was happening now, regret for not protecting her granddaughter enough after what happened at the Casa de Campo.

"We need to be with Mari. We need to make her know how much we love her," she told the family.

Mari's grandmother and her aunt Pilar sat by Mari's bed every day and placed little bits of food in her mouth, making her drink water, washing her, holding her, and carrying her limp body to the bathroom every day without being able to get a response or recognition.

Alfonso tried desperately to make a connection with his daughter. He avoided overnight stays at the battlefront and was home to see her almost every day in between his trips carrying the wounded to hospitals. After a few days, frustrated with his daughter's lack of response, Alfonso negotiated a bar of chocolate candy from a black-market vendor, hoping that the treat would initiate some response from the child. It did not, at least not the response he wanted. After holding the chocolate in her mouth for a few minutes, Mari assumed a fetal position and, for the first time in all these days, closed her eyes while awake. Alfonso looked at her, not knowing the meaning of what was happening. There was no way he could imagine how the taste of chocolate had transported Mari to another world, to another time when chocolate made her feel safe. She remained curled into herself, remembering the times when cold, sweet chocolate melted in her mouth and the arms of the dark-haired woman wrapped around her as she laughed, wiping some of the cold, sweet cream from her chin. The taste of chocolate lingered in her mouth, and memories of laughter and games returned with the familiar-sounding words *ice cream*.

Mari had felt safe in this dream until the darkness of the night entered the room, and the sound of a hoarse voice whispered, "Help me," and something cold wrapped itself around her ankle. It was the hand attached to the arm attached to the body attached to the face with the wide-open eyes that looked at her and then stared into space. The wine bottle she was holding always dropped from her hands, and broken glass and dark fluid splashed on the face attached to the body attached to the arm attached to the hand holding her ankle. She could not tell how long this dream lasted, but time and time again, someone carried her away from the broken bottle and the face with the wide-open eyes, and a soft voice whispered in her ear, "You are safe. You are safe." Was that the voice of Dolores, the woman with the big teeth? Or was it the young woman with the dark olive skin and the smiling eyes of long ago?

Don Juan watched his grandchild grow less responsive every day. Tormented by guilt and sadness, he realized that the convent turned into a garrison was no place for a small child. After much thinking and planning, he addressed his wife and discussed his feelings as well as his observations of how he thought the present environment in their place of residence was affecting their granddaughter. After a moment of pause, don Juan held his wife's hand and finished what he was saying with a question, "How would you feel about moving out of here to an apartment of our own?"

Maria looked at her husband with surprise and said, "Juan, I thought your job at the garrison was important to you."

"Oh, it is. I am not talking about giving up my duties, just where we live. If we rent an apartment near here, I can come to work on my bicycle, and one of the soldiers can take me back home at night. We just would not see each other as much."

Maria smiled a big smile. Kissing her husband, she whispered, "I love you so much! Of course, you know you are right. This is not a good environment for Mari. I will start looking for a place right away. There are so many apartments empty because of the war that I am sure we will have no problems finding something we can afford."

In two weeks, the family moved into a second-floor duplex near the garrison that had no wine cellars, no tunnels, no dead nuns or priests, and where the passing of flying birds was the only interruption to silence in the early hours of dawn. The duplex was situated next to a row of houses, many unoccupied because of the war, and it faced a wide, unfinished street without trees or vegetation. The apartment next to don Juan and his family was empty, and Maria and Pilar started cleaning and arranging all things in the building, as well as the small garden in the back of the house. The grateful soldiers in the garrison gave a parting gift to don Juan and Maria: a pair of rabbits and a small rooster. Maria made a shelter for the rabbits in the yard, with the hope of many more rabbits to come to aid her cooking in the future. The rooster, still a small bird, was given the freedom of the yard, as he also waited for a dark, thankless destiny in Maria's kitchen.

Dormant morning glories crawled up the walls on the sides of the house, waiting for spring to burst into bright, colorful flowers and cover the entire building. It felt like a real home to Mari after the stressful days spent in the garrison. It was a comfortable home, but a lonely one. She slowly left the bed and entered into solitary games in the backyard, spending hours playing with the rabbits, which made her think of Chata and the little piglet she never got to see. Sometimes, the little rooster jumped and cackled, and thinking the rooster was laughing, Mari jumped and laughed with him. The grandmother watched her play with the rooster from the kitchen window, wondering why her granddaughter laughed with the rooster but never with the family.

Everyone soon adjusted to the new routine in the new apartment. The grandmother was gone for most of the day, looking for any edible staples available in the black market around Madrid. Sometimes she returned with a handful of potatoes and sometimes with a couple of beef bones to flavor the rationed lentils. She made salads with the edible weeds she picked on empty lots, using drops of oil from a bottle of oil she hoarded from before the war.

Don Juan spent every available moment away from work behind his typewriter, furiously battling the injustices suffered by Spain at the hands of other countries. He was angry after France banned the shipments of help to the Second Spanish Republic at a time when the German Condor Legion persistently bombed supply ships, cutting off all needed food to the civilian population. As the food supply kept dwindling and as the fall of Barcelona became more of a reality to the people of Madrid, a wave of suicides swept across the city, encouraging more and more Fascist sympathizers to come out of hiding and preach surrender without a peace treaty.

Madrid was in the midst of chaos and hopelessness, yet groups of people gathered almost every day and continued to march in the streets behind the Republican flag, shouting, "¡No pasarán! ¡No pasarán!"

The defeat of the Second Spanish Republic in northeastern Spain was imminent after the fall of Barcelona into enemy hands. Along the coast of the Mediterranean, the mood was heavy among a weary and fearful population. Each hour of the day increased the hopelessness and despair of a defeated people who forgot victory and concentrated on survival. Barcelona had been the heart and soul of the province of Catalonia. With the sound of enemy heels marching down in perfect military precision through its now silent streets, refugees crowded in the port, hoping for an escape by sea. But the continued air raids had destroyed all available ships or boats docked in every port along the western coast, leaving a terrified people unable to flee and doomed for impending prison, torture, and death once Franco's Fascist army secured and dominated the city.

Almost immediately after Barcelona, the pride of Spain, fell into the hands of the enemy, hope had given way to fear and anger all over the northwestern coast of Spain. Municipal workers gave up going to work, government offices closed their doors, uncollected trash filled the streets, and shops were invaded by hungry mobs looking for food or anything of value. Eventually, every street of every town and every city along the coast gave in to the silence of a hopeless people overwhelmed with terror and desolation after their desperate efforts to flee to the French border or by sea to any other country failed. The illusion of a free democratic peninsula had died.

In the meantime, the Republican militia in Madrid continued to oppose the Fascist army, while the civilian population crumbled under daily bombings from German airplanes and from starvation. The militia fought, and civilians continued to put up barricades, but the morale was on a spiral of disintegration after the news that the last government officials, including La Pasionaria, had boarded planes from an airport in Dakar, the capital of Senegal in Western Africa, and had abandoned Spain and all the people who followed them, many to their deaths.

Conflict between political parties disrupted the unity of the army and civilians in Madrid, and eventually, internal wars sprouted among themselves, even while they resisted the enemy's efforts to enter the city. Unannounced air attacks flew over the city during the day, creating large numbers of casualties among the civilian population, especially the unaware children caught playing in the streets. Overwhelmed and unable to counterattack these enemy air raids, the government converted abandoned church buildings into shelters to protect the children during the day when the bombings occurred and called the shelters "day schools." It was a desperate plan that, in addition of offering protection for the children, also freed adults to attend the increased number of wounded in the city. Soldiers began knocking on doors asking for children to be taken to the nearest neighborhood "day school." [I found this discussion of political situation etc. to be intrusive, and to slow the story. Stay with emotions and perceptions.]

When Maria shared this information with her granddaughter, Mari yelled and screamed, threatening to run away with gypsies rather than go to school in a church. She had heard about these places where nuns beat children with the wooden map pointers and sometimes locked them in small, dark closets for days without food or water. Her grandfather said so. It happened to him when he was a small boy, and she was willing to roam the world homeless and away from the family with the gypsies before being beaten and locked in small, dark closets by the nuns. Mari's immovable attitude changed when her grandmother offered to make *cocido* for lunch on her first day of school. This was one of Mari's favorite foods, a meal she had not had for a very long time. She remembered days gone by when she ate delicious noodles made into a soup with the broth of tender meats cooked in olive oil and sweet spices. She forgot all about spending the day abandoned and beaten by nuns. Her head filled with pictures of chickpeas served with large pieces of beef, pork, potatoes, and red cabbage bathed in olive oil served after the noodle soup. These visions made the beatings by nuns seem insignificant. This was her food, the food of long ago. It was the food when her father was home every night, the food when her grandfather told her stories about Spain, a food well worth a nun's anger.

After her grandchild agreed to go to school in return for her cooking, the grandmother tried not to think of what this meal would cost. It would cost her leather shoes, which was what it would take in the black market in exchange for meats to make the cocido. Potatoes, red cabbage, chickpeas, and potatoes could still be purchased with money, a lot of money, but that was of no importance. Giving up her leather shoes was a bit harder; all leather goods had been confiscated to make boots for the army, and one pair of leather shoes was all that was allowed to each person. It was her last pair of shoes, but it was well worth the sacrifice when she stood in front of the school building with her granddaughter.

Mari was smiling and seemed happy as she tucked an orange into the pocket of her apron and pointed a shaking finger at her grandmother. "Don't forget, Abuela. You promised me cocido when I get home from school!" The child's voice was serious and authoritative, and the grandmother had to pucker her lips in an attempt not to laugh and instead nodded her head, signaling assertion and understanding as her granddaughter turned from her, walking toward the door of the abandoned church.

A tall woman with dark hair tied into a bun on the back of her head greeted Mari with a smile and held her hand as they walked through the front doors of the abandoned church into an empty reception room with tinted glass windows and an empty altar at the back of the room. The woman, still holding Mari's hand, pushed a door on back of the altar and followed a long, dark passage to a narrow hallway slanting downward and ending in front of a large room without windows. It was a large, ugly room with wet, unfinished walls. Drops of water trailed into small puddles at the edge of the floor. It seemed as if religious statues and pictures that had once looked down from the walls, now gone, had left empty niches and outlines on the wall. There were no furnishings in the room other than rough, long benches made of unfinished wood, where nuns had once gathered to pray.

Now these benches accommodated a group of frightened children staring at a movie screen. It was a dark room, a damp, dusty-smelling room where the whispering of prayers by nuns could almost be heard above the voices coming from the movie screen. Cowboys and horses dashed around in front of the children, shouting incomprehensible words and making strange sounds. Spanish subtitles flickered at the bottom of the screen, confusing the children, who never learned to read or write because their parents and teachers were too busy killing each other.

The woman with the dark hair tied into a bun on the back of the head continued to smile as she addressed Mari. "I am told that you are an American. Maybe you can understand what the cowboys are saying and later can tell the other children."

Mari did not know what to say. She did not know anything about Americans. "I am—mm," she stuttered and stopped talking, remembering her grandfather's voice the day she had asked him if she was Spanish. "The blood of the Iberians, the Celts, the Greeks, and the Romans is in your veins. You may also have a drop of blood on the tip of your nose from a Moor, a mixture that makes you a Spaniard. It matters not where you were born. There is nothing but Spanish blood in this family. Don't you ever forget it."

She wanted to believe her grandfather, but this woman had called her an American. In all of her grandfather's stories and history about different people, he had never mentioned Americans. What was an American? She sat on one of the wooden benches with the other children without hearing or seeing what was on the screen in front of her. The sound of bombs whistling through the air came from outside the building, echoing inside the room and lingering in the air before the bombs exploded. Each time a bomb whistled through the air, the children sat erect, as if hypnotized, and waited for the bomb to explode.

The children cracked and chewed sunflower seeds from small cones made out of newspaper given to them by the woman with the dark hair tied into a bun on the back of the head. The chewing and the cracking became faster and louder as each bomb exploded somewhere outside the room. The sound of an explosion was still resonating on the walls of the room when a little boy seated next to Mari noticed that she did not have any sunflower seeds and shuffled his body closer to her. His face was wet from tears, and liquid from a runny nose dripped down his chin as he extended his shaking hand holding sunflower seeds.

Mari smiled and reached to accept the boy's gift, when everything in front of her changed. The little boy with the sunflower seeds was Manolito with a runny nose and tearful eyes. He looked the same as the day the mortar shell exploded, the day he and the twins Conchita and Rosa Maria were killed in Casa de Campo. The same Manolito to whom she had lied about the Pasionaria leaving a message. Now Manolito was here, sitting next to her, staring across the room into a darkened corner as the figures of Conchita and Rosa Maria slowly appeared through the wall and silently stared back at him.

Mari's arms went limp. Her hands spilled the sunflower seeds the little boy had given her. She lost control of her bladder. *Whiz, bang, click, snap*; the walls resonated with the noise of falling bombs outside the room and the sound of the children's rapid cracking of sunflower seeds inside the room.

"Are we dead yet?" whispered Manolito.

"We are all dead," whispered Conchita, while Rosa Maria nodded. The twins looked directly at Mari as their images slowly vanished into the shadows of the room while whispering, "You lied, Mari. There was no message from La Pasionaria."

"I am sorry, Manolito. I am sorry, Conchita. I am sorry, Rosa Maria."

The orange her grandmother had given her rolled onto the floor without a sound, and at the same time, Manolito's head flew over the room, quietly disappearing into the opposite wall, leaving headless body sitting next to Mari.

The sound of a voice in the room stopped the spinning inside Mari's head. It was the woman with the dark hair tied into a bun on the back of her head. She was reading the subtitles at the bottom of the movie screen in whispering tones. She was no longer smiling. Every time a bomb exploded, her eyes searched the room to confirm that every child was safe. After Mari's attention returned to the room, Manolito's body was gone, and the little boy next to her with the runny nose was staring at her.

The children continued to look at the screen with empty eyes while listening to the *whiz! bang!* of the falling bombs outside the building and the *click, click, snap, snap* of the cracking sunflower seeds inside the room. They did not notice that the wheezing sound of falling bombs had stopped until the woman with the dark hair tied into a bun on the back of her head stopped talking. The room was silent. Fingers holding the paper cones froze in midair.

The woman with the dark hair tied into a bun on the back of her head rearranged herself, pushing back some hair that had fallen in front of her eyes. She looked around the silent room and walked around the benches, smiling at the children as she turned on the lights, trying to be cheerful. "That was a wonderful movie! Don't you think that it was a good movie? We are just in time to go home and eat lunch. Don't forget to take a nap after you eat. That was such a good movie! Yes, my brave soldiers, we are just in time to go home to eat and take a nap. Soldiers have to eat and rest to be strong."

When the children did not talk or move from their seats, the woman gently ushered them ahead of her, waving her hands and repeating, "Was it not a good movie?" Before leaving the room, the woman asked the children to line up and walk in pairs, holding hands. To avoid anyone noticing her wet skirt, Mari lagged behind, going last in line and holding the little boy's hand. There were no more tears in his eyes, and he was now smiling at her, but his nose was still running. Mari took a small handkerchief from her apron and cleaned his face.

The woman with the dark hair untied the bun on the back of her head as she walked in front of the children, and they followed her in silence. Only the shuffling of the small feet could be heard as the children moved up the slanted hallway until they reached the front of the building and stood quietly by the door. No one seemed to have noticed the large wet spot left behind by Mari on one of the benches because there were many other wet spots left behind on other benches by terrified children.

Outside the church building, a young woman who wore overalls and the pointed cap with a tassel in the front worn by Republican soldiers was waiting for the children. She pointed to a truck parked in front of the door and smiled. "Hurry up! Let's see who can jump into the truck first. We don't want to be late for lunch."

Mari looked at the woman's pointed cap with the tassel in the front and remembered the one given to her by the Andalusian soldier on the trip back to Madrid from her grandmother's village. Preoccupied with thoughts about the cap, Tio Miaja, and Chata, the pregnant pig back in the village, Mari was too distracted to hear a voice calling her name until the voice called her name over and over again. It was Dolores, the woman with the big teeth. What did she want? Why was she suddenly always around?

Mari turned and noticed that her father was standing next to the woman, with his arm around her shoulders. Mari's upper lip twisted as she looked away. She did not want to go anywhere with this woman. The bitter taste of jealousy and anger rushed from the bottom of her stomach, and she ran away from Dolores and her father and jumped into the truck. Trying to smile, Dolores moved away from Alfonso and reached into the truck, attempting to hold Mari's hand and help her come down.

Mari moved farther into the truck, waiting for her father to lift her and hold her up in the air, as had been his usual greeting to her since she was a baby, but her father did not move. He remained standing, once again holding on to Dolores's shoulders. It was Dolores who, moving away from Alfonso, lifted Mari from the truck up into the air and then placed her on the ground as she held her hand. "Don't you remember me? I am Dolores, your father's friend. I would also like to be your friend. We are here to take you home."

Mari lifted her eyebrows and began walking backward. She said, "Yes, I remember you, but my grandmother said the school truck would take me home. I'd rather go home in the truck with my friends."

Dolores smiled, trying to hide her growing disappointment. Alfonso said nothing, which further disappointed Dolores. Holding back her feelings and realizing that Alfonso was not going to take charge of the situation, she walked toward Mari, holding her hand, and softly directing her words in an effort to gain the child's trust. "I know, I know. We were at your house, and your grandmother said that it was all right with her for us to take you home so that we can talk a little and get to know each other."

Why did they need to know each other? Mari watched the school bus leave without her. Holding her head down to avoid looking at them holding hands, she walked behind her father and the woman with the big teeth, hoping that her underwear would soon dry. She would gladly choose death than to have the woman with the big teeth notice that she had wet herself. After they boarded the trolley car, Mari sat next to Dolores and kept her head straight but at the same time gave occasional glances at the woman with the big teeth who was wearing a heavy woolen jacket over a printed dress made of a soft material that accentuated her small, well-shaped breasts. Dolores did not wear an apron or ugly black skirts like other women. Her small feet were neatly tucked into high-heeled shoes, not in worn flat shoes, like Mari's aunt and grandmother. Her smooth, long legs were barely covered under the dress, a much shorter dress than the usual skirts worn by mature women.

Looking at Dolores, Mari felt unkempt in her own tired, well-worn clothing, which was full of patches and torn elbows. Mari's toes stuck out of holes in her cloth-and-rope alpargatas, which she had outgrown. Her feet were almost larger than Dolores's feet, and instead of full, curvy legs, she had a pair of straight, skinny sticks with knees full of scratches and scabs incurred during her playful hours with her grandmother's rooster and rabbits. Mari noticed the people in the trolley looking at Dolores with admiration and her father's arm around her shoulder with the pride of ownership. No one looked at Mari. She hated this woman.

Dolores tried to make some sort of contact with the sullen child sitting next to her. "Your alpargatas don't fit you anymore. You are growing fast, and your feet are getting bigger. Maybe your father and I can help you find more comfortable alpargatas to fit you."

Big feet. The woman with the big teeth had said that Mari had big feet. The trolley car rolled and rocked through the streets under the cloudy sky of a chilly afternoon as Mari escaped her hated reality by drifting into daydreams that gave her power and control. She imagined a castle situated on the top of lofty cliffs made of living rock. It was her castle, a castle she had constructed from the remains of her dreams, her fantasies, and her nightly journeys into other realms. A castle constructed out of loneliness. And now, instead of sitting in a trolley car next to the woman she hated, she was galloping toward the castle, mounted on a white stallion. The sound of her whip snapped through the air, urging the horse to go faster as she watched the stallion flare his nostrils and race ahead at incredible speeds. The stallion galloped along the high cliffs overlooking a series of dramatic, dangerous rocks below. The rush of the wind was blowing through Mari's cape, a cape made from the finest of Arabian cloth, a cape embroidered with golden threads. A turban made of the finest of silks glittered with precious jewels and miraculously hugged Mari's head, undisturbed by the strong force of the horse's pace against the wind. A big and majestic castle appeared on top of the highest rock. Trumpets echoed in space, heralding her arrival. Heavy chains clanked as the bridge from the castle was lowered over a crocodile-infested moat that protected the entrance.

Mari galloped across the wood-and-iron bridge. Tall, muscular men servants rushed to hold the reins of her horse. Mari jumped off the steed without effort and rushed toward the gigantic opening doors of the castle with clipped, precise military steps. Deep winding tunnels led to dungeons within the very bowels of the castle. The woman with the big teeth was hanging by irons, spread-eagle in one of the dungeons. She had enormous feet encased in heavy iron boots. Mari looked at the woman. Parading back and forth, Mari hissed and laughed with hatred and disdain. "You have big, ugly feet! Big, ugly feet are not allowed in *my* castle. Off with your feet!"

The trolley car ride ended just as the woman with the big teeth was screaming for Mari's forgiveness.

The promised meal was not as good as Mari remembered eating in the days when there was no strange woman stuffing food between her large white teeth and taking the small moments of her father's attention away from her. She sat at the table, dangling her feet and nervously twisting her ankles. She pointed her toes to better feel the holes in her alpargatas. She was facing her father and Dolores. Mari watched them laugh as they ate and poured wine down their throats from a leather bota; she felt totally unloved by her father and spent most of the mealtime fighting not to cry. No, the noodle soup was not as tasty as she remembered. The chickpeas stuck in her throat. The meat made her want to vomit. She wished for her uncles to be there so that they could tease her and notice her, but her uncles were still fighting the final battles at the edge of Madrid. There were only her grandparents and Aunt Pilar at the table, and they were all entertaining her father and the woman with the big teeth.

After the meal was finished, Alfonso announced that he soon would have to leave on his way to the front lines to bring back the wounded and the dead before morning. He looked at his mother, knowing how she dreaded his trips in fear that one day Alfonso might transport back the body of one of his brothers. He got up from his chair, and gently placing his arms around her shoulders, he said, "You don't need to worry so much anymore, Mother. Soon this will be all over."

There was silence in the room. Don Juan tried to break the sad mood by asking Mari about her day in school. Before Mari could answer, the woman with the big teeth interrupted, and smiling a forced smile as she squinted, she looked at Mari. "You must have had a good time with your playmates, because when we went to pick you up, you did not want to leave your friends and come home with us. I almost felt like you did not like me."

An uncomfortable tension traveled through the room, and ignoring Dolores's comment, don Juan poured a little wine in a glass of water and asked his granddaughter to sit on his lap as he offered her the mixed drink. The child sipped from the glass, and her eyes filled with tears as she listened to her grandfather in between sighs. Her grandfather said, "The bombs were very loud today; it made me feel good knowing that you were safe in school, and I hope that it was fun to be with other children instead of being stuck at home with old people. Did you play games?"

Throwing her arms around her grandfather's neck, Mari cried openly. She was about to tell her grandfather about Manolito, but instead, she whispered, "The woman in school said I was an American."

Without hesitating, don Juan took a large handkerchief from his pocket and began wiping his granddaughter's face. "Oh, Mari. You know she made a mistake! Someone must have told her we once lived in America for a short time, and she got confused. Don't you remember what I told you about our family? We are the descendants of Iberians, Romans, Greeks, and Vikings, and let us not forget the drop of Moorish blood on the tip of your nose."

Mari stopped crying. Taking the glass from the table, she sipped a little of the liquid without looking at anyone.

The discomfort in the room was mounting. Dolores felt drops of sweat sprouting from her forehead, and Alfonso looked at his wristwatch, got up from his chair, and addressed his father. "I must go. Sanchez and his cousin Martin are going to pick me up at the corner and take me to the garage." He kissed Dolores on the cheek and asked, "Do you want a lift home?"

Mari wondered whether Dolores would stay and ruin the rest of her afternoon. "No, thanks, Alfonso. I am going to stay for a short time talking to your folks about us while Mari takes a nap."

Alfonso took his daughter's hand, gently helped her down from her grandfather's lap, and walked her toward the bedrooms. He told his daughter, "I will miss you tonight. Tomorrow, I will pick you up after school, and we will go for a ride in the ambulance, just you and me. You know you are very special to me; I do not want you ever to be unhappy."

Mari let her father cover her with a light blanket. She envisioned a little baby reaching from the bed to a woman with dark curly hair and sad eyes.

Her father kissed her on the forehead and left the room.

Mari waited for the dark-haired woman to come and hold her in her arms, but no one came, and there was no sound in the room other than her own sobs.

After Alfonso left his parents' apartment, Dolores sat talking to don Juan and his wife. They listened to her while sipping a cup of chicory, the make- believe coffee of wartime.

Pilar sat at the table for a short time, but with the conversation in the room going fast and mouths frequently engaged in drinking the chicory, she was unable to lip-read what was being discussed by her parents and Dolores. Excusing herself, Pilar gathered the dishes from the table and took them to the kitchen and washed them. Neither her mother nor Dolores offered to help her, but she preferred it this way. Hearing people could be uncharitable and unkind toward each other without apparent reason, and at times, she was almost glad of having lost her hearing; her deafness had rewarded her with powers to read people's bodies, a skill that seemed to improve with the passing of time, and today she was able to clearly read the masked anger in her parents' faces toward Dolores.

Yes, deafness was almost a reward; she did not have to hear bombs exploding, the moaning of wounded soldiers, or the crying of mothers who had lost their children fighting in the war. Unfortunately, she also could no longer hear the chirping of birds, the crackling [crowing?] of her mother's rooster in the morning, the laughter of her brothers, or her father's powerful voice. She could not hear the sound of a gypsy guitar. These sounds were now a distant memory in a vast universe of silence, but it was a silence that gave her special power and refinement of her other senses. She could now see, taste, smell, and feel with amazing accuracy. Sometimes, she could feel the approaching planes half an hour before they reached the city, smell and taste the gunpowder of guns fired in the streets, and above all, interpret the body language of people, animals, and sometimes even birds and insects.

Now, as she returned to the dining room, her special powers flashed alarm as she quickly interpreted the interaction between Dolores and her parents; it was strained. Pilar offered to make more chicory, but everyone refused. This brief interruption was followed with silence in the room. Dolores looked down and played with her fingernails, Maria stared ahead at the balcony, and don Juan began rolling a cigarette. Because she was standing and everyone at the table was either looking down or away from the table with a slight turn of the head, Pilar found it hard to read their lips. She pulled a chair next to her mother and sat at the table, openly staring at everyone, waiting for them to speak.

Only Dolores's lips moved, and Pilar read what she was saying. "Alfonso can't get a divorce from Rosa; she is refusing the divorce because of the church. We can't wait anymore and have to get married in a civil ceremony before the war ends and the church regains its powers. Rosa will probably have Alfonso excommunicated, and this would present problems if we wait until the war ends and the church gets involved in marriages again. We must do this now, because I am pregnant."

Pilar played with her apron, making unnecessary adjustments and brushing imaginary crumbs from her lap. Don Juan and his wife said nothing as they looked down and played with the empty chicory cups. After a short uncomfortable time, Pilar ignored the last of Dolores's words about her pregnancy and asked, "Will Mari live with you and my brother?"

Dolores smiled. "Of course. Alfonso is her father. But we thought Mari could spend weekends here with the family until she gets used to the changes—that is, if this is all right."

Maria and don Juan looked up, trying to soften their face muscles. After an uncomfortable pause, don Juan spoke slowly and carefully. "Of course; it will ease her anxiety, and we will try to spend more time with her. My problem is the fact that you and our son will not really be married unless he gets a divorce from his wife, and if he does not get a divorce from Rosa, all of my future grandchildren with you will be bastards, leaving Mari as my son's only legitimate child."

Dolores looked at don Juan and forced herself to smile. "Well, the word *bastard* is a little rough, but for a time, our child will not be old enough to know the circumstances of our marriage; I am sure everything will be all right in the years to come. We are not rich. There is no property. Legitimacy is really nothing other than a paper and a signature. Alfonso is going to declare himself as single, and no one is going to look for a divorce decree."

Don Juan stood up. He excused himself and walked out of the room.

Shortly after don Juan left, Dolores made her excuses. Hugging Maria and Pilar, she verbalized the necessary formulaic courtesies and went home.

The siege against Madrid by Franco's army and allied Italian troops in the last days of the war became a daily horror of human casualties too large in number to count. In the midst of confusion, hunger, and exhaustion, ambulances and medics were used as daily targets by the enemy, making it almost impossible to care for the needs of the wounded as they lay bleeding and unattended behind the trenches. Each day was a nightmare. Each day, more officers deserted from the Republican army, or were killed, leaving soldiers behind trenches with little or no leadership to watch helplessly as most of their comrades abandoned the front lines or died as the enemy gained momentum. With most of the officers gone, there was no hope for resistance. Hour after hour, the powerful Fascist army pushed back the rapidly vanishing Republican soldiers and soon reached the outskirts of Madrid, signaling the end of the war and the defeat of the Second Spanish Republic. Fearing that Madrid would soon became an extended battlefield, terrified civilians trapped inside the city disappeared inside their homes, drawing blinds across balconies and windows that faced the street and leaving behind silent streets, empty shops, abandoned trolley cars, and dark, empty subways.

Alfonso had listened to the horrifying and frightening accounts of inhuman treatment received by both civilians and soldiers following enemy occupation of towns and cities all over Spain. These accounts included vicious headhunters looking for any and all persons who might have been in favor of the republic. Horrifying stories kept coming into Madrid and were passed on by friends and relatives, making Alfonso fearful not so much for himself but for his father and brothers. He knew that his father, as a well- known Marxist, and his brothers as members of labor unions, if caught, would be questioned, tortured, and killed in front of a firing squad if they refused to divulge information. But the most brutal rumors Alfonso feared were the rumors traveling throughout the city of plans formulated by Franco's ruling party, the Falange, to use the underground chambers remaining in Madrid from the days of the Inquisition to question prisoners after the war ended.

Horrifying images of human extremities being torn away from bodies as prisoners lay on the Inquisition's famous racks, where bodies were stretched beyond endurance, plagued Alfonso. He knew that he had to convince his father to leave Madrid before the peace treaty was signed. It would not be an easy task to ask a man like his father to abandon his city, his friends, and his fight against Fascism, but it had to be done, and if necessary, Alfonso was prepared to abduct his father by force with the help of his brothers. Or Alfonso would use guilt by explaining how his father was placing the family in danger by staying in Madrid. Alfonso was willing to try any type of coercion, even if he had to use his mother and the family for leverage. With these thoughts of concern for the safety and survival of his father and brothers, Alfonso met with his family a few days before the peace surrender was signed.

Alfonso arrived at his father's home with Felipe and Carlos, Dolores's brothers. Both men were widely known to be members of the Spanish Communist Party, as well as to be close friends of don Juan. The family greeted these men in the kitchen with hugs and kisses on the cheek, followed by animated conversation about recent experiences and the present situation in Spain. Leaving the group, Alfonso walked out of the kitchen toward the dining room to arrange chairs for the meeting. As he passed an open balcony, he stopped for a moment and looked into the last sunrays before they left a silent and empty street below. There were no children jumping rope, no boys chasing each other, no women gossiping or sharing their concerns about the war or their fears for loved ones.

Alfonso closed the balcony doors and drew the curtains. The end was soon to be, and all of Spain knew it, but the reality of losing freedom and equality had not yet been accepted. Sitting next to the table and staring at a calendar hanging on the opposite wall, Alfonso let out a deep sigh. It was March 1939. The people of Spain had aged three years since the war began but did not get three years wiser. Much blood would still be shed. One by one, the family and the two guests came into the room and took their seats around the table.

Pilar smiled and placed napkins and a skin bota filled with red wine on the table. She explained, "I was saving this wine for the day of victory, but we can now celebrate and hope for a safe and peaceful end to our war, a war between Spaniards, family against family, fathers against sons and daughters, and sons and daughters against fathers. How sad."

As Pilar was passing by him, Chato tapped her on the shoulder and spoke slowly to make it easier for his sister to read his lips. "Thanks for the wine, sister. Yes, it is sad that we have treated each other like savages, but the reality is that as sadistic and cruel as we have been to each other in this war, there will be no safe and peaceful end to this mess. My gentle sister, I will gladly drink your wine. Thank you."

Alfonso cleared his throat. Looking directly at his father, he spoke in quiet but firm tones. "This brings me to the reason for this meeting. As we know, the war will soon be lost and finished; we now must concentrate on new kinds of survival, because it is without a doubt that the new regime will imprison and probably execute all members of the Communist Party, as well as all members of the workers' unions." His voice grew shaky. Blowing his nose, he tried to hide the beginning of tears before continuing. "Father, you are a well-known Marxist. So are Carlos and Felipe. Max and Pascual are members of UGT and the CNT workers' unions. You are all in danger. With luck, the new government will just imprison you for many years. If you are not lucky, they will execute you after days, maybe weeks, of torture to get information.

"Because of this, Carlos and Felipe have made a very wise decision and are leaving to their family's village in Estremadura tomorrow morning. The town is small and isolated; the people in the village seldom come into contact with the outside and are politically not one way or another. Because the town has been of no political or strategic importance because of its isolated location, the war never separated them from each other. Their young are still alive, and the old are still cranky and wise. Everyone in the village knows Carlos and Felipe, their family still owns a house and land in the area, and their mother and father have worked the farmland every summer for years. It will be a safe place for now, and Father, we want you and Mother to go with them and take Pascual and Max. Chato and Pilar are Americans, so nothing will happen to them until I arrange something through the American embassy to get them to America. We'll see."

Shouting and pounding his fists against the table, don Juan shouted at Alfonso, "Son, I hope you are not suggesting that I run like coward! Doesn't anyone remember the stories about Spaniards of Jewish faith who, after centuries of living in Spain, were made to run from their homes by the Catholic kings? What kind of life did they have after that? They were persecuted and tormented; many were murdered. I'd rather not prolong my misery. I'd rather die fighting."

Alfonso raised his eyebrows and shook his head. "You did not let me finish. Taking a step back and exploring the alternatives is not running away. This war may be lost, but not the fight. At this moment, plans for future guerrilla attacks are being made, and men and women from those provinces have stashed arms in places behind the northern mountains. These plans will go into effect when Hitler and Mussolini withdraw all air and ground troops from Spain. After things settle down, Franco will probably offer pardons, and almost everyone will be able to travel freely, so we can join them. If not, we will have to travel to the north any way we can."

Don Juan stood up, his face contorted by anger. "Offer pardons? I will be damned forever if I humiliate myself by accepting a pardon from a Fascist dictator! How many times were the Jews pardoned if they switched their religion to Catholic? When they did or said they did, it did not stop them from being treated like lepers. I have no intention of switching my beliefs in exchange for a pardon."

Alfonso ignored his father's anger and continued talking. "Father, you never let me finish. After Hitler and Mussolini withdraw their air and ground troops from Spain, we hope to gather enough momentum from every province to help initiate guerrilla attacks, beginning in the north, to debilitate Franco and weaken the regime until we can get help from Russia and foreign volunteers. We'll go from there, one step at a time. We need you not only to fight but also to write and inform the world about the efforts of the Spanish people against Franco. You can swallow your pride for the good of your motherland and pretend to accept a pardon and then go north and fight with the guerrillas. Mother can stay in the village, return to Madrid if Chato and Pilar are still there, or go with you. For these plans to become a reality, all of us need to stay alive to fight against Franco. Being able to move freely would help. I am not asking you to accept a pardon; I am asking you to pretend that you accept a pardon so that you can stay alive and help. This time, it *will* be a people's war, without parties and politics. There will be no Germans and Italians to help Franco. What do you think, Father?"

"That is still dishonesty, Alfonso. I am not a dishonest man. Accepting a pardon, if only for a short time, would require me to declare my beliefs as having been harmful to Spain."

"It is not dishonesty, Father. It's called strategy, and strategy is always used during wars. It is a plan to distract the enemy and attack in places where and when they least expect it."

Still standing and holding on to the top of his chair, don Juan leaned toward his wife and reached for her hand. "Maria," he said. "We have been together for a long time, and you are the only person who knows me well. You know what I want to do, but I will do whatever you think will be best for our family."

Maria squeezed her husband's hand and cleared her throat before answering. "I do not always know how well I know you, but what I do know about you has always been wrapped with honor and love and concern for the workers in the world. Staying alive, for whatever reason, is not cowardly. You owe it to me and to your country to stay alive and to continue to fight. I will be next to you, and I promise to hold and use a rifle when the time comes."

"All right, woman," answered don Juan. "Make sure to pack some winter underwear. I hear the nights get cold in Estremadura." The conversation between don Juan and his wife was interrupted when, almost all at once, they both remembered their son Alfonso. There was no mention of him or his wife and daughter in the plans they were making for everyone else. "Alfonso, you have said nothing about what you are going to do! My son, what about you? What are you going to do?"

Alfonso sat next to his parents, holding their hands. "I am not going to do anything. I have no need to run. I do not belong to any party. I have never carried a gun or been in battles. I am not important enough. I'm just an ambulance driver. Ambulance drivers are not supposed to be considered dangerous or held as prisoners of war. We have often given first aid to enemy soldiers and applied tourniquets to stop their bleeding. They have done the same for us. This is the humanitarian law of medics. But if things get bad, I will join you in Estremadura."

"I hope you are right, son," don Juan muttered. Lifting the wine bota, he pressed a stream of wine into his throat and then passed the wine on to the others, bending his right arm in the Loyalist salute and letting out a loud "¡Salud!"

One by one, eight strong and separate voices responded, "¡Salud!"

The next morning, the sun barely visible behind the mountains, Carlos and Felipe's small and battered truck backfired, bouncing on the street's cobblestones until finally stopping in front of don Juan's home, wrapped in a cloud of smoke from the engine.

The family was ready. Don Juan, his wife, and their two sons had been waiting by the curb with three small suitcases and a large typewriter. Carlos and Felipe placed the suitcases on the back of the truck and smiled at each other when don Juan refused to surrender his typewriter. Carlos sat on the driver's side as his brother and don Juan's sons jumped on the back of the truck and sat on top of the suitcases.

Making a space for herself between Carlos and her husband in the front seat, Maria frowned with discomfort after her husband placed his typewriter in the small space in front of her. She complained, "Did you have to bring the typewriter?"

"Look, Maria, this typewriter goes where I go."

Carlos cranked the engine, and the truck moved.

Maria looked at her husband and pinched his arm playfully. She said, "Things would be much easier had you learned to use a pen!"

Bumping and backfiring, the truck picked up speed. They tried to avoid contact with the enemy by moving on the back roads, made of dirt, in between hills once used by nearby farmers to take produce into Madrid on market days.

After weeks of fighting a losing war behind the trenches with little food and less sleep, the men who had protected Madrid from the Fascist invasion for three years were told by their immediate commanding officers that the war had ended. The officers ordered the men to place all arms on top of the trenches as an act of surrender. The war was lost, and the dream for a free Spain was gone. The soldiers, emotionally numb, felt relief as they gave up their arms in silence and watched German tanks, followed by Franco's foot soldiers and Italian ground troops, march past to the other side of the trenches, shouting and singing words of victory.

Shortly after the troops passed, trucks carrying machine guns and trailing cannons followed. In the spotless blue sky, German airplanes flew in perfect formation toward Madrid. Afraid of being shot by the passing troops or machine-gunned from the airplanes, the hungry and tired soldiers of the defeated Republican army huddled together next to their wounded comrades inside the trenches, but neither the passing troops nor the airplanes fired at them. No shots were fired by anyone, and the now less terrified soldiers began to climb out of the trenches. They carried the wounded into supply trucks that were parked with keys in the ignition and sped away into little-known back roads used by shepherds.

Franco had been sick in bed with influenza when the signed treaty of surrender was delivered to him. Almost immediately, another war started all over Spain, a far more painful war than the one that had just ended. The new ruling party initiated manhunts. Men bearing guns, dressed in blue shirts and red berets, searched home after home, looking for anyone or anything related to the exiled Republican government. Nothing was safe as they invaded all municipal and government buildings, tearing through files to look for the names and titles of persons who had worked for the Republican government. Personnel files and records from the war years were confiscated. Desks were forced open, and all documents were examined for the identity of members of the opposition.

Travel in Madrid was monitored, and every exit road was carefully guarded by Spain's oldest rural police, the Guardia Civil, who stood everywhere, dressed in old-style uniforms and patent-leather hats, holding rifles, waiting to arrest anyone who attempted to leave the city. Soldiers returning home hid wherever they could find safety from the hunts: under bombed buildings, in abandoned churches, and in underground wine cellars. Some were able to reach caves left by gypsies in the outskirts of the city. Despite efforts to save themselves, most soldiers coming into Madrid fell into the hands of the Falange or the Guardia Civil, who, drunk with power, beat, mutilated, and tortured their prisoners, regardless of age or sex, before throwing them into jail or executing them.

From that day on, the Reconquista was a time of subordination and torture for the thousands of Spaniards who did not support the new regime. Most of them were shot immediately, while others were transported to prisons or concentration camps to await the disposition of their fate, a fate that could be anything from torture followed by lifelong imprisonment at hard labor to death in front of the firing squads as their families were made to watch. The higher-ranking Republican prisoners disappeared into subterranean cells beneath the streets of Madrid. Before they died, they fell victims to the same methods of torture used by the Spanish Inquisition to extract information almost five hundred years before. Franco conducted this sinister war against the Spanish people in the name of a "united Spain," while the rest of the world watched without taking action. From his throne in the Vatican, the pope cheered and blessed Franco.

From the day Franco's army entered Madrid, the city remained silent, with empty streets where there was no cheering or waving of flags. Madrid was ready to die before kneeling to the enemy; the people had lost their military power but not their belief in a democratic Spain where everyone was equal and everyone was free to express personal beliefs and worship their own gods. The people in the city existed under an almost religious austerity of silent discipline and self-denial under the fearful scrutiny of the Falange's enforcement of a now Fascist state.

Madrid did not return to the different sounds and the different smells that once characterized the city streets before the war. There was still no smell of freshly baked bread in the mornings, no vendors announcing their arrival with fresh vegetables and fruit, no scent of Spanish cooking in the early afternoons. Women did not chatter and laugh as they waited in line for the family's food rations. Every neighborhood was wrapped in a silence and stillness that seemed to come from a sphere of time and space unrelated to the daily activities of the people's present lives.

Inside their homes, families gathered to wait for their husbands, wives, sons, and daughters to be released from prison as they shared their pain and sorrow with each other in low tones and closed windows, afraid of being heard by neighbors and denounced to the Falange. It was a painful, interminable wait that sometimes ended in despair when their loved ones were killed, sent to Africa to work at hard labor, or locked behind inscrutable prison walls and denied contact with the outside world. [This is excellent journalistic writing. In a book like this, it's better to bring out information through the perceptions of a character, perhaps Alfonso.]

There had been very little time for Mari to adjust to her life with Dolores or to any other aspect of her new environment. In the middle of the night, there was heavy pounding on the door. Tall young men of the new order, wearing red berets and armed with rifles, stood in front of the door of the apartment, dressed in immaculately clean and well-pressed blue shirts that bore the Falange's symbol embroidered on to the shirt pockets: a red yoke and five arrows. The young men clicked their heels and stood at attention in the hallway, holding rifles and shifting their feet inside shiny black ankle boots over which they had folded the top of white socks and neatly tucked in their black pants.

The young men stood looking ahead without expression and waited as their leader stood by the doorway and looked at Alfonso and Dolores, who held the door open. "Alfonso Martín Gonzalez?" asked the oldest-looking Falange militant.

"That would be me," answered Alfonso.

"Alfonso, we have information that you know where to find some members of the Communist Party."

Alfonso looked at the man and smiled. He said, "I am not a Communist. How would I know about members of the Communist Party?"

"Because one of them is your father, don Juan Martín Villaverde. The other two members of the Communist Party for whom we are looking are your brothers-in-law, Carlos and Felipe."

Alfonso said loudly, "Ah, my father! I have not seen that son of a bitch for a long time. He did not approve of my wanting to marry my wife, so we parted ways more than a year ago. I have no way of knowing where he or the others may be. I do not know my wife's family too well—"

He was not allowed to finish his sentence; the butt of a rifle across his face broke his teeth. Mari stood in the doorway of her room, paralyzed with fear as she watched bits of her father's teeth and blood splatter on the wall before he was once again hit across the face by the leader of the young Falange militants. After staring into space for a moment and taking a step backward, Alfonso fell against the wall and spat more blood and pieces of broken teeth. Two other men kicked him onto the floor and held him down while one of the standing Falange youths pressed the heel of his boot against Alfonso's hand and cracked the bones.

Dolores threw herself against the young man, slapping and punching his face. She shouted at him and scratched his face. "You're breaking my husband's hands, and that's not going to help him remember something he does not know!"

The man grinned and stroked the scratches on his face as he attempted to touch Dolores's abdomen, where her pregnancy was beginning to show. "Having a baby, uh? Making little Communists for us to eat?"

Dolores grabbed the man's arm and bit it. The young officer pulled his arm away from Dolores, furiously sucked his wounds, and screamed, "¡Hija de puta!" (Daughter of a whore) as he pointed his rifle at her.

Mari jumped in front of him. For the first time in her life, she was proud of her father and in awe of Dolores's courage. This gave Mari strength. She was no longer afraid. Mari hissed at the officer, "Leave her alone!" She grabbed the barrel of the rifle and pushed it to one side. "I'll tell you where they are!"

Alfonso lifted himself from the floor, looked up, and said thorough swollen lips and a bloody mouth, "No, hija. No!"

Mari pretended not to hear her father. "You are not going to like hearing this, but my grandfather and his friends left for the French border a long time ago."

Alfonso slumped to the floor as the blue shirts pushed Mari against the wall and out of the way. They tied Alfonso's hands together as they kicked and pushed his body down the steps and into the street. A moment later, the wailing of a siren trailed away into the night. Alfonso was gone.

Dolores sat in the kitchen and motioned to Mari to sit down on the floor next to her. Dolores stroked Mari's hair in silence. They didn't talk for a long time after the Falange officers left. The night dissolved itself into dawn. Dolores bent down, held Mari's face between her hands, and looked into her eyes.

"You were brave tonight. I am proud of you. Always remember to have an honorable reason for telling a lie. Tonight, you had to lie to save our lives, but you could have been killed, beaten, or both. That was a courageous thing you did."

Mari looked toward Dolores's waist and whispered softly, "The man said you were pregnant. I did not want the baby hurt. Are you going to have a baby like my friend Chata?"

"Chata? I did not know you had a friend named Chata."

"She was a very nice mama pig who was pregnant when I left my grandmother's village."

Dolores stood up and helped Mari stand next to her. "Yes. I am going to have a baby soon. It will be your brother or maybe your sister. Come on. We have only a couple of hours to sleep, and there is nothing we can do about your father tonight. Tomorrow, we'll to go to Franco's victory parade and pretend to enjoy it. They will be watching us, and if they think we support their victory, it may help release your father from jail a little sooner."

As they walked together toward Mari's bedroom, Dolores's optimism made Mari feel as if she was Sancho Panza walking next to a delusional Don Quixote. Parade or no parade, she knew that nothing she or Dolores did would change how, when, or whether her father would be released from jail. Everyone knew that once in jail, few prisoners were released alive. It was kind of Dolores to pretend that the parade would help her father come home. Mari was not a stupid kid. Sure, she would go to the parade and pretend, but it would be very hard not to wish Franco was dead.

Soon after Dolores left her bedroom, Mari's eyelids became heavy. She drifted into a troubled sleep, thinking of her father, how brave he had been, how he never once cried or screamed like the wimpy blue shirt man did after Dolores hit and bit him. Mari replayed the night's scene when Dolores slapped and bit the Falange man. Mari's stepmother became the proud Queen Isabella seated on a beautiful white stallion stomping over thousands of Moors who were wearing blue Falange shirts. These thoughts of admiration for her stepmother clashed with the angry and resentful feelings Mari had felt since taken away from her grandparents and had been forced to wear funny-looking skirts and tight, uncomfortable shoes on Sundays. She had hated Dolores and the new rules and regulations, except learning to read and memorizing the multiplication tables. Learning things had been worth wearing funny-looking skirts and tight shoes, darning socks in the afternoons, and doing dishes. But Mari had hated Dolores until that moment.

Long after Dolores left the room, as Mari drifted into a deeper sleep, a soft but vibrant flamenco cry drifted from the clouds above, and Dolores's strong voice transported Mari into dreams where she was standing on the tower of her make-believe castle, watching gypsies sing and dance as Dolores straddled a white stallion and galloped through the plains of Castile next to the Cid Campeador. At the end of her dream, and with tears in her eyes, Mari had to chain Dolores and hang her to the wall inside one of the dungeons below the castle and pace in front of her, dressed in wide Moorish pantaloons, a turban, and a flowing cap, snapping a whip and yelling, "You are not my mother! What have you done with my mother?"

The next morning, Mari and Dolores, together with thousands of other people—dark, silent people resembling shadows—stood watching the beginning of Franco's victory parade as the Guardia Civil walked through the crowds to make sure that everyone knew when to extended his or her arm in a Fascist salute and shout, "Franco, Franco, Franco!" It was a bright and pleasant morning in May, and the sun shed rays of happiness and warmth toward the earth down below, except in Madrid, where the dark and hungry shadows standing on the sidewalks of the Paseo de la Castellana felt cold and abandoned by God.

The splendor and obvious cost of the parade was an insult to a people who had been surviving on small rations of noodles in watery broths without meat or flavor, boiled chickpeas, and yellow bread made out of corn normally fed to caws and cattle. The noise, the movement, and the music of the parade was intoxicating for Mari, making her forget the decision she had made the night before not to like or support the parade in any way.

She participated by practicing her newly learned skills in mathematics by counting the men, the horses, and tanks as they appeared in front of her. The first count was that of 150 Italian Royal Carabineers mounted on beautiful white Spanish horses, playing military marches as they passed in front of a tall tribunal built to accommodate Franco and other government officials for the parade, a tribunal just as impressive as the parade itself. The word *VICTORY* was written across the tall arch behind and above in golden letters, and Franco's name repeated three times was displayed on either side of the tribunal. The ancient shield of Castile and Aragón, Spain's symbol since the Catholic kings united their two kingdoms, was displayed prominently against a dark background below the arch with the yoke and arrows of the Falange added below a corner outside the shield and above, behind the eagle's head. Franco's cry, "Spain, One, Big, Free," was painted on a strip like a waving scroll.

At the foot of the tribunal, soldiers stood holding flags representing every province of Spain, and Franco's Moorish guards stood in front of them, holding rifles with hands inside white gloves and wearing flowing white pants and shirts with a wide purple sash around the waist. The white turbans that covered their heads and the full-size red capes that fell to the ground behind the shoulders accentuated the Moors' impressive presentation. Franco's Moorish guards presented a menacing and impressive addition to his theatrical presentation of victory and power.

The Italian marching band passed the tribunal. Mari counted 150 infantry soldiers, followed by 200 members of the artillery with cannons and 150 tanks. After the display of five hundred motorcycles roaring down Paseo de la Castellana, Mari lost count and grew bored. She complained that she was tired and wanted to go home.

Leaning down and squeezing Mari's hand, Dolores whispered in her ear, "Shh! The Guardia Civil is looking. Don't talk. Just watch the parade. You don't have to count anymore."

Planes flew in the sky and threw flowers down at the marching troops. This distracted Mari for a little longer. Hundreds of cannons and thousands of cars and trucks followed through the afternoon, followed by more planes, including fifty-four Fiats and eight German Heinkels. The planes at first filled the immediate sky with smoke fumes that spelled the name *FRANCO*, followed by a perfect formation in the sky above the tribunal that used the planes to spell VIVA FRANCO.

The demonstration was colorful and vibrant, as well as being an intimidating and a decadent show of power to control the people who had spent three years fighting against the very ideals paraded in front of them on this day, ideals they were forced to pretend to accept to stay alive.

On the way back home that afternoon, Mari imagined herself wearing a colorful Falange uniform and marching in front of hundreds of people holding a flag. It could be fun. She did not have to believe in whatever it was that the Falange represented, just pretend that she did, and maybe get more food to eat, as well as help her father out of jail and bring her grandparents home. She missed all of them.

As the days and weeks passed, Alfonso remained in jail, with no visitors or any other contact with the outside world, and if any official charges had were made, these charges were never disclosed. The only information Alfonso received was that of having to remain in prison without visitors until the case was reviewed.

In the first few weeks after Alfonso was imprisoned, Dolores made daily trips to the prison, having to walk long distances through the old neighborhoods with cobblestone streets and narrow sidewalks before she was able to reach one of the main avenues where the crowded trolley cars stopped, the closest transportation to the prison from where they lived. The daily walks through the old streets were hard on her feet now that she was beginning to feel the added weight of her pregnancy, making it harder to step on the uneven cobblestones with high-heeled shoes. In addition to the physical stressors, there was also what she felt was harassment from men who, having escaped prison and unable to find work, had nothing to do all day but make remarks at the passing women.

These men spent hours leaning in doorways, trying to make light of their present situation by returning to habits of long ago—habits of younger happier days, making flirtatious remarks to women as they passed by, such as, "¡Olé, *guapa!*" followed by "¡Viva la *mujer de España!*"

(Hey, good looking! Long live the woman [women?] of Spain!)

Dolores had been used to these comments for as long as she could remember. They had been flattering and amusing in the past when she was able to walk the streets with the grace and the arrogance of a flamenco dancer, but now she was pregnant and found these comments offensive, which added to the discomfort of her daily trips to the prison. Once she reached the trolley stop, regardless of the time of day, every trolley was above capacity, forcing Dolores to push and squeeze herself between the bodies of the people standing on the rear platform. She could barely hang on. In spite of the discomfort and in spite of the long hours that it took to get to and return from the prison every day, Dolores continued to make the trips, hoping to see Alfonso or at least to be able to get some information.

Every day, her attempts were aborted with abruptness and rudeness from the prison guards. Dolores would return home, quietly controlling her anger, afraid that any protest on her part would make things worse.

After so many trips, and after so many times failing to see Alfonso, Dolores grew tired. Sometimes, she experienced abdominal cramps, accompanied by traces of vaginal bleeding. These episodes forced her to limit the trips to the prison in an attempt to avoid possible problems to her unborn child. The additional time at home allowed Dolores to spend more time with Mari and to establish easier communications with her. This helped build a daily routine, some sort of normalcy in their lives.

After resolving to avoid attention to protect their sons in hiding, Dolores's parents decided not to spend the summer in Estremadura. Dolores was able to visit her family often, usually on Sundays, when no one had to stand in the morning lines for food rations. Together, they had discussed all available possibilities to inform don Juan of Alfonso's imprisonment, but after a time, they decided that there was no safe way to make contact with anyone in the village without endangering their safety. Safety issues had grown worse since the unexpected guerrilla attacks from the north of Spain, which made matters more difficult for those in hiding or anyone associated with them. Because of the attacks and because Franco had issued no pardons, it was impossible for don Juan and his sons to leave the village without endangering the lives of the entire village.

Fear was evident everywhere. Madrid now was changed to a city of silence and fear, a world of suspiciousness and anger following the lack of food that made it hard to guess who would be reported to the

Falange with real or sometimes invented charges in exchange for a piece of bread. Everything had also become different for Dolores since Alfonso was arrested; her friends avoided her or limited their contact with her to greetings and comments about the weather, afraid of being singled out as possible Communists. Alfonso's younger siblings, Pilar and Chato, who sometimes used to spend evenings at her home, had to ask asylum from the American embassy after Alfonso was arrested. They now waited to embark on a Portuguese ship to the United Sates, leaving no adult in Madrid with whom Dolores could interact other than her parents.

Dolores spent most of her time with Mari, who every day was becoming a surprisingly more alert reader and kept Dolores in awe with her questions and remarks. After standing in line every morning to secure their daily rations of food and bread, Dolores had made a habit of sitting with Mari on the balcony in the afternoon after eating. Dolores would sew or knit and listen to Mari recite the multiplication tables or the alphabet in preparation for writing. Mari already could read simple children's stories.

Mari frequently interrupted her lessons with one of her many questions, such as, "Dolores, who loves Spain the best—those on the right, or those on the left?"

These questions always made Dolores smile. Some questions were hard to answer, but not this one. "Ah, Mari. There is no Left, and there is no Right. We are all from the same fierce and noble race, and that is probably part of our tragic legacy."

Mari was silent, without follow-up comments, and Dolores realized that she had not answered in a way that the child understood, so she leaned forward and tapped the child's hand.

"Let me explain it better. All of those who fought and died in our war fought and died because they loved Spain. It does not matter now on what side of the trenches they fought and died; all did what they believed was best for their country."

Mari thought for a moment about what Dolores had said and wondered about all of those who survived the war and then left Spain. Did they love their country? She lowered her eyes, fearful of the answer, and asked Dolores whether she would ever leave Spain.

The reply came without hesitation, mixed with a little giggle. "¡Que no, *guapa!*" (Gosh, no, cutie!) "Spanish blood is like Spanish wine—it becomes bitter vinegar in other countries."

Vinegar? Mari thought of France, where most of the Spanish refugees had fled, now probably overrun with vinegar, but she was happy with Dolores's answer. Her blood would never turn to vinegar, and Mari wanted to be like her—a pure Iberian, but her grandmother had said that she had bad blood, like her mother. Holding her breath in silence for a moment and trying not to cry, Mari finally asked, "Am I a fierce and noble Spaniard?"

There was a short silence, during which Dolores pretended to look down the street, but in reality she was trying to understand the question and the child's tears before answering. She placed the sewing basket on the floor. Holding Mari's face between her hands, Dolores whispered, "All the children of Spain are noble Spaniards, but, you know, a person does not have to be fierce to be noble. You, my dear, are noble and very brave."

Mari was noble and she was brave, but was she a Spaniard? Mari wanted to ask about the bad blood her grandmother said she had; she also wanted to ask about what the woman in the school shelter meant when she said that Mari was an American, but before she could ask, Dolores stood up and picked up her sewing basket, so Mari knew that the conversation had ended.

On her last trip to the prison, Dolores had been escorted into an office where an obese Falange officer informed her that Alfonso would be released as soon as his papers were reviewed and filed with the proper authorities. She was given no dates or explanations. When she asked to see her husband, the man looked annoyed. After blowing his nose and sticking the handkerchief into his pants pocket, he told Dolores that her request was not a good idea.

Dolores knew that she had to accept the man's answer without questions. Alfonso would be coming home soon, and all the humiliations she had endured from the prison guards would end. The news of her husband's freedom was the most exciting news she'd received since learning that she was pregnant.

The next day was Sunday. After convincing Mari to wear her funny-looking skirt and squeeze her feet into the tight shoes, Dolores and Mari ate a piece of toasted yellow bread, drank a cup of black chicory, and hurried to share Alfonso's coming home with Dolores's parents. They rushed through the same cobblestone streets Dolores had walked on during her trips to the prison, but on this day, the streets felt smooth and friendly, and Dolores felt free to once again let her body assume the arrogant air of a gypsy dancer. She threw her shoulders back, pointed her chin, and hummed Spanish folk songs of long ago. Her now full breasts and well-rounded pregnant figure no longer seemed to inhibit the pace of her steps. Her walk was fast and rhythmic as she clicked her high-heeled shoes on the cobblestones. Women smiled at her, and she no longer objected to what she now accepted as complimentary comments made by men.

Mari continued to skip behind to keep up with her stepmother and protect her from the men leaning in doorways. Mari imitated her stepmother's walk by throwing back her shoulders and exaggerating a pointed chin to the extent of sometimes blocking her immediate vision and stumbling. Her mission was sacred, so after each stumble, she always continued her self- appointed guard duties behind Dolores.

The street finally came to an end, emptying into a bustling avenue filled with people going to church or rushing somewhere while trying to avoid the many beggars who asked for a few coins. Dolores stopped and waited for Mari to catch up. Taking Mari's hand, Dolores prepared to cross the avenue. A troop of adolescent girls, members of the Falange Youth called Flechas, or Arrows, from the Falange's symbol of arrows held together by a yoke, appeared in front of them, marching on their way to church. The young Flechas carried banners, beat on drums, and stomped their ankle boots on the ground in unison as they chanted, "¡*España unida, España grande, España libre!*" (Spain, united, big, and free!)

Mari stood on the small sidewalk, holding on to Dolores's hand, totally mesmerized by the uniforms, rhythms, and banners, by the young girls' dramatic presentation of military training. Oh, yes, she knew that the chanted words were not true; Spain was not united, Spain was not big, and Spain was definitely not free, but the red berets, the impeccably clean and starched blue shirts tucked into black skirts, the beating of the drums, and the waving of the flags were exciting to her.

Mari wanted to be a Flecha. She wanted to chant and carry a banner, but above all, she wanted to be Spanish like the girls marching in the street, and if she were a Flecha, she would really be a Spaniard. Mari's heart beat with the same resonance and timing as the sound of the drums as they passed through the intersection and disappeared into a side street. Mari stood transfixed, envisioning herself standing at attention and extending her right arm in Spain's new Fascist salute.

Dolores pulled Mari's hand to cross the street. Long after they had crossed the intersection and long after the sound of drums had faded, Mari continued to obsess with thoughts of becoming a Flecha and walked behind Dolores, stomping her feet on the ground with military precision and in her mind reviewing all the benefits of becoming a Flecha: new friends, school, food, new clothes, and the admiration of other children. She knew that becoming a Flecha would change her world, and all she had to do was to convince Dolores of this before her father came home.

Mari's plans to approach her stepmother and regale her with the benefits of being allowed to join the Flechas were interrupted at dawn the next day when Mari was awakened by unfamiliar sounds, strange, low, throaty, gasping sounds that she had never heard before. She stood up, frightened and confused. She followed the sounds to Dolores's room, where Mari found her stepmother covered with sweat and rolling from side to side on the bed. Her face muscles retracted, showing her large white teeth in between gasping breaths. Mari stood by the bedside, wide eyed and terrified. She asked the restless woman, "Where did they shoot you?"

"I am not shot," Dolores responded. "I am not shot," she repeated. "I am having a baby. Don't be afraid. Get me some towels."

Mari felt helpless. She had no knowledge of how to deal with the situation. She knew about bullets, and she knew about the wounds that bullets made. She had seen the devastating bullets from machine guns across bodies, and she knew how the explosions of mortar shells could decapitate and kill people, as it had done to her friend Manolito and the twins, Conchita and Rosa Maria. But Mari knew nothing about having babies. Well, she knew a little from Chata the pig, but she had already left her grandmother's village before Chata had her baby. Pigs had baby pigs, but people's babies were born in France under a cabbage plant and flown to Spain by huge storks. She had at times heard that human men and human women made babies together, but how was that possible? When women were pregnant, it only meant that they were making arrangements while waiting for the stork from France to bring them a baby. Or was the story about babies being born in France under a cabbage plant and flown to Spain by a stork another lie?

Mari gathered the towels and placed them on the bed. She watched her stepmother cry out and make blowing sounds with her breath as she threw the bedcovers aside and asked Mari to place the towels under her legs. A rush of warm, viscous fluid flooded the towels, and Dolores's face became completely distorted as she held on to the top of the bed while pushing and straining between quick panting breaths. She told her stepdaughter, "Hold a towel in your hands, and grab the baby with the towel when it comes."

Mari waited. It seemed like a very long time of holding the towel and watching Dolores cry and push. Just when Mari was almost expecting a piglet to appear in between her stepmother's legs, a mass of bloody something with yellow hair surfaced; it was a very small head, a human baby's head, not a piglet's head. As sweat poured from Mari's face, something that looked like a tiny bluish body followed the head with the yellow hair. It was a baby! Holding the towel in her hands, Mari took the incredibly small creature from the bed, but after she tried to move away with the baby, she felt a strong resistance, a pull from a grayish rubbery-looking cord coming from between Dolores's legs and attached to the baby's stomach.

Mari looked at her stepmother. Not knowing what to do, Mari tried not to cry when a smiling Dolores told her to put the baby on the bed and fetch a ribbon and a pair of scissors from the dresser.

Dolores said, "Everything is going to be all right, Mari. Don't be afraid; this is called the baby's umbilical cord. It is how the baby ate and grew inside me, but the baby does not need it anymore. We are going to cut and tie the cord, and after we cut the cord, the baby will be completely on his own. Well, not really on his own; he will have us to love and care for him."

Mari watched with fascination as Dolores lifted herself halfway up on the bed and tied a piece of ribbon around the glistering cord that came out of the baby's belly. She instructed Mari to cut the cord a little below the ribbon.

Mari cut the cord. Blood mixed with fluid came gushing out from the other end.

Dolores explained, "We are almost finished, Mari. Bring me some more towels, and see if you can clean the baby a little with a towel. Then wrap him in a blanket."

With the baby in her arms, Mari noticed that the baby was making soft choking sounds. Again not knowing what to do, she looked at her stepmother with tears streaming down her face.

"Turn him upside down," said Dolores. "Stick your fingers in his mouth, and clean out the mucus."

Mari followed her stepmother's instructions. As if by a miracle, a shrill, piercing cry filled the room. Mari stared at the little person in her arms. She realized that "he" was a she, and she was breathing and crying! It was a tiny sister, a small, grouchy, potbellied sister with blonde hair, ten fingers, and ten toes, with a mouth that would not shut up.

Exhausted, Dolores lay back on the bed and closed her eyes. She told Mari to leave the baby next to her and go to the apartment upstairs and tell Lucia's mother that the baby had been born and that everything was good.

Mari gave the good news to Lucia's mother, Paquita, who then let out a little scream and ran down the steps from her apartment. After checking on Dolores and the baby, Paquita immediately left to fetch Dolores's parents. She left Mari in charge of looking after her stepmother and the baby for the rest of the day.

Dolores slept on and off, touching the baby's face when awake. She would then smile and go back into a peaceful sleep, filled with good dreams. Her child had been born healthy and whole. Her husband was coming home. She and her stepchild had established a strong and loving relationship. Life would return to normal as soon as all the family could be together again.

Before leaving, Lucia's mother had showed Mari how to use a baby bottle and asked Mari to give the baby water every two hours. Paquita said she'd be back with Dolores's family as soon as possible. Mari had already given the baby water two times, and still no one came. When the sun flooded the apartment at high noon, she fell asleep at the foot of the bed, holding the baby in her arms.

Mari woke up when she heard Dolores's parents, as well as Lucia's mother and several other neighbors, gather around Dolores's bed, talking and laughing. Steamy bowls of soup and cheese sandwiches made with fresh bread suddenly appeared, and small glasses of red wine were passed around the room. Mari was bewildered, wondering where all the food and wine came from.

Dolores sat up in bed, gleaming, talking, and answering questions about the child's birth. When the baby cried, Dolores held the baby against her breast, making the first attempt at nursing her. The baby clutched at the breast and began sucking as Dolores held her tightly, humming rhymes from her childhood.

Mari watched the scene with fascination and mixed feelings. Her own tongue reached for the roof of her mouth, simulating small sucking movements. Her mind flashed pictures of a woman with curly black hair holding a baby and kissing the baby's face. She suddenly remembered the woman and the woman's name. Her name was Mommy, and the child Mommy was holding and the face the woman was kissing was the face in the baby pictures of long ago, her face. She ran to her room. She closed the door and muffled her cries with a pillow for a long time until Dolores's mother came into the room.

Dolores's mother removed the pillow and offered Mari food. "Eat, child. Today you helped a young soul come into this world. This makes you part responsible for the baby, and the responsibility should make you proud. You are growing up, and your sister is going to need you to help her grow up smart and nice like you."

Mari ate in silence. When the woman left, Mari stood and looked out the window until the last rays of sun disappeared. From that moment on, she never again felt like a child. [This is good.]

As time passed without news from Madrid, don Juan tried to be patient and realistic. He lived his life day by day, working in the fields until late afternoons. In the evening, he sat in the town's plaza, discussing the weather and the day's work with family and neighbors, sharing bits of ham and sausage and passing a wine bota around. At night, when everyone was tired and had retired, don Juan sat behind his typewriter, writing in a journal he had started when he had arrived in the village. In this journal, he outlined the many problems that led to the defeat of the Second Spanish Republic.

"It has always been the same," he wrote. "We have always been a stubborn and politically immature people without the emotional ability to accept our shortcomings and modify our issues to be able to come together into a peaceful form of democratic understanding of our needs that would permit Spain to self-govern. We have always allowed cruel and tyrannical rulers to set us apart, without rights or the means to educate ourselves. We have known all of the time that leaders with strength and education are necessary to lead a country out of oppression, leaders with the strength and the intelligence to implement education for the people, leaders with the strength to let go of personal gains and encourage the growth and independence of their country until the people themselves can come together and govern themselves."

Don Juan wrote in his journal every night. The entries resembled a political bible to guide and educate a society toward self-discipline and responsibility to build their own government and rid themselves of kings and dictatorships. Writing in his book and sharing the townspeople's way of life had helped don Juan to be less impatient after the long and unexpected stay in the village without news from Madrid or from the rest of Spain. He now studied how the village had survived for generations using methods taught to them from past generations of farmers. They had been taught how to grow their own food, make their own soap, make their own wine, and how to keep self-governing leadership. All of this fascinated don Juan.

In an area where droughts were common, this village's water supply was plentiful. Water flowed into town from the river and from the mountain's melted snow, channeled into ditches for irrigation, an art learned from the Moorish occupation, and into a fountain in the plaza from which women filled jugs and from which horses, donkeys, and mules drank every day. Cattle, pigs, and sheep were plentiful. Hundreds of chickens roamed the fields after laying their eggs in the henhouses built next to every home.

The evening conversations of those gathered in the plaza each night never included politics. This had been a tacit agreement since the war ended, an agreement not to identify anyone's political beliefs or position during the war years. This silent agreement avoided arguments and the making of enemies. The town had survived for many generations following the simple rule of minding one's own business, a lesson learned from the terrible days of the Spanish Inquisition. Now, hundreds of years later, after another round of brutal and self-destructive carnage, to blame others was no longer important. Through all the changes and conflicting beliefs, and with a possible Jewish heritage, the villagers silently renounced the Vatican, remaining Catholic under the advice of their priest, who had also separated himself from the Vatican. This priest worked the fields during the week and on Sundays translated the services from Latin into Spanish. He performed marriages and baptisms wearing rolled-up baggy pants without questions or criticisms from the villagers.

The men of the village had always run the town's finances and services. They took turns assuming the responsibilities as part-time mayors, assisted by volunteer council members. The village had no doctor. A self-educated midwife attended pregnant women with giving birth, as well as pre- and postpartum health issues. Family health care was assigned to wives, mothers, and grandmothers, who attended the families with natural herbs and the will of God; no medical person had ever lived in or visited the town.

Mesmerized by the independence of the self-governing people of the village, don Juan wrote about them in his journal. He admired the loyalty that each person felt toward others and the ability to govern themselves without political treachery or religious persecution. Everyone was a landowner and traded with each other. This was the closest arrangement to a Marxist society he had ever known, making it a pleasure to participate and work in this ideal environment that had given him the initiative to write in his journal. Every time he felt that too much time had passed without news from his son or what was happening to the country, he thought of making a clandestine trip to Madrid, but his wife and sons always voted down this idea.

His wife would say, "We have heard absolutely nothing, and hearing nothing can only mean that going to Madrid is not a good idea. We may have to settle down here for the rest of our lives, but settling here is better than ending our last days behind iron bars, tortured and killed. Be patient, and finish your book."

Don Juan continued his life and writings, unaware of the serious changes taking place in his family, such as his youngest son and daughter's departure for New York, his oldest son's imprisonment, and the birth of his granddaughter.

Almost a year and a half had passed since Dolores had been informed that her husband would "soon be released from prison." After that, she was told that there had been a delay from the main office with reviewing the case of her husband's release.

Alfonso's freedom came just two weeks after Dolores's last visit. Two guards escorted Alfonso to the front gate and told him that he was free. They mentioned no further conditions, reasons, or details. They simply handed him a book of food stamps and an ID card that had his name and his date of release from prison. Alfonso put the ID and food stamps in his pants pocket. He stood in front of the prison, confused by the sounds and movements of an outside world to which he was no longer accustomed.

It was early morning. Having no money for fare, when a trolley stopped in front of him to allow the boarding of passengers on their way to work, Alfonso walked to the back, ready to jump on the trolley's rear bumper, where the conductor collecting fares could not see him, but when the trolley pulled away, Alfonso was still standing on the street, looking at the ground, ashamed of the dishonest action he had considered. Looking around, he identified Madrid's center, miles away from his home. For a moment, he thought of stopping someone to explain his problem and ask for a few coins, but he was so ashamed of this plan that, instead, he began walking.

Alfonso continued walking for six hours under a hot sun. With his throat and lips swollen and parched from thirst, Alfonso followed the road. He made a sharp turn around the statue of a lion, the miracle of a fountain. From the open mouth of the lion water poured into a small circular pool. He drank from the pool and was soaking his face in the water when he spotted a trolley car slowly passing the fountain, following the curve on the street and stopping at the other end.

After so many hours of walking under the burning sun without food or water, Alfonso decided that he no longer could afford to play the game of right and wrong. It was a matter of survival. Feeling no shame, he ran toward the trolley car just as it began to move. He jumped on the rear bumper and held on to the edge of a back window for support. He closed his eyes to avoid having to see the possible looks of disapproval from the trolley's passengers or the people walking the streets, but there were no such looks. Everyone in Madrid was used to seeing someone on the back of trolleys unable to pay the fare or there because the trolley was too full. It was an uncomfortable but relatively short ride. The trolley arrived at an intersection that crossed the street where Alfonso lived.

Alfonso took just a few steps on the familiar cobblestones, when he was suddenly stopped and searched by two uniformed Guardia Civil police. With Alfonso's ID card and food stamps in his hands, one of the officers walked around Alfonso and looked at him from head to toe, growling, "Another Red walking the streets like a ragged beggar without a tie and jacket. I know you Reds like to walk around with rolled-up shirtsleeves to look like honest workers, but we have laws against that kind of display. These laws will be enforced and obeyed. Do you understand?"

Alfonso was confused by this question until he remembered something he had heard in prison about new laws for clothing in the city—men had to wear jackets and ties, while women had to wear skirts below the knee and have their arms covered just above the elbows, but he pretended not to know this. "I don't know what I have done wrong. I don't have a jacket and a tie because I have just been released from prison, as you can see on my ID card, and—"

Before Alfonso could finish his sentence, the officer pointed his finger at the ID card and hissed, "You are a Communist, no? We are no longer going to allow Communists walking around, dressed as they please. If Franco says you need to wear a tie and a jacket, you will wear a tie and a jacket. We ought to throw you right back in prison, but I don't want you to freeload off the government anymore. You must have been in prison for a while, comrade, because there has been a dress code mandated by Franco himself for a long time. It's not a new thing."

Aware that any further excuses or comments on his part would be dangerous, Alfonso lowered his eyes and addressed the officers in a low voice. "Yes. I was in prison for a long time, but I am not a Communist. I will dress properly as soon as I get home, where I have my clothes."

Returning the ID card and food stamps to Alfonso, the officer wrote something in a small notebook. He said, "I have taken your name and address, and I want you to report to the Guardia Civil Headquarters here in Cuatro Caminos within a week, wearing a jacket and a tie. Understood?"

Choking with anger and humiliation, Alfonso nodded. "Yes, sir. I'll be there."

Dolores opened the door. Alfonso stood on the other side and smiled. Laughter and tears followed. They embraced and kissed each other, oblivious of the world around them.

Mari stood by the door of her room, watching them and waiting for her father to notice her. After waiting and feeling totally excluded, Mari went back to her room.

Unaware that a man had come to the apartment, Mari's little sister, Candra, now almost two years old, sat on the floor, playing and showing no interest in or awareness of what was happening.

Mari lifted her sister from the floor, held her hand, and walked with the small child to the kitchen to greet Alfonso, who was still holding on to Dolores as she laughed and cried, unaware of anyone or anything around them.

Candra frowned. She looked surprised to see a strange man holding her mother and making her cry, and she looked up at her sister. Candra got no response to her look from Mari, so she ran toward the man and struck his legs with clenched fists kicked him on the shins and yelling, "Mamá, mamá!"

Alfonso let go of his wife and looked down with amazement at the fearless, tiny warrior who defended her mother with such courage. He said, "You must be Candra! Come over here, Candra. I am not hurting your mamá; I love your mamá! Tell her, Dolores. Tell her that I am not hurting you. Tell her who I am."

The young child looked at her mother with tearful eyes.

Dolores knelt down in front of her and said, "It's all right, little one. He is not hurting me. I am crying because I am happy. This is your papá. Come, let's say hello. Show him how glad we are that he is home."

Alfonso picked up his daughter. He laughed, kissed her cheek, and danced around the room. "You are so grown-up and so beautiful! Look at you! Blonde hair and green eyes like your papá. Ah, little woman, you and I are going to have a lot of fun together." Alfonso sat and held his daughter. He told her of his unhappiness over not being home when she was born but how happy he was finally to be next to her.

Candra did not really understand what her father was saying and was bored, slid down from her father's lap and ran to her sister, who was standing by the doorway. Candra looked back at her father. "This is my sister. She takes care of me and is teaching me how to count, and today we are going to bury treasures."

It was not until Candra grabbed Mari's hand and pulled her toward the front door that Alfonso let out a loud cry of surprise. "Ah, my strong, beautiful Mari! You were standing there all of this time. Why didn't you say something? Come here. Let me hold you. I have missed you so much!" Kissing her on the cheeks, Alfonso wrapped his arms around his daughter for a long time before telling her how brave she had been the day they took him away. He said that he had known all the time in prison that she would take care of Dolores and little Candra. "Dolores told me how you helped her the day your sister was born. I am proud of you!"

Crying and trying not to show her tears, Mari took a long time to answer her father, but when she was finally able to talk, she told him how he had been the brave one the day they took him to prison. He never cried when they broke his teeth or when they hit him with the rifle butts. She had always loved him, but she had loved him much more after that day.

Dolores sat next to them, and the three of them shared the passing of sad days, the lonely days without each other, and the infinite joy of being home together, safe.

Beginning to lose her patience, Candra pulled on Mari's hand, wanting her sister to go with her to bury treasures as she had promised.

Mari smiled and walked toward the front door, holding Candra's hand. "We will back before dark. I am sure you both have a lot of things to share."

Mari showed her sister how to dig small holes in the ground, fill the holes with bits of colored broken glass, cover them with a larger piece of plain glass, throw dirt, brush the dirt from the middle of the glass, and expose a treasure of multicolored "jewels." Mari shared the moment by watching Candra jump up and down, uttering cries of joyful playfulness. This made Mari feel safe, loved, and worshipped by Candra.

The day after Alfonso returned, he and Dolores decided that it would be good for Alfonso to go to the nearest headquarters of the Guardia Civil as he had been instructed to do by the officers; both he and Dolores thought it best to do this as soon as possible and avoid any further problems or have the Guardia Civil use it as an excuse to search the apartment. After finishing dressing and before leaving the apartment, Alfonso gathered from a folder kept in the bedroom some documents that he thought the Guardia Civil might ask to see.

Dolores asked Mari to stay home with Candra until they returned and promised that afterward, they would all go to Dolores's parents to visit and celebrate Alfonso's return.

Mari agreed to stay home with her sister and walked Dolores and her father to the door. After kissing them good-bye, she walked back toward her room, where Candra had been playing, but when she got there, Candra was in her father's bedroom and was playing with the pictures and papers Alfonso that had left on top of the bed. Mari began gathering the papers, but before she could return them to the folder, a picture fell out—the picture of a small baby who sat on the grass next to a smiling woman whose large dark eyes looked at the baby. The baby was Mari, and she recognized the woman sitting next to her, the woman she had called Mommy, the woman her grandmother said had bad blood. Mari looked for more pictures, but there were no more pictures, just letters, many written in Spanish, signed "Mommy," and one written in a language she did not understand, signed "Joseph."

The letters had been addressed to her father. All were stamped from a place called New York City and began with "My sweet baby girl" and ended with "Mommy." These letters said that she would return to Spain as soon as the treatments for her illness were completed. The postmarks were 1933, 1934, and 1935, then a break in dates until 1939, with a letter in a foreign language signed by someone named Joseph and addressed to her father. No other letters were in the folder, only two small documents written in the same foreign language as the letter written by Joseph. Mari recognized one of the documents as her birth certificate, because it had her name and the date of her birth on the top and her mother's name, as well as her father's name, on the lines below. The date was 1936, and the name of a place called New York City was stamped inside a round seal. Mari still remembered when her grandmother used to tell her that her mother was Ethiopian, and the bad-blooded Ethiopians came from Africa.

Mari looked at the envelopes again and decided that New York City must be in Ethiopia, where they had bad blood, but none of this mattered; what mattered was not being pure Iberian. In all her short life, blood had been the essence of life as well as the unquestionable indicator of a person's worth and honor. "*La sangre Española*," Spanish blood, had been the theme in every childhood lullaby, in every folk tune, in every tale of past Spanish grandeur. Purity of blood had been the message seared into her consciousness. It was the identity that she had always wanted, the safety she needed from the nightmare with which she had existed since the beginning of her remembering, a nightmare from which she had hoped to wake and find her blood cleansed from the impurities associated with non-Iberian blood.

Mari placed the birth certificate inside the folder and looked at the other certificate. It had a large black cross on the top and her mother's name. Again, Mari did not understand the language, but she understood the meaning. The woman with the sad eyes, the woman with the curly hair, the woman she now remembered holding her and humming until she went to sleep, had died. She felt a pull inside her chest, but before the tears could reach her eyes, she felt the heavy weights she had carried on her shoulders disappear. If her mother had died, her connection with Ethiopian blood was broken, and she was now Iberian, like her grandfather, like Dolores, the same as the girls marching in the streets wearing the Flechas uniforms.

Dressed in an immaculate suit, shirt, and tie, Alfonso went out looking for work every day. Dolores and Mari, after spending the morning cleaning and standing in line for the daily food rations, spent the afternoons on the balcony, sewing and reading as little Candra entertained herself, waiting for her sister to be finished with her chores and the reading so that they could go to play with friends in the street until dark.

Mari did not mention finding the letters to anyone, but since finding them, she had been reserved and moody. Dolores and Alfonso attributed this moodiness to hormonal changes and chose not to address the issue. The moods continued.

Two months after he came home, Alfonso found work driving a truck, and the added income made life less stressful, because the food sold in the black market was now more accessible.

At breakfast one morning, Dolores talked about Mari attending school, given that Alfonso was working, so they could afford a modest school fee.

Mari listened to Dolores and Alfonso's discussion for a time without taking part in the conversation until Dolores asked her if she wanted to go to school. The answer was quick, sharp, and emphatic. "I want to join the Flechas. They have real schools with real teachers, and it will not cost anything."

Alfonso stopped eating. He shook his head with a look of surprise in his eyes. "Why, Mari? Why do you want to belong to a Fascist group?"

"I know my mother is dead. I don't have to be Ethiopian anymore. Now I can be a true Spaniard with good Iberian blood like the Flechas."

"Ethiopian? Who is Ethiopian?" Alfonso demanded to know.

"My mother. Her parents came from Italy, and Italy is in Ethiopia. My grandmother Maria said so."

Alfonso turned to Dolores with a look of hopelessness in his face and pleaded, "Help me. Please help me, Dolores. I have no idea what she is saying."

Dolores got up and walked over to Mari. Dolores knelt next to Mari and gently stroked her face. "Your mother was not Ethiopian. Grandmother Maria sometimes made up things when she was angry. Your mother was American, and you were born American. Your father is Spanish. Therefore, you have Spanish blood and don't have to join the Flechas. When you get to be eighteen years of age, you can change your citizenship to Spanish."

Silence followed. Dolores returned to her chair.

Suddenly, Mari shouted, "I want to join the Flechas *now!*"

It was dangerous to deny his daughter membership into the Flechas without being labeled a Communist and an active enemy of the regime. Before going to work the next morning, Alfonso took his daughter to the Falange headquarters and let her apply for membership in the Flechas.

It had been almost a year since Mari joined the Flechas. She was supervised by older members of the Falange through long hours of rigid military discipline, daily drills, enforced academic standards, and constant reminders of the need to help the motherland attain unity to once again become "the empire where the sun never sets." Every morning before school, a Falange officer carefully inspected the Flechas, starting with the red beret properly set and firmly secured on top of the head, a clean and pressed blue shirt neatly tucked into an equally clean and pressed black skirt, followed by a flipping of the Flecha's leather strap across the chest with his finger to make sure that the strap was secured and went under the shoulder epaulet and ran down the back, secured by the belt. The leather strap and leather belt had to be polished and scratch-free. If everything was clean and in place, the officer ended the inspection after his approval of the shine on the Flecha's ankle leather boots and the white wool socks folded over them.

Having to force the back to remain erect for long periods of time and having to be serious and immaculately clean had been difficult for Mari. It had been hard work, but the sound of the drums, the flapping of the flags, and the newly owned sense of responsibility were addictive. The new rhythms in her life prepared her to give her love and obedience to the motherland without questions or doubts.

At home, Dolores watched Mari's ability to follow and obey orders. Taking advantage of this, Dolores set a daily regime for Mari to do her own uniform washing and ironing, as well as shinning her boots, and, in the absence of a tub or shower in the apartment, attend to her daily personal hygiene using the kitchen sink during weekdays and a more comfortable, large, portable round metal laundry tub on Sunday mornings before breakfast.

Candra was fascinated by her sister's uniform and her sister's seriousness when wearing it. She sometimes sat in front of the mirror, fashioning Mari's red beret on her head and tipping it into various angles while moving her body from right to left, mimicking her sister's seriousness and stiffness of facial muscles when she was wearing the beret. "When can I join the Flechas and wear a uniform like you?" she had asked her sister.

"On your one hundredth birthday," intercepted Dolores before Mari could answer.

"And how many years is that, Mamá?"

Dolores smiled, picked up the child in her arms, and whispered, "It's a secret, but it is not too many years, and with your smartness, you will be one hundred years old pretty soon!"

Mari's responsibility to care for her own clothing and personal hygiene without help did not include her nightly homework. Because the assignments were long and at times difficult, Dolores helped Mari every night by explaining and clarifying reading and mathematics assignments.

Dolores liked helping Mari; it felt good to once again review academic issues and equations and to remember things she thought she had forgotten. It felt like the return of her school days and at the same helped Mari finish her homework and be able to get a full night's sleep. Sometimes Dolores and Mari took a rest from homework to talk about issues worrying or confusing Mari—home issues, academic issues, or about what was happening everywhere in general.

Mari said, "Papá said only Fascists belong to the Falange, and my grandfather told me that Fascists hated other races and people who were not Catholic. The Falange leaders who talk to us are not like that. They are always reminding us that all the people of the world are brothers and sisters. They say that we must all work to find unity of heart and spirit, even if sometimes we don't agree with each other."

Dolores looked at Mari, smiled, and lowered her voice. "I would like to give you my opinion, and I will if what you and I talk about when we are alone stays with us, making it a secret we share because we love and trust each other. Do you agree?"

"Yes, Dolores. You are my only true friend besides my grandfather, and I love you both very much. I will never give away our secret talks."

"I love you too, Mari. What the Falange is telling you is in essence very beautiful, if it were true, but you know that every day since the war ended, hundreds of people have been executed because their beliefs did not agree with the beliefs of the present regime. When they say we are all brothers and sisters, they mean those who believe what they believe, which no one in our family does. There are millions of different people in Spain, and it is impossible for everyone to think the same."

In school or standing at attention with the other Flechas, Mari continued to listen to the daily speeches exalting the greatness and purity of Spain. "We are all brothers and sisters, and we must work together toward encouraging some of our brothers and sisters to rid themselves of fear, come out of hiding, and return to their homes and families."

Dolores and Mari continued to spend many evenings together discussing issues confusing to Mari and sometimes to Dolores. During the day, Mari continued listening to teachers and military officials mention the "brotherhood of Iberians" together with "the war has been over for three years, we are now at peace, and all has been forgiven." Mari carried these messages to Dolores, and Dolores discussed these messages with Alfonso.

"I am afraid," Dolores whispered to Alfonso one night after they were alone in their bed. "It seems that Mari believes more and more of the lies she is being fed by the Falange. She's now talking about going to Estremadura with me to convince your father to come to Madrid."

Alfonso jumped out of bed and stood over Dolores with wide eyes. For a moment, he was unable to talk. Then he said, "Dolores, for heaven's sake. Can't you see what they are doing?"

"What do you think is going on?"

"They are brainwashing Mari. That is what is going on. Eventually, she is going to tell them where to find my father and our brothers."

"I'll see if I can get at what she is really feeling. She may just miss your father. She loves him a lot. It has been a long time since she has seen him, and it must be hard for her to be away from him after they had been so close."

"Everything is hard these days. Too much suffering," muttered Alfonso before drifting to sleep.

After three years under Franco's Fascist dictatorship, if not executed, political prisoners died every day from hunger and diseases or from the barbaric treatment in prisons, concentration camps, or hard labor. The harshness of these three years was felt all over Spain. Those who had survived without going to prison wrapped themselves in silence and distanced themselves from others. If tourists asked them about the war, they usually replied, "Yes, we had a war. It was bad for both sides," and offered no further comments. The free Spaniard went to work during the week and watched soccer or bullfights every Sunday. But after the game, the old habit of stopping at a local bar or outside restaurant for a glass of wine and a lively discussion of the game was gone.

To the occasional tourist, Spaniards were happy watching soccer or attending bullfights, but what the tourist could not and did not see was how almost every one of the Spaniards watching soccer or a bullfight on Sundays was at the same time apprehensively looking over his shoulder, fearing someone would suddenly accuse him of war crimes and take him to prison. Sleep was poor since the war had ended for those who fought against Franco and were still alive. They woke up during the night, thinking that they had heard the sound of a rifle butt breaking the door, and they experienced nightmares, during which Falange officers invaded their home, raping the women and taking the men away to prison.

Life was difficult for those who lived and had fought in areas loyal to the Second Spanish Republic during the war. The older generation attempted to find some unity and agreement with their neighbors during routine daily activities by remaining silent about the bloody discord that had killed their sons and daughters. In schools and in the Flechas training camps, the younger generation grew up accepting the concept of rights that only allowed total obedience to the dictates of the motherland.

Growing up in this confusing environment, Mari found it easier to accept what everyone said without questioning or challenging either side. She offered no comments, and that made her life easier and less complicated than the life of the adults in her family. This casual attitude was not broken the day she was called to the Falange headquarters. She went without fear or preconceived ideas. A Falange officer was sitting at a large desk decorated with small flags. On the desk was a picture of a well-dressed, attractive woman holding the hands of two boys in Flechas uniforms. The officer noticed Mari looking at the pictures and smiled. "That's my family, my wife and my sons."

As she was not given permission to talk, Mari stood at attention and looked straight ahead, remaining silent. The officer signaled Mari to take a seat on the empty chair in front of him. "At ease, cadet. At ease." Reclining on the back of his chair, the officer looked benign and comfortable, his face relaxed and friendly, as he chewed on a pencil. He told Mari, "You are a very good cadet. A memo has been sent to me by your lieutenant naming you for the rank of sergeant, and I support the nomination. Tell me, soldier, do you think that you can teach and practice the principles directed by the laws of this nation and if necessary give your life for the good of your country?"

Mari took a deep breath. A sergeant. And he had called her a soldier! Ah, yes. She could function as a sergeant. She could lead an army, if that was necessary, or even if it was not necessary, and she was certainly ready to give her life if it was for the good of the motherland. Because she was totally engrossed in her excitement, Mari did not reply to the officer's question.

Slowly returning his chair to an upright position, the officer placed the pencil he was chewing on the desk. Looking at Mari, he asked again, "Well? What do you think? Do you have enough training and loyalty to be a sergeant?"

Mari stood up. She shuffled her feet and looked ahead at attention. She gave the officer a right-hand salute. "Yes, sir! Thank you, sir."

"All right, cadet. Congratulations. You will get your stripes next week in this office. One of your parents needs to be present. If your father works, bring your mother. Who else lives in your house?"

"I have a little sister."

"Where is the rest of your family?"

"My mother is dead, but I have a stepmother, and her parents live here in Madrid. The others of my family are farmers."

The officer leaned forward with a smile. "I have always admired farmers. They are the heart of a nation, and we would not be able to exist without them. It is sad that so many of our good farmers went to France after the war. Some areas of France have poor soil, and farming is very difficult. Where in France is your family's farm?"

"My family is not in France, sir." Mari was immediately horrified by what she had said. Blood drained from her face, and she stumbled over her words, trying to correct herself. "They went to America during the war, and they have not returned since then, sir."

The officer shook his head. "No need to dishonor yourself with lies, cadet. There is nothing to fear. Your family and all the Spaniards who fought on the side of the Republican government are just as honorable as the Spaniards who fought with our Caudillo Franco to liberate Spain from the Communists. We are all brothers, and all has been forgiven between us. No need for members of your family to hide in silence somewhere in Spain anymore."

Mari felt helpless and totally suffocated by two ideologies fighting inside her. She wanted so much to believe the Falange officer. If what he said was true, it was beautiful, as Dolores had said, and maybe there was no one else being thrown into prisons anymore. She had not heard of anyone taken prisoner for a long time. In the silence, she heard a clock tick. Time passed. She had to make a choice. She said, "My grandfather has been in Estremadura. He has never hurt anyone; he likes to write and knows nothing about guns."

A week passed, and having been told to attend Mari's ceremony, Dolores was making coffee before getting ready for her trip to the Falange headquarters where Mari was to be given the sergeant stripes that morning. It was early, and Alfonso was still home dressing to go to work. Mari was quietly finishing the last details of her uniform.

The silence in the apartment was interrupted by knocks on the front door. Dolores opened the door, and Alfonso's mother and a young man wearing a black beret and dressed in the baggy pants of farmers stood in the doorway, holding a bag. Before the young man could uncover his head, Dolores and Maria at first looked at each other, saying nothing, then embraced and let out loud cries. After a few minutes, Maria stepped back from the door, holding on to Dolores's hand and drying the tears from her face with her apron. "This is Fernando; he is the only one who knew how to drive in the village. He was kind enough to bring me in the truck Felipe and Carlos left behind when they were arrested yesterday."

Hearing his mother's voice, Alfonso rushed from the bedroom. He buttoned his shirt, kissed his mother on the cheek, and asked, "What happened, Mother? After all this time, how did they find them?"

Maria's eyes filled with tears again, and she found herself unable to talk.

Dolores helped her to a chair in the kitchen. "Oh my God, Maria. Come. Sit down. Have some coffee, and tell us what happened."

Maria continued to cry, unable to speak. Young Fernando, holding his beret and looking down at the floor, volunteered information. "They came in the afternoon; we were still in the fields when they came."

Dolores realized that the young man had not moved from the door and interrupted him to say, "Oh, I am so sorry, Fernando. Please come in. Sit, and have some coffee."

Fernando walked into the kitchen, sat next to Maria, and held her hand. "Well, we were still in the fields when they came. Felipe was carrying a bale of hay to the cart when they stuck a gun in his back and told him to kneel down. Carlos came from behind and hit the Falange guy on the head with his fist. It was all over in moment. Felipe was shot in the leg and Carlos was shot in the shoulder before two more blue shirts came running from a truck parked on the side of the road. After they stopped the bleeding and dressed the wounds, they tied Carlos's and Felipe's hands and took them to their truck. Later on, they found don Juan walking home with his wife and sons, and they arrested the men. They are all in custody here in Madrid, pending a hearing.

"I don't know what else to tell you. I am sorry for what happened to don Juan and the boys, but I swear by the Holy Mother, no one in the village had anything to do with it." After he finished speaking, Fernando made the sign of the cross on his chest and went back to the door. He picked up the package he had left there when he went into the kitchen. He looked at Dolores and said softly, "We brought you a ham and some bread."

Maria stopped crying. She stood up and helped Fernando with the sack. She patted his hand and said, "No one from the village would ever think such a thing, Fernando. I am not even sure if anyone had anything to do with it. Maybe the police went to Estremadura in one of their happy routine hunts."

Fernando emptied the bag, leaving a big smoked serrano ham and several loaves of crusty bread on the table.

Maria turned to Dolores and explained, "Fernando has to get back to the village. There is no one in his family left that can do the irrigation. He needs your permission to use Felipe's truck to get back and keep the truck in the village until you need it or until Felipe is released. In the meantime, I would appreciate it if I could stay here with you until we find out what is going to happen."

Alfonso put his arms around his mother and kissed her forehead. "Dear God, Mother. Do you have to ask? Of course you can stay here!"

In all the confusion and sadness that had been shared by the family in the kitchen, everyone had forgotten about Mari. She walked back to her room, unnoticed, flattening and dragging her body against the floor, sliding under the bed and trying to hold her breath. They had lied. They told her that the war was over and that all had been forgiven. What was going to happen to her grandfather?

After bringing a suitcase with Maria's clothing into the apartment and finishing his cup of coffee, Fernando left for Estremadura. The apartment became quiet. When Maria asked her son whether Mari was in school, he looked at his wife, and both of them, as if directed by invisible hands, walked together to Mari's bedroom. Mari was not visible, but Candra was waking up. Maria picked up her granddaughter and kissed and hugged her all the way back to the kitchen.

"Blessed Virgin, Jesus, and the Holy Spirit!" shouted Maria to her grandchild. "You are the most beautiful princess in the entire world!" Candra looked at the unknown woman holding her and tried to pull herself free. Maria laughed and held her closer. "I am your grandmother! Your grandmother Maria, the mother of your papá."

Putting his arm around his mother, Alfonso asked her to let Candra down. "Let her go, Mother. She is too young for all of these changes. One day, she will get to know you, and she will get to love you soon. She is a very special child."

Candra became more agitated before her grandmother could put her down on the floor and managed to free herself. She ran to the bedroom to look for her sister. One of Mari's feet was sticking out. Candra crawled under the bed next to her.

Unable to find Mari and unable to explain his daughter's disappearance, Alfonso apologized to his mother, but before he could say anything, he was interrupted by Dolores as she pointed under the bed, where Mari's shiny boot was sticking out.

The grandmother approached. She knelt and looked under the bed, staring straight into a very pale and frightened face. "Mari, it's me, your grandmother Maria. Come out, my love. Let me see you! It has been such a long time since we have been together."

Mari moved toward her grandmother, who was now sitting on the floor, reaching for her. Mari cried.

Still lying under the bed and unable to understand what was happening, Candra shouted at her grandmother, "Leave her alone! You are making my sister cry."

Before anyone could say or do anything, three rapid knocks came upon the front door. They were there, the Falange police, in blue shirts, red berets, and shiny boots. They were holding rifles. One of them announced, "Sergeant Mari was absent from the Flechas for today's morning drill, as well as not being available to receive her sergeant stripes at headquarters. She is now to come with us, because her grandfather is in prison and has requested to see her before his—" He looked at everyone's face and decided not to finish the sentence, which everyone guessed would have been "execution."

The next few seconds passed like remnants from a bad dream. Mari stepped forward and saluted the officer.

After he called an "About face!" and a "Forward, march!" Mari followed the group to the steps and into the street. She did not look back.

Alfonso, Dolores, and Maria stood by the door, unable to move. Each wore a look of disbelief as they watched Mari leave.

Mari sat by herself, erect and silent, in the back of the truck. The Falange police traveled through streets busy with people. Mari glanced straight ahead, paying no attention to what was happening around her. Cars and trolleys passed, and people stared at the truck with blank faces, unaffected by the sight of a small child seated among full-grown armed Falange police. Quiet and afraid, Mari began exploring all kinds of ways to explain to her grandfather how she had been tricked into disclosing his hideout in Estremadura. She hoped that he did not know that she was responsible for his arrest. How could she explain being as gullible and naive as to believe that the Fascist government could bond with liberals and forgive them for having fought against the Fascists during the war? There was no way to explain. Hiding under the bed and running from the apartment with the Falange police without greeting her grandmother or saying good-bye to her father and Dolores was unforgivable.

The Falange police took her out of the truck and into a room in the headquarters, where Mari was startled to see her grandfather. There was nothing else in the room except two chairs and a small table, plus a bright lightbulb that hung from the ceiling, attached to a long cord, making shadows across the bare walls. Mari's grandfather was unshaved and unkempt. He sat on one of the chairs with a faraway look that disappeared as he stood up and saw his grandchild walk through the door.

He exclaimed, "My love, my love, my most wonderful grandchild, how have I missed you!" He put his arms around Mari before looking at her face with admiration. "You are growing up. I missed you every day. Seeing you again is the best thing that has happened in my life for a very long time."

As they embraced, Mari was unable to hold back the tears. She whispered, "Abuelo. What's going to happen to you now?"

Don Juan shook his head and squeezed Mari's hand. "I will be going somewhere, and I will wait for you, no matter how long it takes you to get there. I suspect that it will be a long time. If there is a typewriter available where I am going, I will keep on typing words to encourage a peaceful, love-filled universe for all beings." He took a deep breath. "Mari, your grandmother will be giving you a diary of the days I spent in Estremadura. Eventually, when you are a little older, I want you to read it, inspect it, analyze my words, and take from them only that which feels honorable and comfortable to you. Promise me that you will never allow anyone or anything to tell you what to think or what to feel. Promise!"

Two guards entered the room and approached don Juan. They announced, "It is time."

Don Juan stood up. Before leaving the room, he placed a hand over his heart and blew a kiss in his granddaughter's direction.

When Mari tried to leave with him, a female Falange officer stopped her. The officer said, "Your grandfather gave himself up and has admitted being an active member of the Communist Party. I am sure that you, as a loyal Flecha, understand that this cannot be tolerated in the New Order. Your grandfather is to be executed, and you are to be present at the execution as a reminder of the seriousness of keeping Spain undivided and a devoted Catholic country willing to follow and obey the mandates of the church and state."

Mari did not hear anything the woman said. Mari was confused. She did not understand the meaning of what was happening or what was being said until she found herself in the prison's courtyard, where she saw Dolores's brothers, Carlos and Felipe, standing next to her grandfather in front of a concrete wall that faced the back of the prison. A row of soldiers armed with rifles looked straight at them from the other side of the courtyard, awaiting orders. A young officer stood next to them with his right hand over the pommel of a sword attached to his belt. Mari was told to stand at attention, and she watched the young officer draw his sword and order the soldiers to fire. Carlos looked at her and smiled. His eyeglasses slid from his face to the ground. Life left him. He fell on top of his eyeglasses. As if in a dream, Mari watched Felipe slowly fall to the ground like a ragged doll with a bended arm making a fist, his one last salute to the Second Spanish Republic. The nightmare took her breath away when her grandfather slid to the cement floor after blowing a kiss in her direction. She ran toward the concrete wall. She yelled, "Abuelo! Abuelo!" and fell onto her grandfather's inert body.

The sun was hot against her red woolen beret. Hot and cold thrust back the bitter fluids her empty stomach was pushing upward against her throat.

Mari had been in the prison's first aid office all afternoon. Now she waited in front of the prison building for her father and Dolores to pick her up. With the sun against her eyes, seeing nothing and hearing nothing, she sat on the curb, almost in a trance, unaware that her father, Dolores, and her grandmother knew what had happened and were inside the prison, signing for the release of the bodies.

When Mari heard Dolores calling, her heart flipped wildly inside her chest, obstructing her breathing. How could she ever look at her stepmother without experiencing Carlos and Felipe's executions and knowing that their deaths were her own fault? How could Dolores ever be able to look at her without remembering who was responsible for her brothers' deaths? How could she live day by day with her father and grandmother, knowing that she helped the Fascists to execute her grandfather?

Jumping from the curb in a panic, Mari ran blindly and without direction until she found herself skipping over steps that led to streets and alleys of Old Madrid. The day was fading when she reached the Plaza Mayor, busy with strolling couples and groups of young people talking and laughing. She crossed the Plaza. After walking through narrow cobblestone alleys, she entered the courtyard of an abandoned old chapel with a well hidden in a weed-covered vegetable garden.

Mari looked around this beautiful place with no people. She took a deep breath and removed the beret from her head and the boots and socks from her feet. Using the chest strap and belt from her uniform, she tied everything into a package and placed it on the edge of the well. She did not want to belong to anything anymore. Not to Spain, not to Queen Isabella, not to the Cid Campeador, not to her grandfather's world of happy workers or the Second Spanish Republic, not to the Flechas. She did not want to belong to this world. She now belonged to no one and to nothing. She did not want to think about people who had been shot because they did not think or believe the same as the people who shot them. She did not want to think of the people who shot other people and who eventually got shot because they too did not think or believe the same as the people they shot. Death seemed to be the reward for trust, for believing or belonging. Regardless of ideology, they all had something in common: asking the children to die for their country. Did anyone ask children to live for their country? Riddled with these thoughts, Mari sat on the ground and leaned against the wall of the well.

Mari let a row of rapidly traveling red and black ants carry bits of food across her feet. Even ants traveled in different colors, but these ants were neither all red nor all black; they were both colors. Ah, smart ants, smarter than people. A gentle breeze blew through the trees. The fading sun flickered through the branches around the chapel, making Mari feel peaceful. As she was about to close her eyes, the life-size statue of Jesus with a bullet-ridden face from stray fire during the war faced her from behind the trees.

Jesus of Nazareth with extended arms was looking at her. Jesus, the Jewish messiah of whose words the Jewish rabbis had been afraid. Her grandfather said so. Jesus, the son of Mary and Joseph, was a Socialist the crooked Jewish rabbis had the Romans kill on a cross. Her grandfather had explained to her how Jesus's death was a political issue for power and financial gain, having nothing to do with sins or salvation. Mari's grandfather was almost always right. Not always. She remembered the time he said Queen Isabella and Columbus were lovers and were getting ready to flee from Spain when King Ferdinand had Columbus locked in an attic and let him die there. She believed him until her grandmother told her he had made that up just to be funny, but she had believed him at the time.

Mari's grandparents argued a lot about everything, especially about God and Jesus. They seemed to have the same problem as the rest of Spain, different ideas and believing that things happened for different reasons. "Jesus never said he was the one and only Son of God," her grandfather would argue. "If there is a God, it is the Infinite, a Thing, not a person, and we are all parts and bits of that Infinite. Jesus has to be respected as the first Socialist who could not be bribed by the rich and chose instead to die for his ideals, for his people, for the poor, for the exploited workers. Oh, yes. He was a martyr, a Socialist martyr killed by the rich and the powerful, not by God, not by the devil, just fat Jewish rabbis with bellies full of matzo balls and a heart full of avarice."

Mari smiled, remembering how the arguments always ended after her grandmother picked her up in her arms and left the room, whispering, "Dear Jesus, Son of God, please forgive my husband, Juan. He is a good man, but sometimes he gets dumb and stubborn and does not know what he is saying." Mari's grandfather had been stubborn, but he had not been dumb. He had been a good writer, a dreamer, the most important person in her life. And she had helped to kill him. She wished he was still alive. She needed to explain to him what had happened. She needed to be forgiven.

Mari's eyes closed once again, and the trees hummed and whispered in a strange language, sending Mari adrift into a dreamless world where everything was dark and everything was quiet until she heard a familiar voice breaking through the stillness and the darkness. It was her grandfather's voice. The voice was coming from the Jesus statue behind the trees. She sat up, surprised, and listened. It was real. She heard it again. The statue was talking, but the voice was her grandfather's voice.

"You did not kill me, child. I chose my own death for reasons that no longer matter, such as the equality, the respect, and the freedom for my country."

Feeling the statue's extended arms reaching for her hand, Mari stood up as her grandfather's voice spoke again.

"Come. Hold my hand. Let's you and I go find the answers to the questions you have been asking since the day you learned your first word. Let's see if I had the right answers."

They climbed to the edge of the well, holding hands, and jumped into the dry darkness of a well that had been without water for a very long time. When Mari reached the bottom, there was no one there.

Her body lay broken and listless on the well's sandy bottom, all alone, except for a hungry rat.

"What was that all about?" asked Jesus.

"Ah, nothing much, my boy," God said. "Just another kid full of questions I will soon have to answer."